the
BLUE
ROAD

the BLUE ROAD
a fable of migration

WAYDE COMPTON

illustrations by
APRIL DELA NOCHE MILNE

ARSENAL PULP PRESS
VANCOUVER

THE BLUE ROAD
Text copyright © 2019 by Wayde Compton
Illustrations copyright © 2019 by April dela Noche Milne

ARSENAL PULP PRESS
Suite 202 – 211 East Georgia St.
Vancouver, BC V6A 1Z6
Canada
arsenalpulp.com

The publisher gratefully acknowledges the support of the Canada Council for the Arts and the British Columbia Arts Council for its publishing program, and the Government of Canada, and the Government of British Columbia (through the Book Publishing Tax Credit Program), for its publishing activities.

Arsenal Pulp Press acknowledges the xʷməθkʷəy̓əm (Musqueam), Sḵwx̱wú7mesh (Squamish), and səl̓ilwətaʔɬ (Tsleil-Waututh) Nations, speakers of Hul'q'umi'num'/Halq'eméylem/hən̓q̓əmin̓əm̓ and custodians of the traditional, ancestral, and unceded territories where our office is located. We pay respect to their histories, traditions, and continuous living cultures and commit to accountability, respectful relations, and friendship.

This is a work of fiction. Any resemblance of characters to persons either living or deceased is purely coincidental.

Proofread by Jaiden Dembo

Printed and bound in Canada

Library and Archives Canada Cataloguing in Publication:
Title: The blue road : a fable of migration / Wayde Compton ; April dela Noche Milne, illustrator.
Names: Compton, Wayde, 1972- author. | Milne, April Dela Noche, illustrator.
Identifiers: Canadiana (print) 20190130660 | Canadiana (ebook) 20190130679 | ISBN 9781551527772
(softcover) | ISBN 9781551527789 (PDF)
Subjects: LCGFT: Graphic novels.
Classification: LCC PN6733.C66 B58 2019 | DDC 741.5/971—dc23

For Senna
– Wayde

For Grandma, Mom, and my nanay.
– April

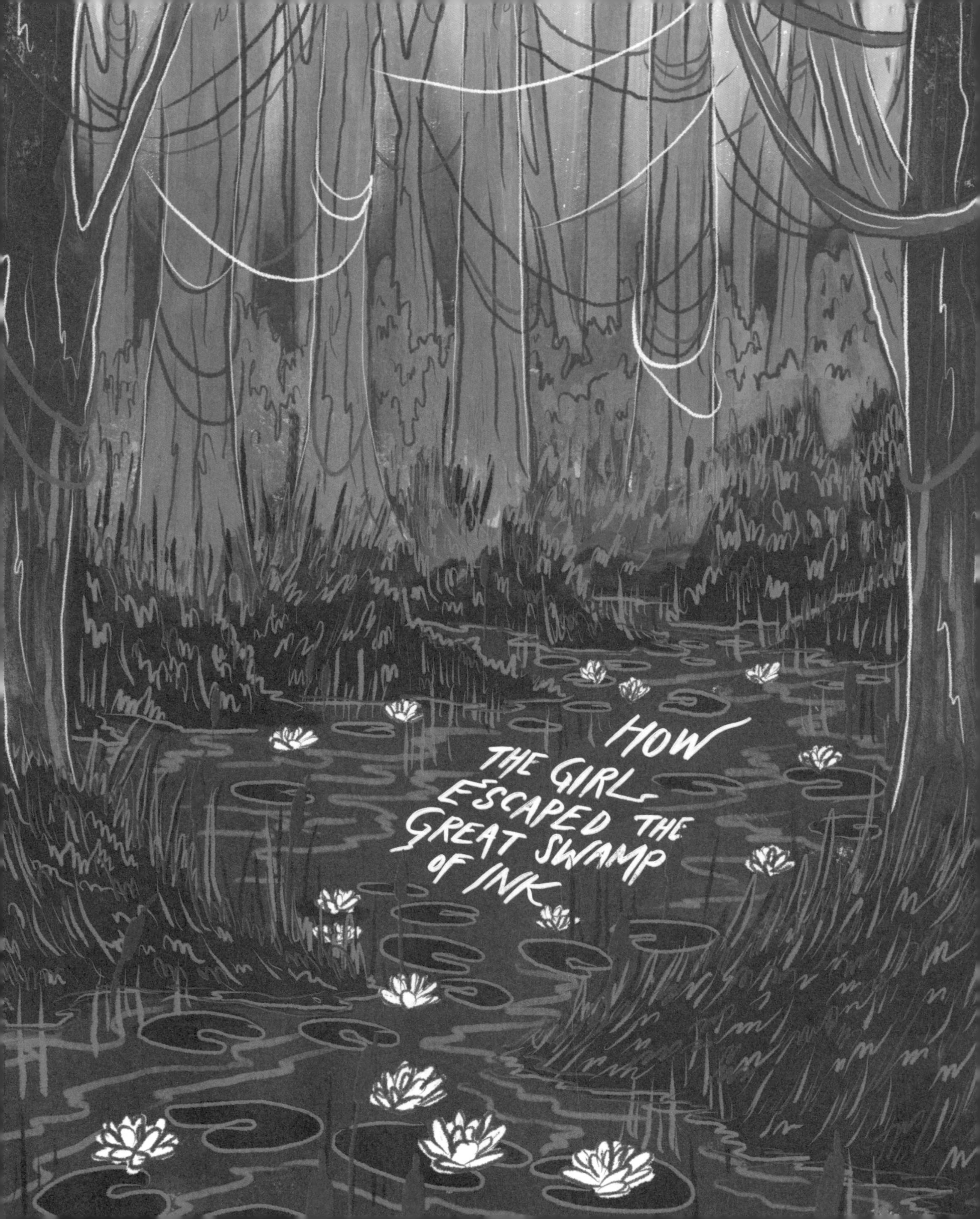
HOW
THE GIRL
ESCAPED THE
GREAT SWAMP
OF INK

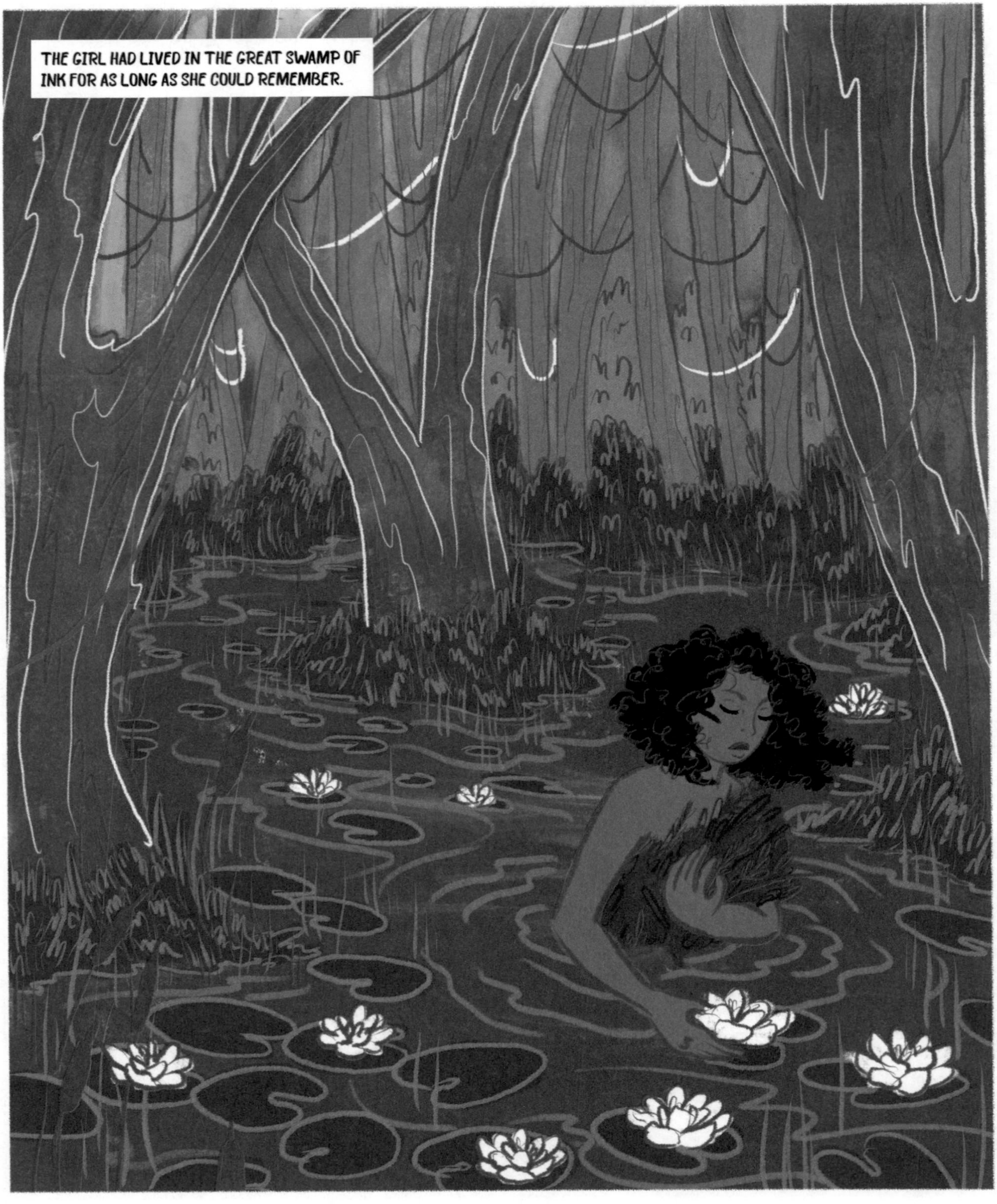
THE GIRL HAD LIVED IN THE GREAT SWAMP OF INK FOR AS LONG AS SHE COULD REMEMBER.

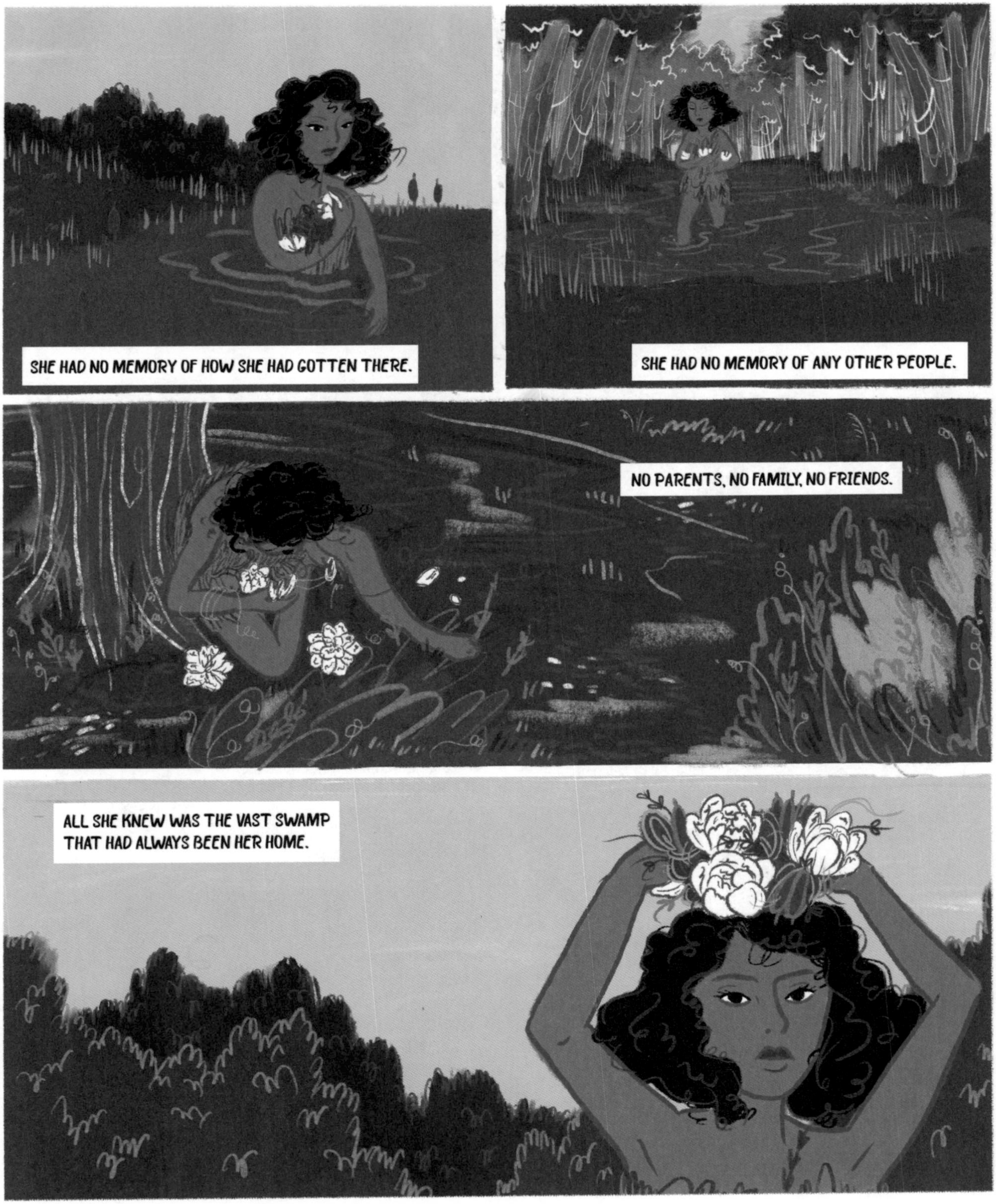
SHE HAD NO MEMORY OF HOW SHE HAD GOTTEN THERE.
SHE HAD NO MEMORY OF ANY OTHER PEOPLE.
NO PARENTS, NO FAMILY, NO FRIENDS.
ALL SHE KNEW WAS THE VAST SWAMP THAT HAD ALWAYS BEEN HER HOME.

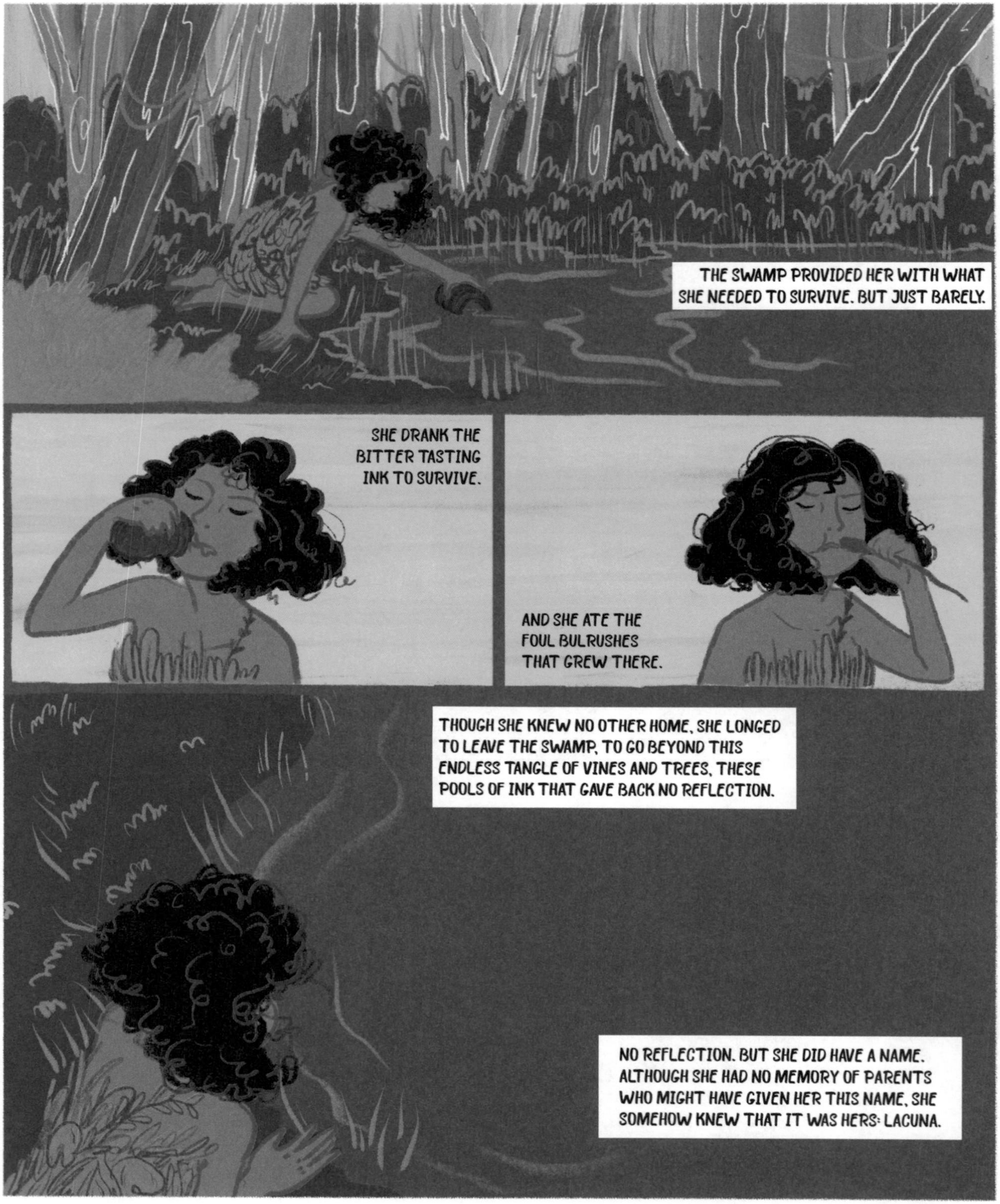
THE SWAMP PROVIDED HER WITH WHAT SHE NEEDED TO SURVIVE. BUT JUST BARELY.
SHE DRANK THE BITTER TASTING INK TO SURVIVE.
AND SHE ATE THE FOUL BULRUSHES THAT GREW THERE.
THOUGH SHE KNEW NO OTHER HOME, SHE LONGED TO LEAVE THE SWAMP, TO GO BEYOND THIS ENDLESS TANGLE OF VINES AND TREES, THESE POOLS OF INK THAT GAVE BACK NO REFLECTION.
NO REFLECTION. BUT SHE DID HAVE A NAME. ALTHOUGH SHE HAD NO MEMORY OF PARENTS WHO MIGHT HAVE GIVEN HER THIS NAME, SHE SOMEHOW KNEW THAT IT WAS HERS: LACUNA.

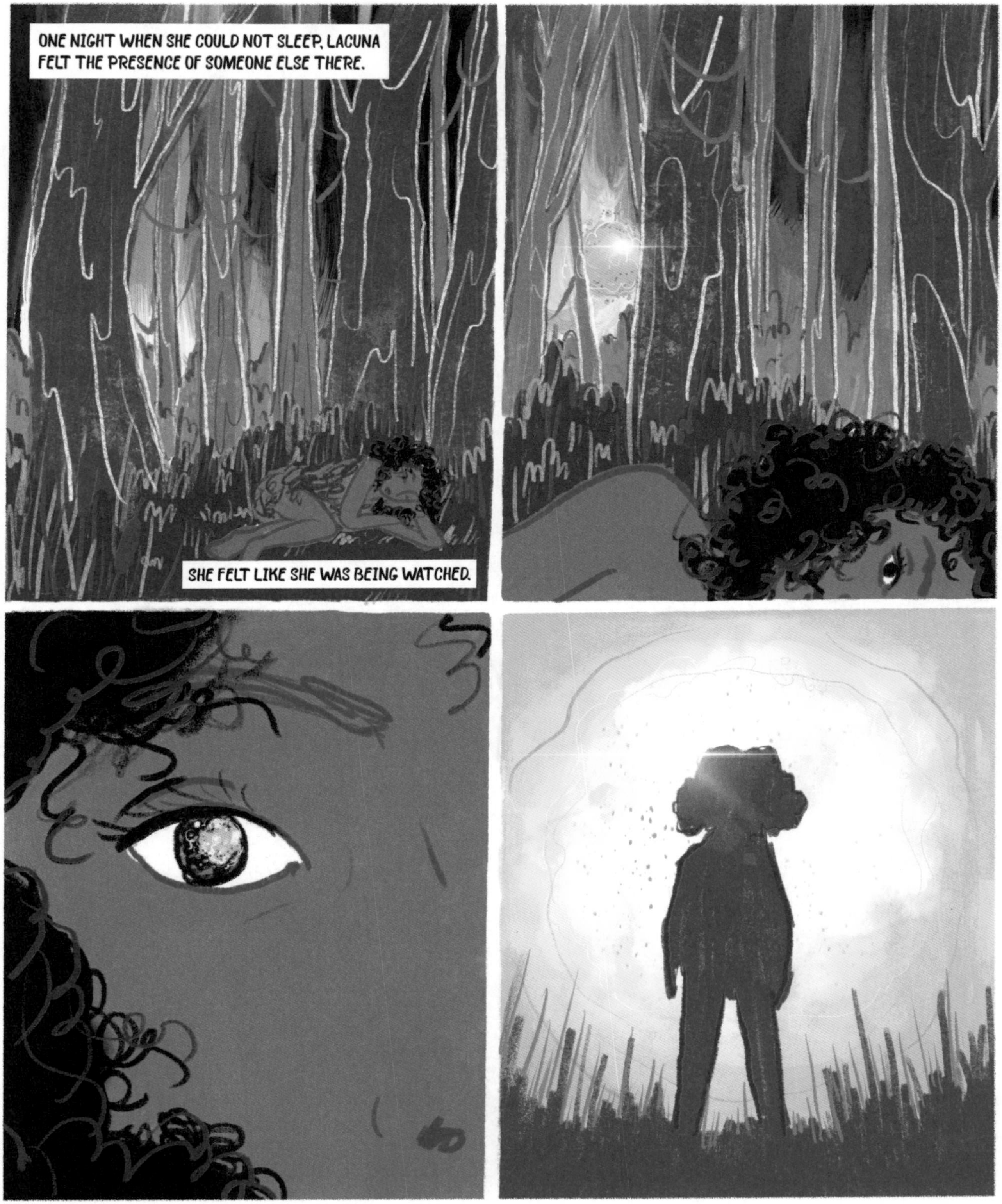
ONE NIGHT WHEN SHE COULD NOT SLEEP, LACUNA FELT THE PRESENCE OF SOMEONE ELSE THERE.
SHE FELT LIKE SHE WAS BEING WATCHED.

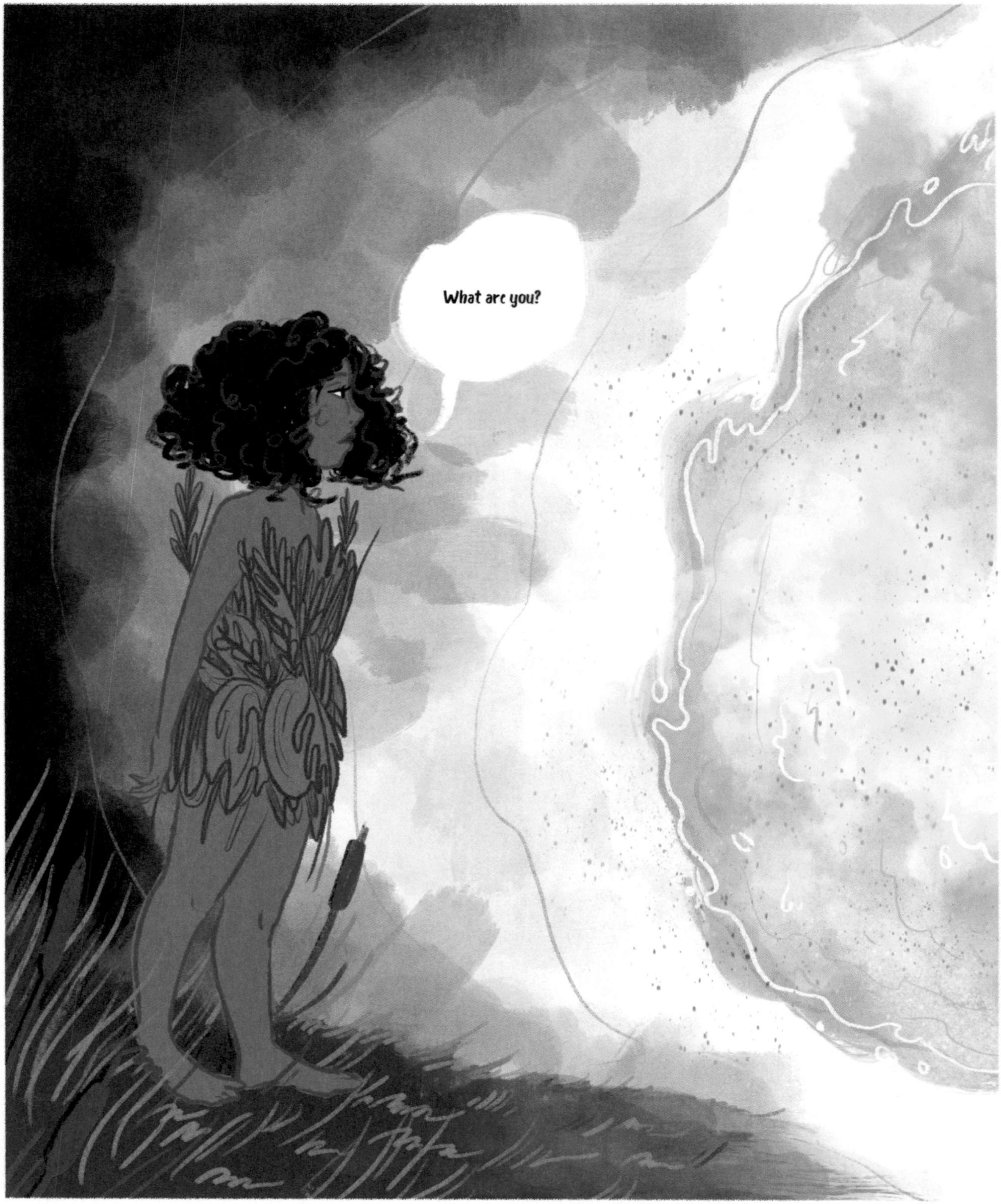
What are you?

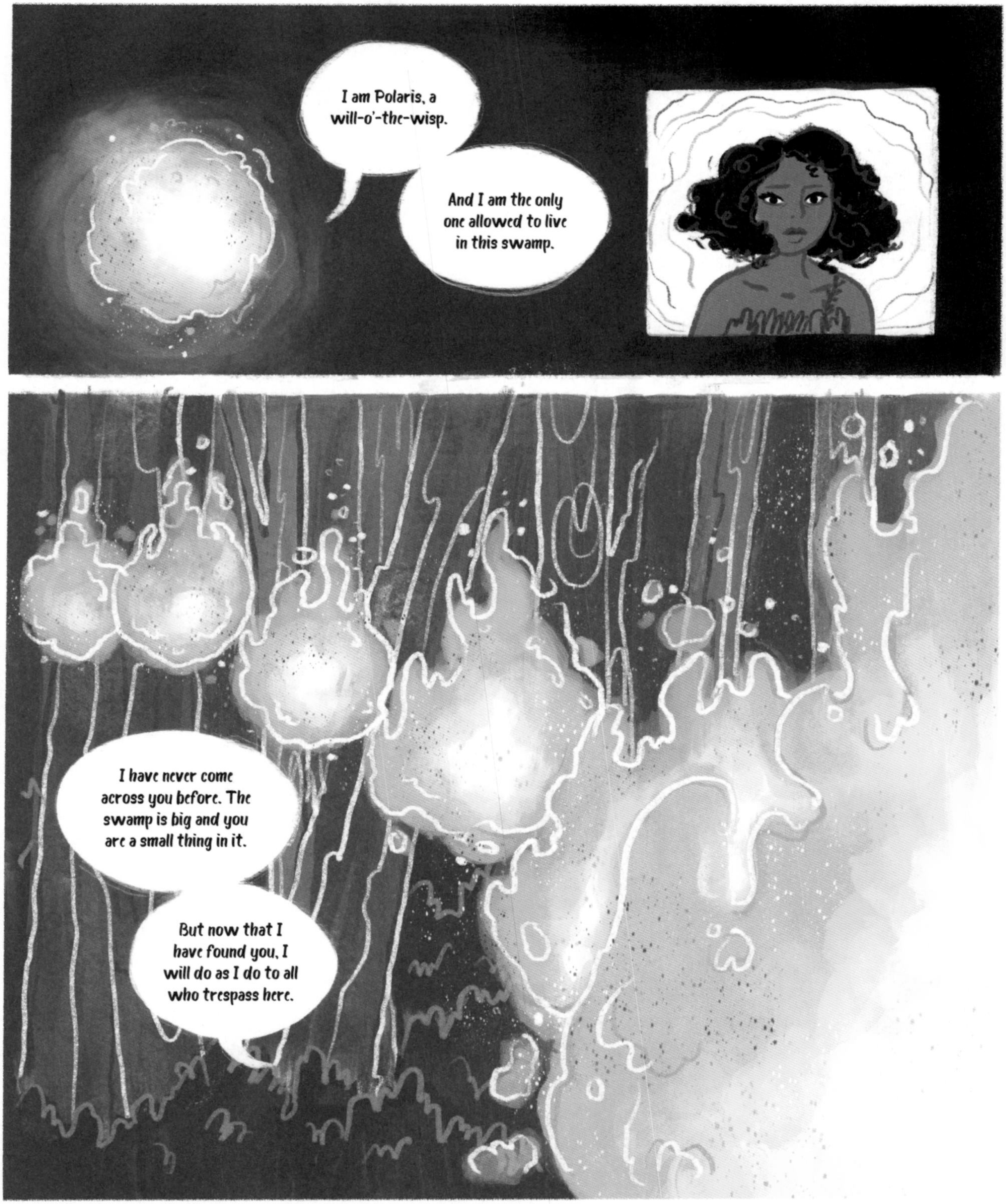
I am Polaris, a will-o'-the-wisp.
And I am the only one allowed to live in this swamp.
I have never come across you before. The swamp is big and you are a small thing in it.
But now that I have found you, I will do as I do to all who trespass here.

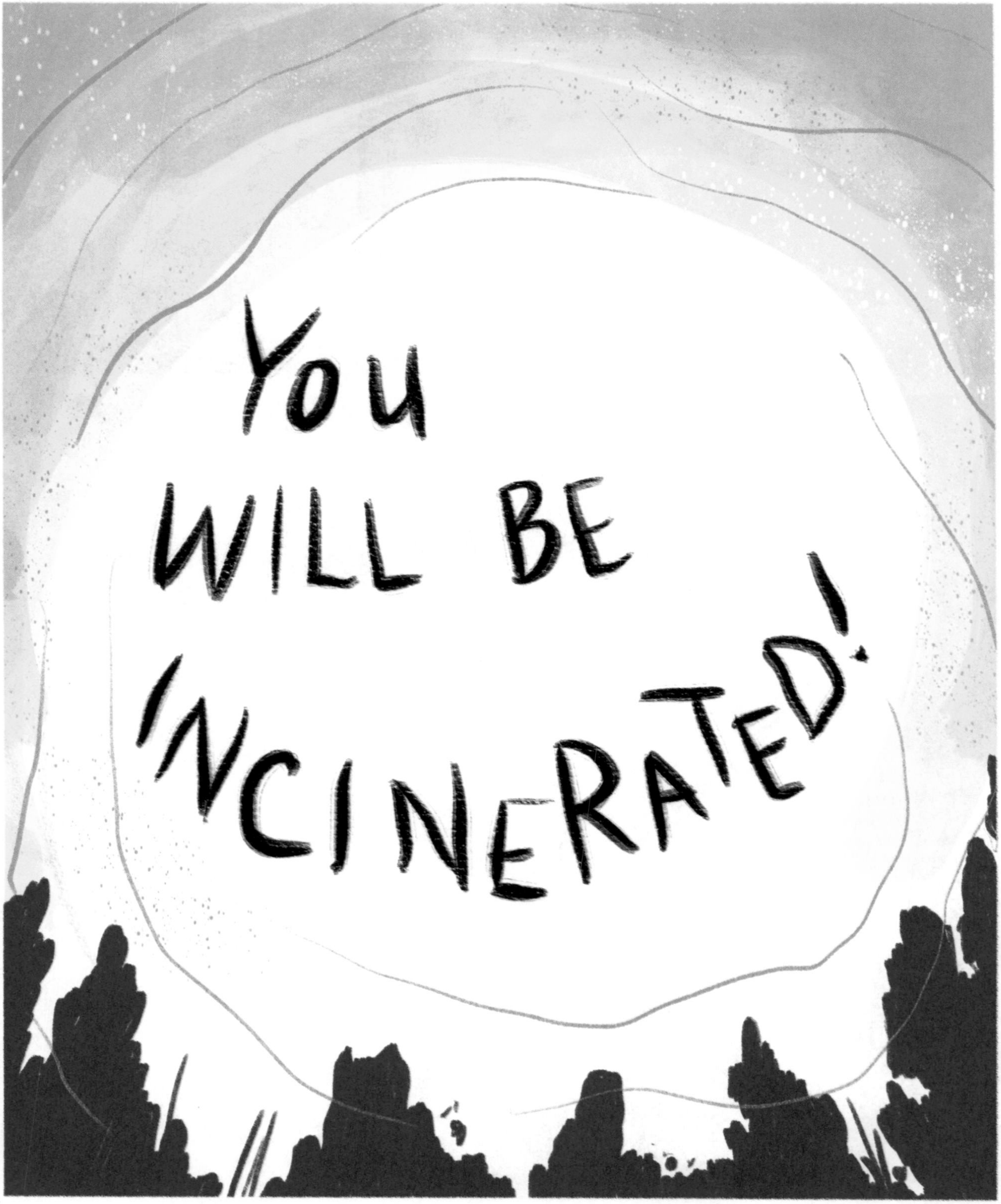
YOU WILL BE INCINERATED!

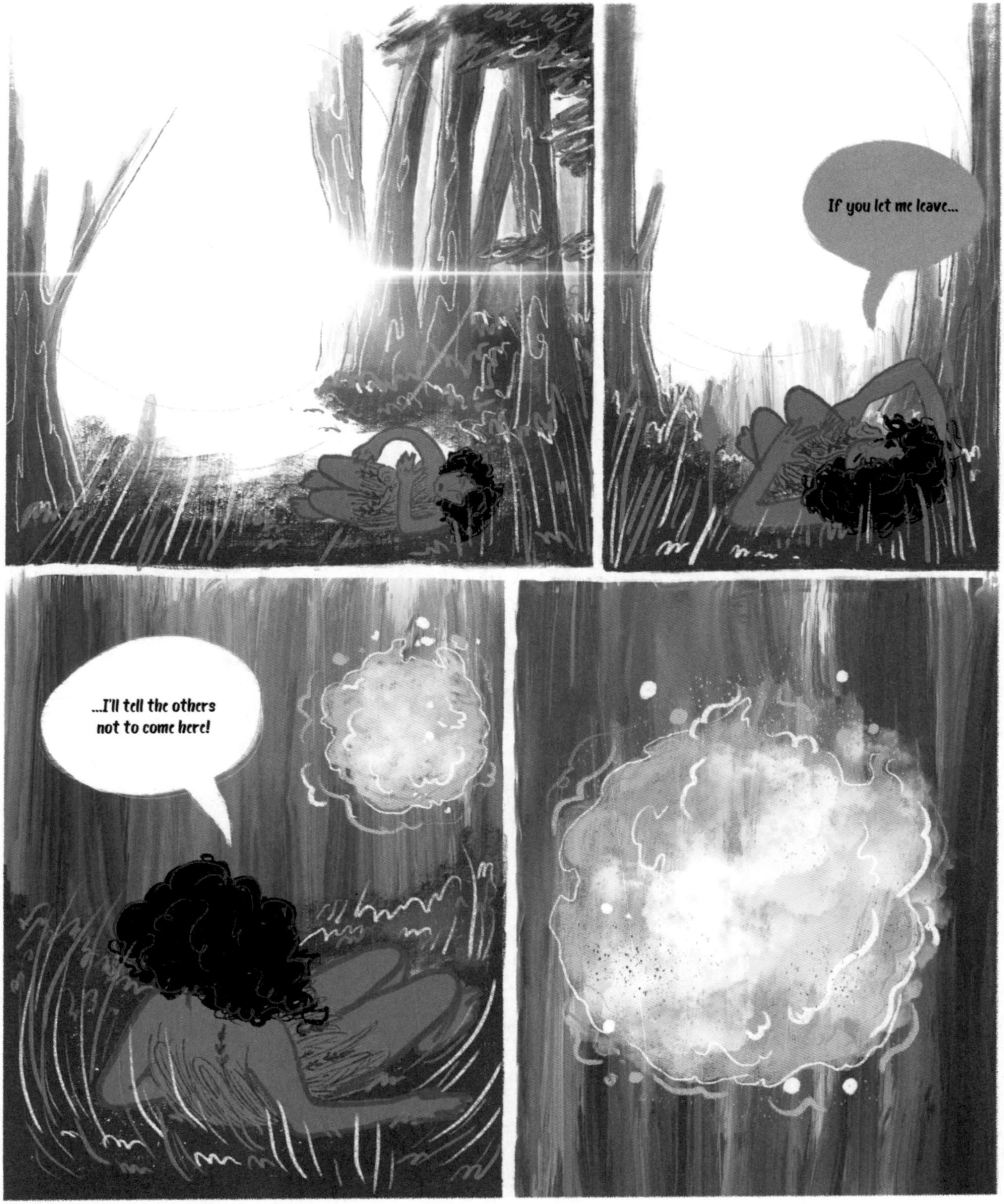
If you let me leave...
...I'll tell the others not to come here!

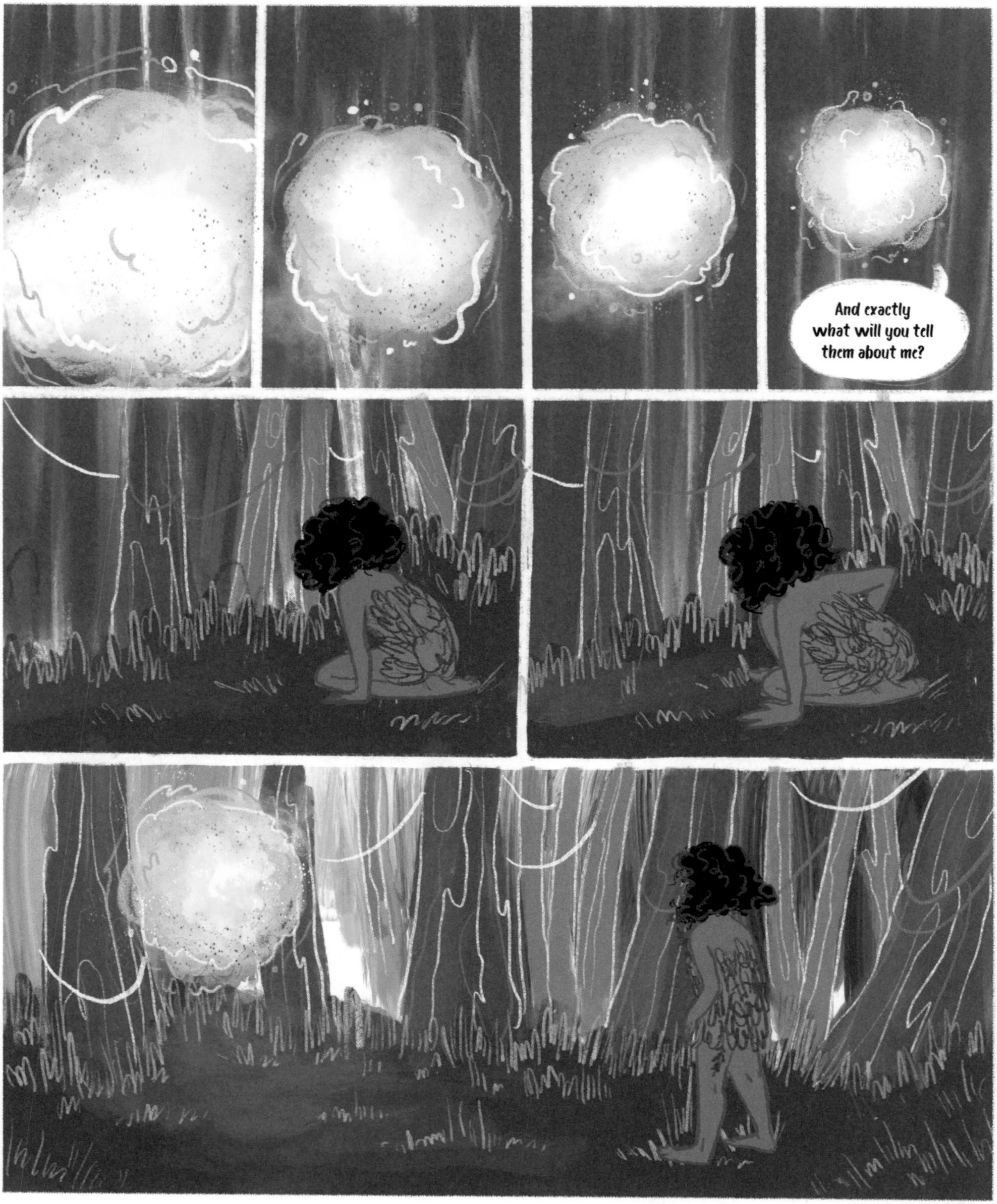
And exactly
what will you tell
them about me?

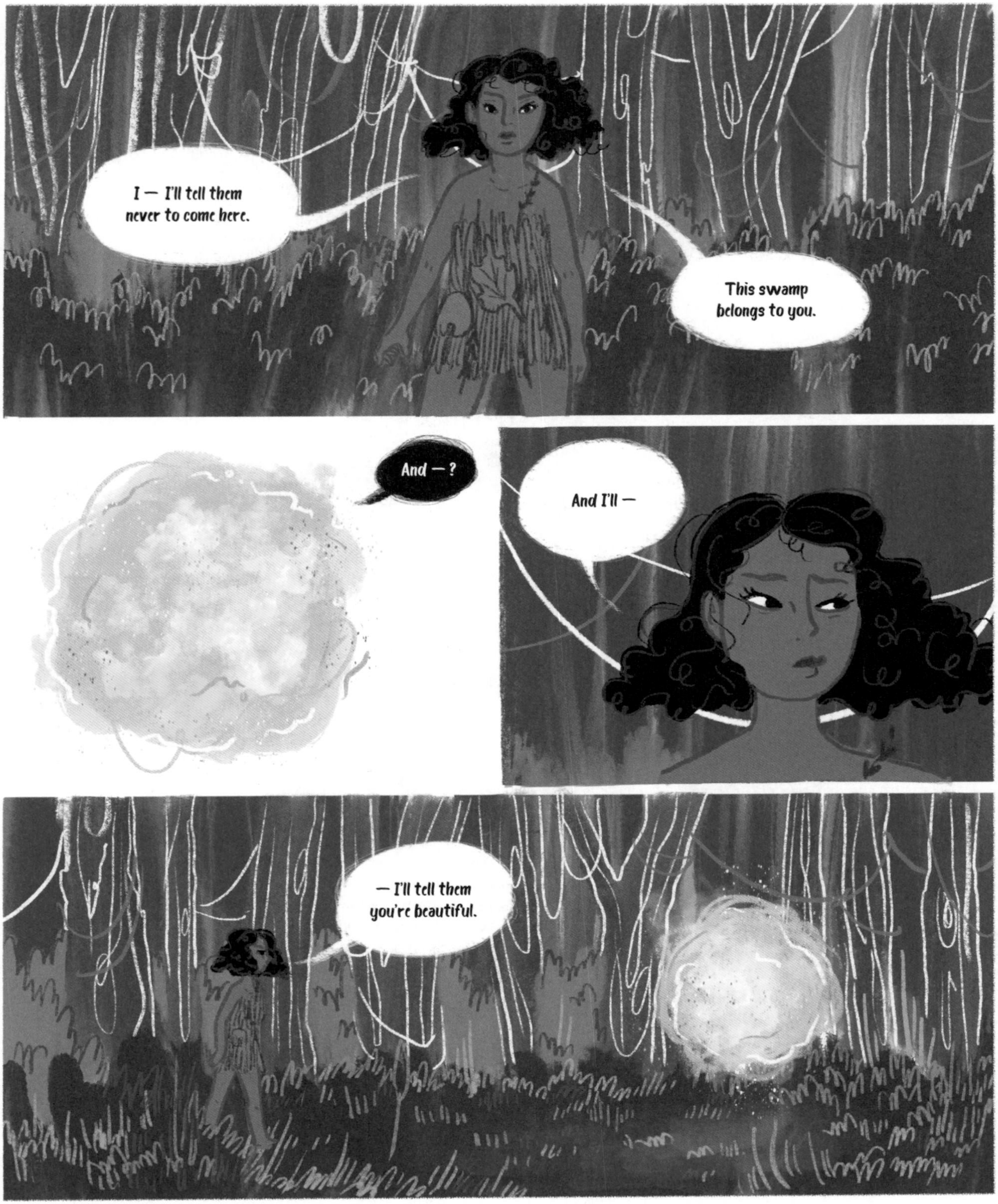
I — I'll tell them never to come here.
This swamp belongs to you.
And — ?
And I'll —
— I'll tell them you're beautiful.

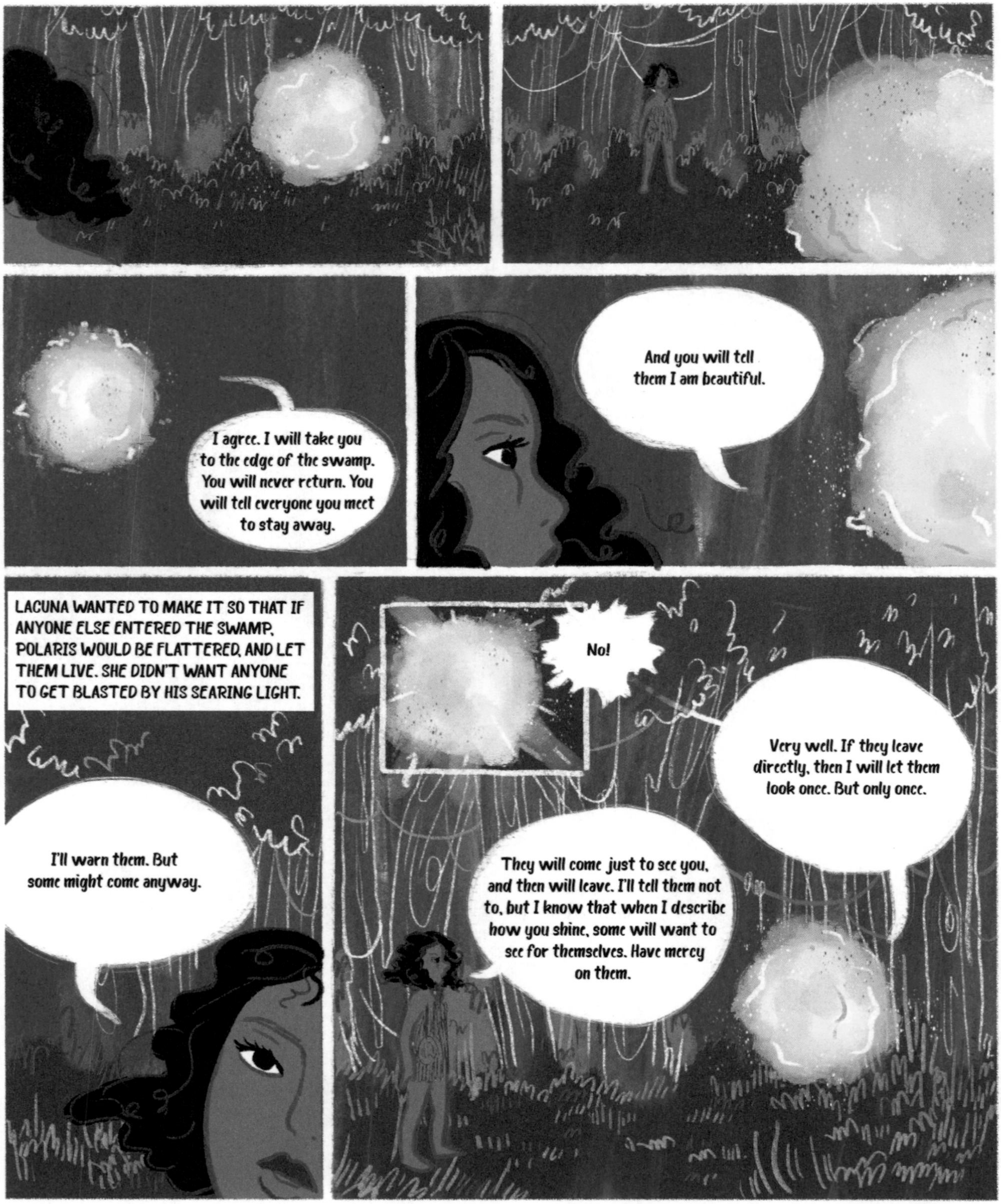
I agree. I will take you to the edge of the swamp. You will never return. You will tell everyone you meet to stay away.
And you will tell them I am beautiful.
LACUNA WANTED TO MAKE IT SO THAT IF ANYONE ELSE ENTERED THE SWAMP, POLARIS WOULD BE FLATTERED, AND LET THEM LIVE. SHE DIDN'T WANT ANYONE TO GET BLASTED BY HIS SEARING LIGHT.
I'll warn them. But some might come anyway.
No!
They will come just to see you, and then will leave. I'll tell them not to, but I know that when I describe how you shine, some will want to see for themselves. Have mercy on them.
Very well. If they leave directly, then I will let them look once. But only once.

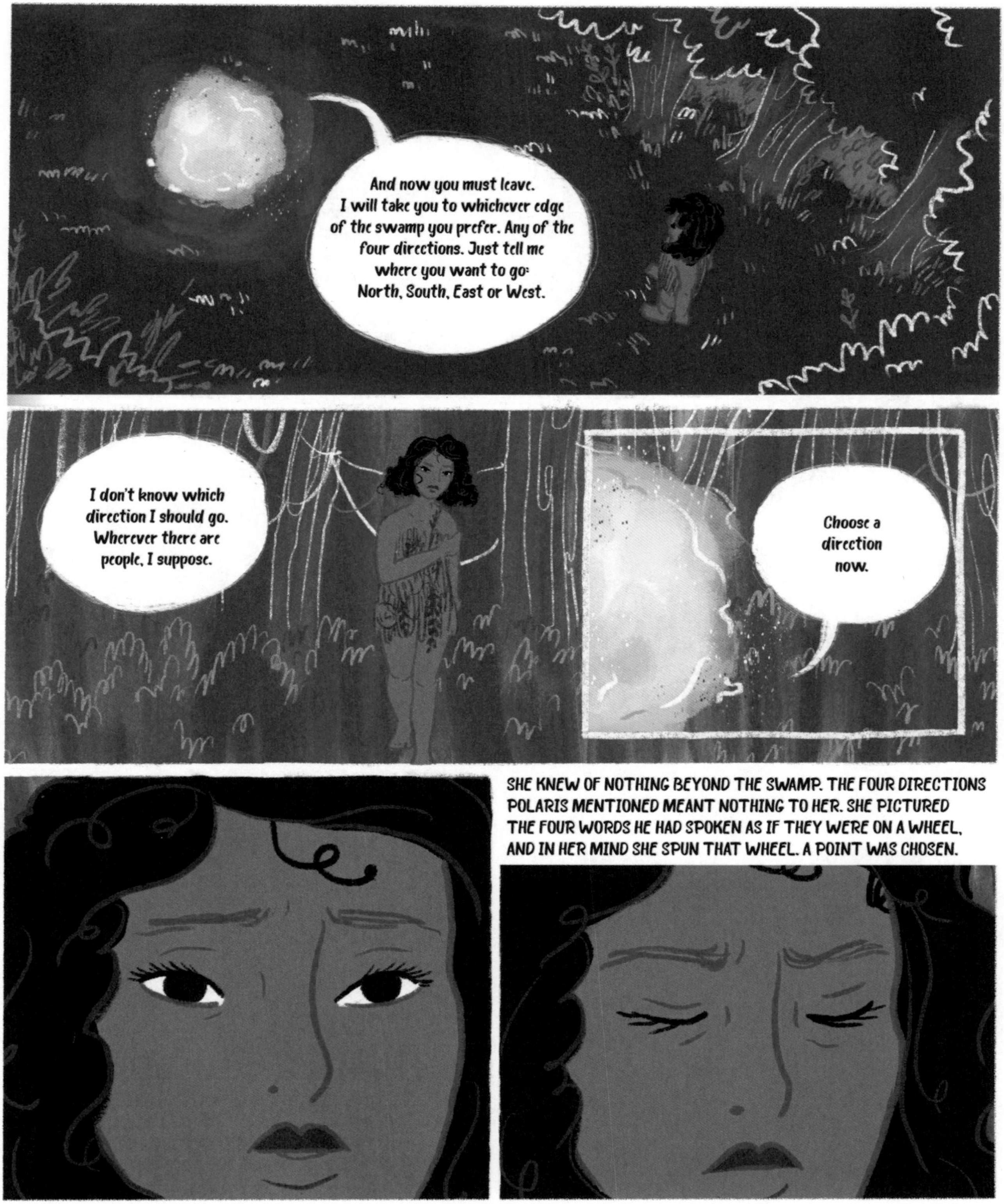
And now you must leave. I will take you to whichever edge of the swamp you prefer. Any of the four directions. Just tell me where you want to go: North, South, East or West.
I don't know which direction I should go. Wherever there are people, I suppose.
Choose a direction now.
SHE KNEW OF NOTHING BEYOND THE SWAMP. THE FOUR DIRECTIONS POLARIS MENTIONED MEANT NOTHING TO HER. SHE PICTURED THE FOUR WORDS HE HAD SPOKEN AS IF THEY WERE ON A WHEEL, AND IN HER MIND SHE SPUN THAT WHEEL. A POINT WAS CHOSEN.

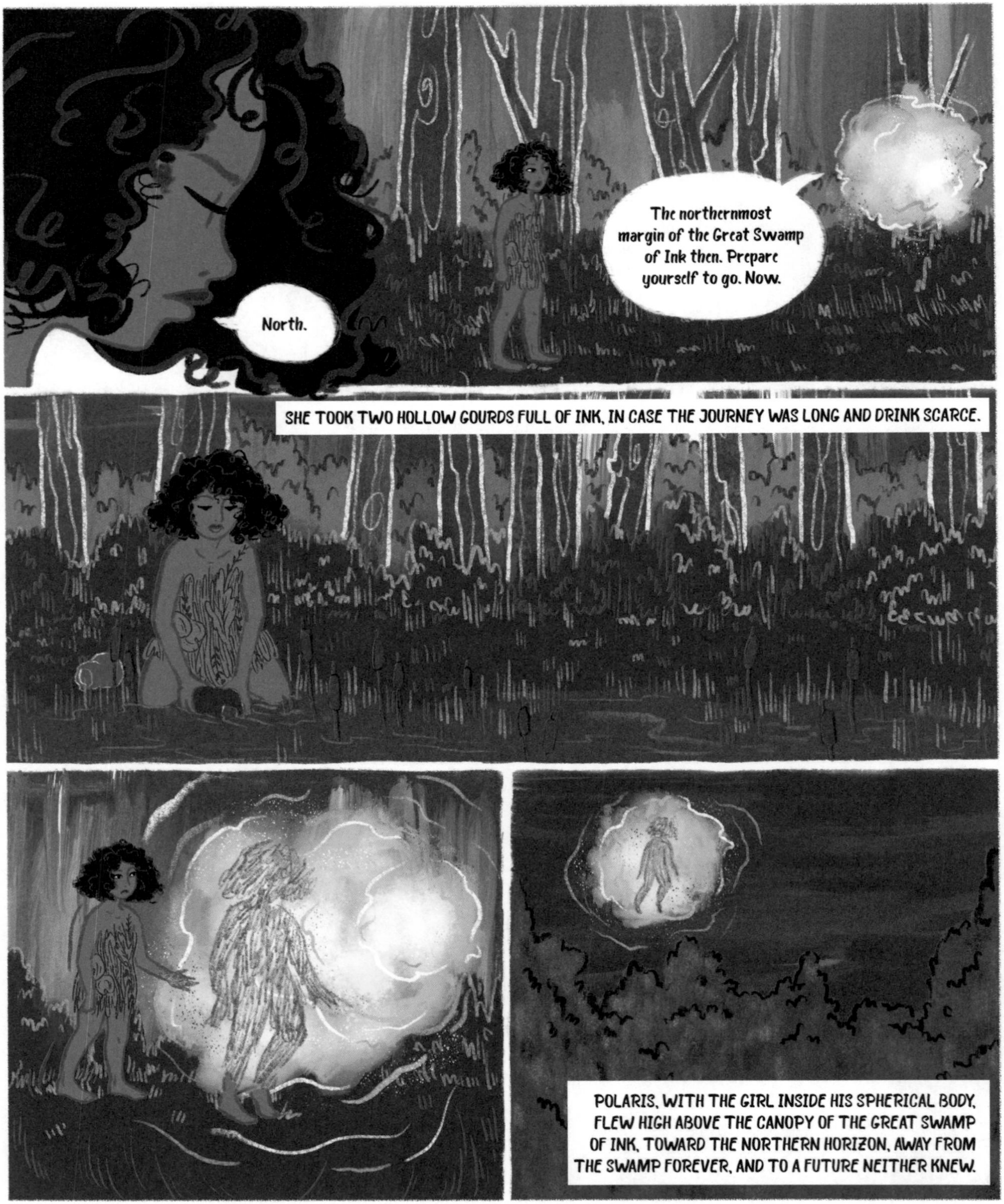
North.
The northernmost margin of the Great Swamp of Ink then. Prepare yourself to go. Now.
SHE TOOK TWO HOLLOW GOURDS FULL OF INK, IN CASE THE JOURNEY WAS LONG AND DRINK SCARCE.
POLARIS, WITH THE GIRL INSIDE HIS SPHERICAL BODY, FLEW HIGH ABOVE THE CANOPY OF THE GREAT SWAMP OF INK, TOWARD THE NORTHERN HORIZON, AWAY FROM THE SWAMP FOREVER, AND TO A FUTURE NEITHER KNEW.

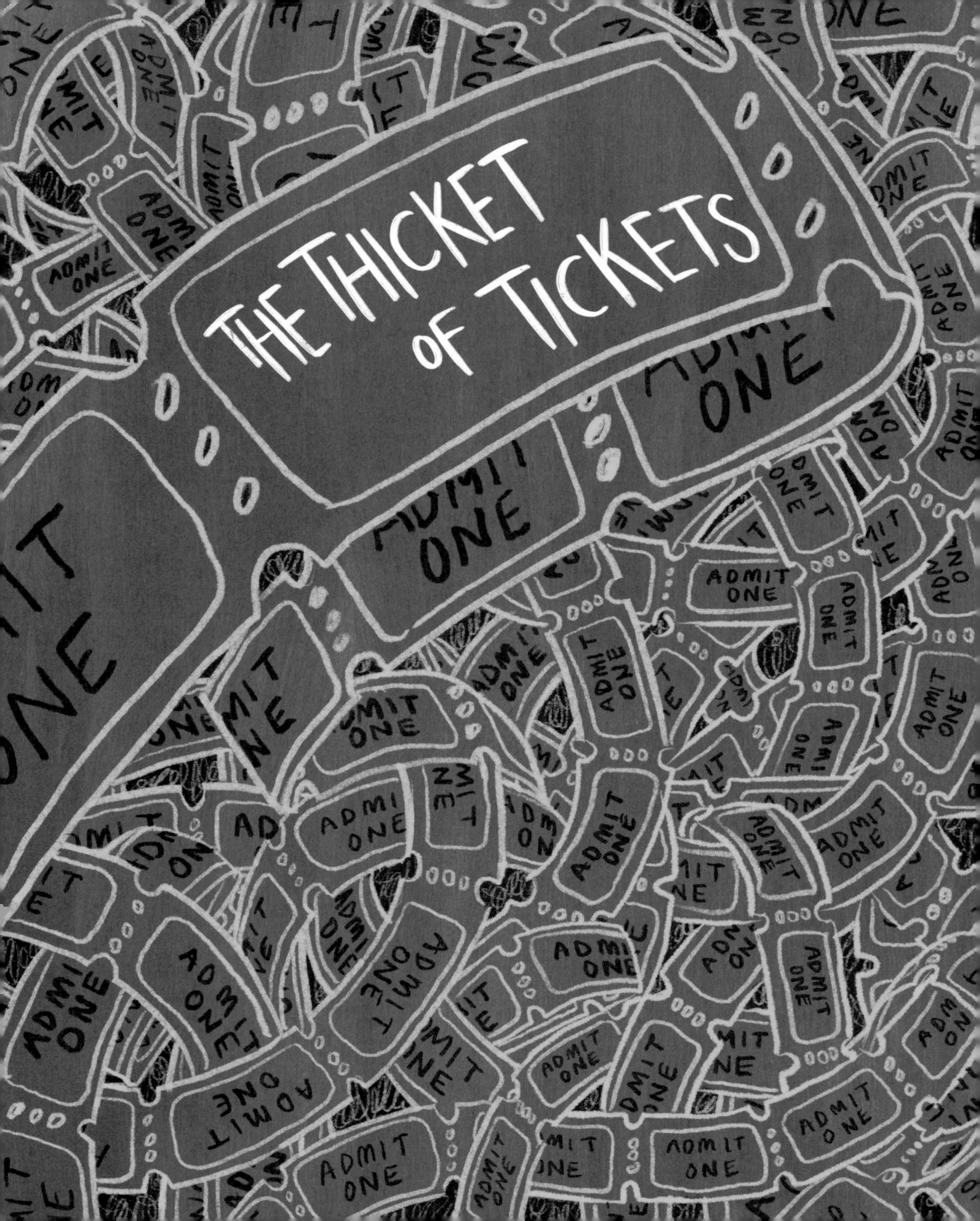
THE THICKET OF TICKETS
ADMIT ONE

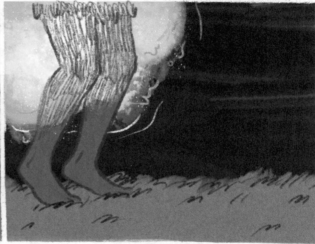

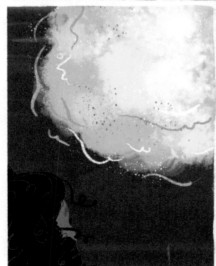

AFTER FLYING ALL NIGHT, POLARIS SET LACUNA DOWN AT THE NORTHERNMOST EDGE OF THE SWAMP.

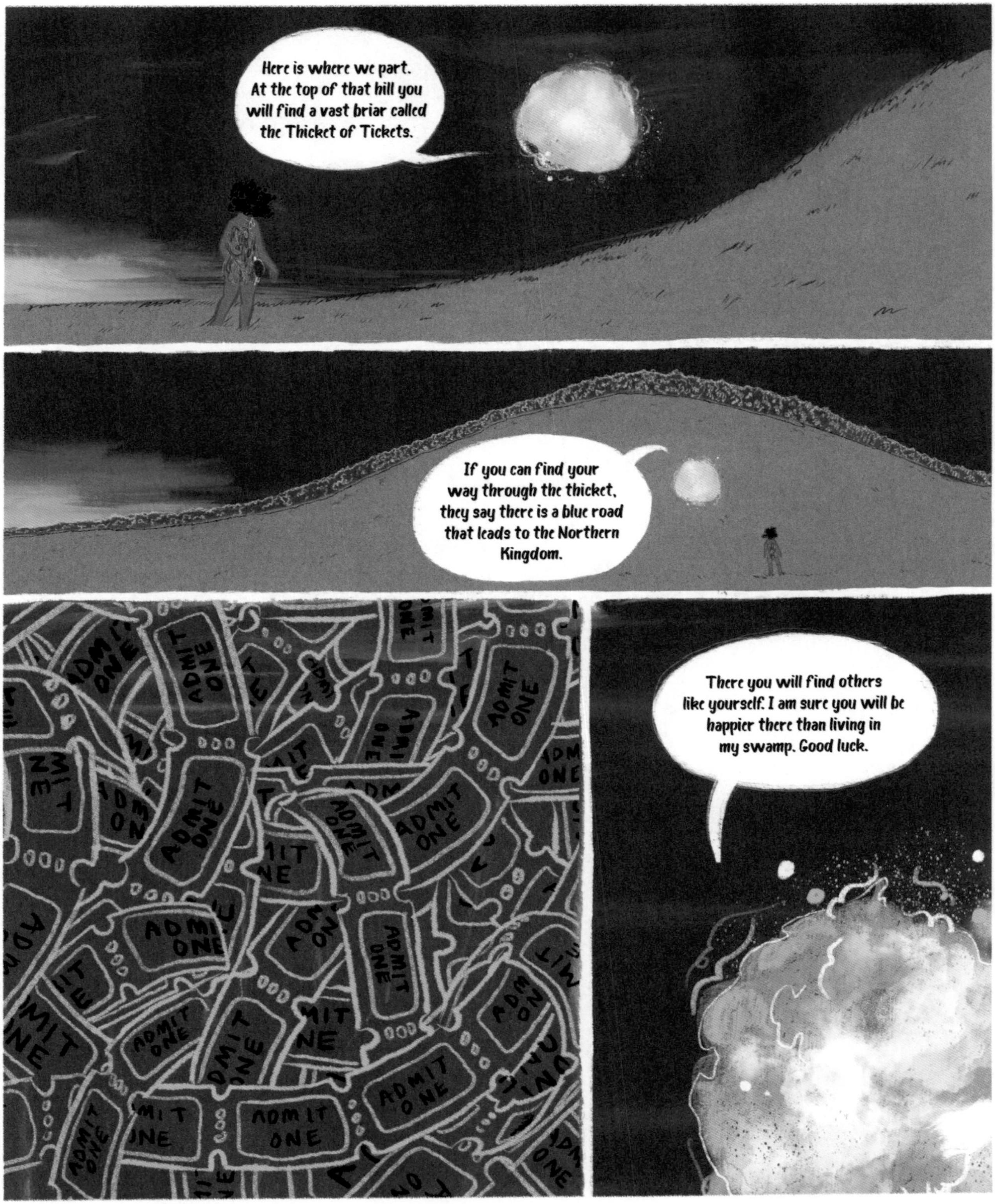
Here is where we part. At the top of that hill you will find a vast briar called the Thicket of Tickets.
If you can find your way through the thicket, they say there is a blue road that leads to the Northern Kingdom.
There you will find others like yourself. I am sure you will be happier there than living in my swamp. Good luck.

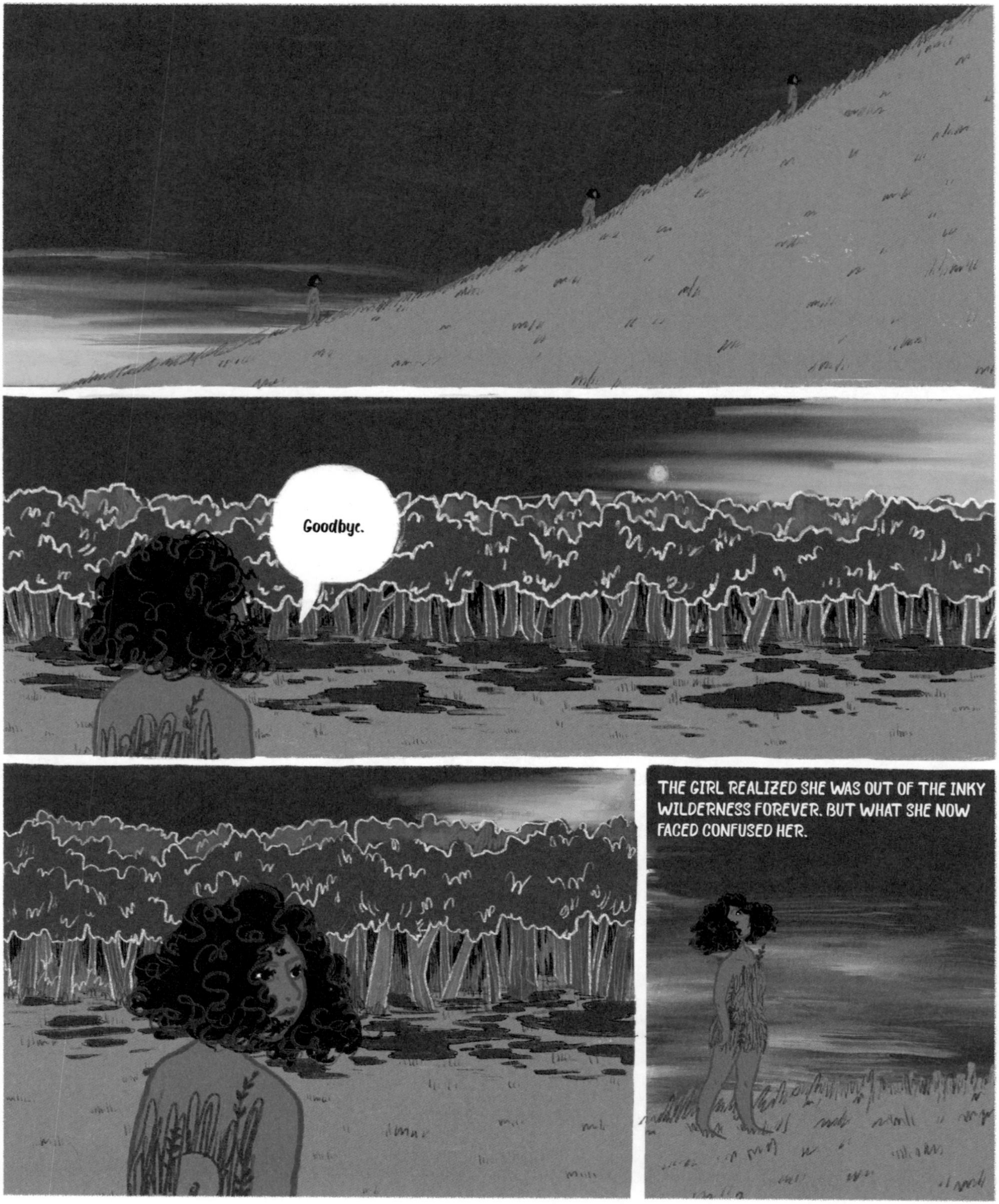
Goodbye.
THE GIRL REALIZED SHE WAS OUT OF THE INKY WILDERNESS FOREVER. BUT WHAT SHE NOW FACED CONFUSED HER.

THE THICKET OF TICKETS — AS POLARIS HAD CALLED IT — WAS THE MOST DENSE BRIAR SHE HAD EVER SEEN. IT STRETCHED TO HER LEFT AND RIGHT ALL THE WAY TO EACH HORIZON.

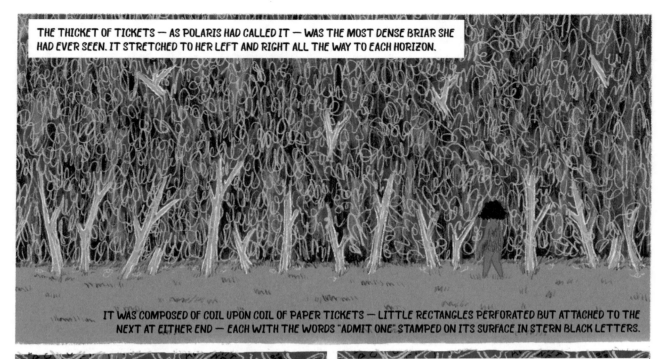

IT WAS COMPOSED OF COIL UPON COIL OF PAPER TICKETS — LITTLE RECTANGLES PERFORATED BUT ATTACHED TO THE NEXT AT EITHER END — EACH WITH THE WORDS "ADMIT ONE" STAMPED ON ITS SURFACE IN STERN BLACK LETTERS.

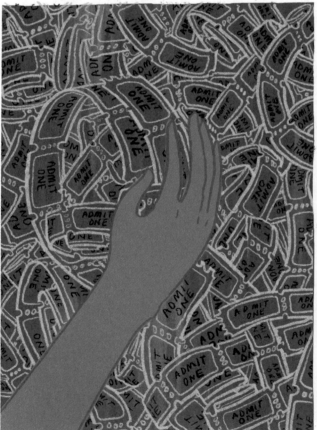

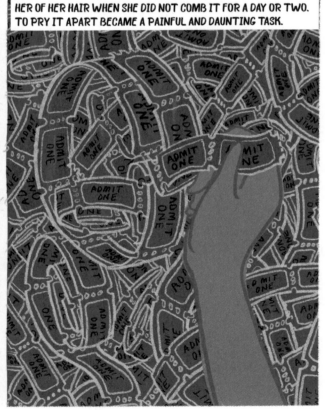

THE COILS OF PAPER TICKETS WERE SO TANGLED THEY REMINDED HER OF HER HAIR WHEN SHE DID NOT COMB IT FOR A DAY OR TWO. TO PRY IT APART BECAME A PAINFUL AND DAUNTING TASK.

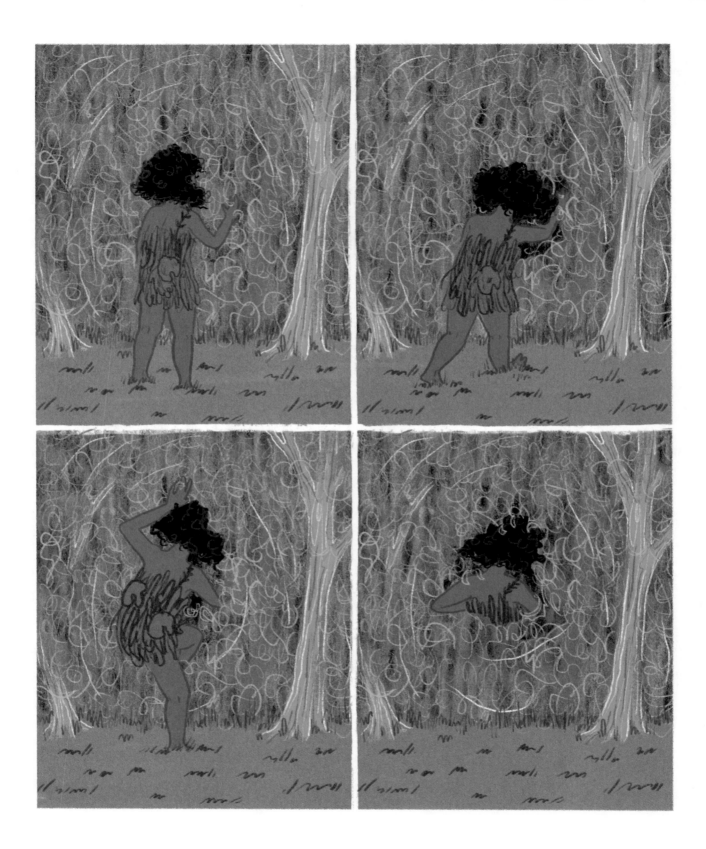

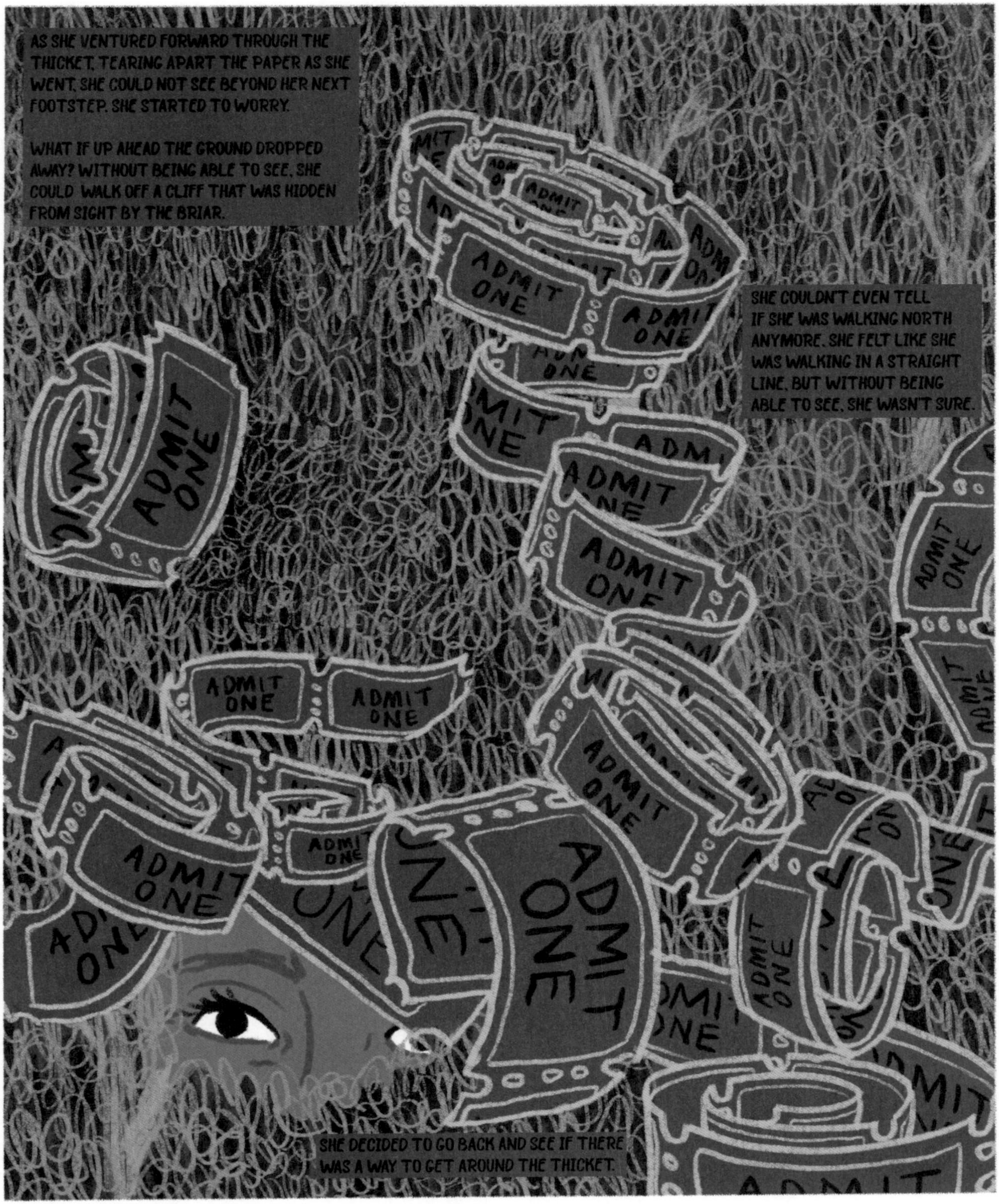
AS SHE VENTURED FORWARD THROUGH THE THICKET, TEARING APART THE PAPER AS SHE WENT, SHE COULD NOT SEE BEYOND HER NEXT FOOTSTEP. SHE STARTED TO WORRY.
WHAT IF UP AHEAD THE GROUND DROPPED AWAY? WITHOUT BEING ABLE TO SEE, SHE COULD WALK OFF A CLIFF THAT WAS HIDDEN FROM SIGHT BY THE BRIAR.
SHE COULDN'T EVEN TELL IF SHE WAS WALKING NORTH ANYMORE. SHE FELT LIKE SHE WAS WALKING IN A STRAIGHT LINE, BUT WITHOUT BEING ABLE TO SEE, SHE WASN'T SURE.
SHE DECIDED TO GO BACK AND SEE IF THERE WAS A WAY TO GET AROUND THE THICKET.

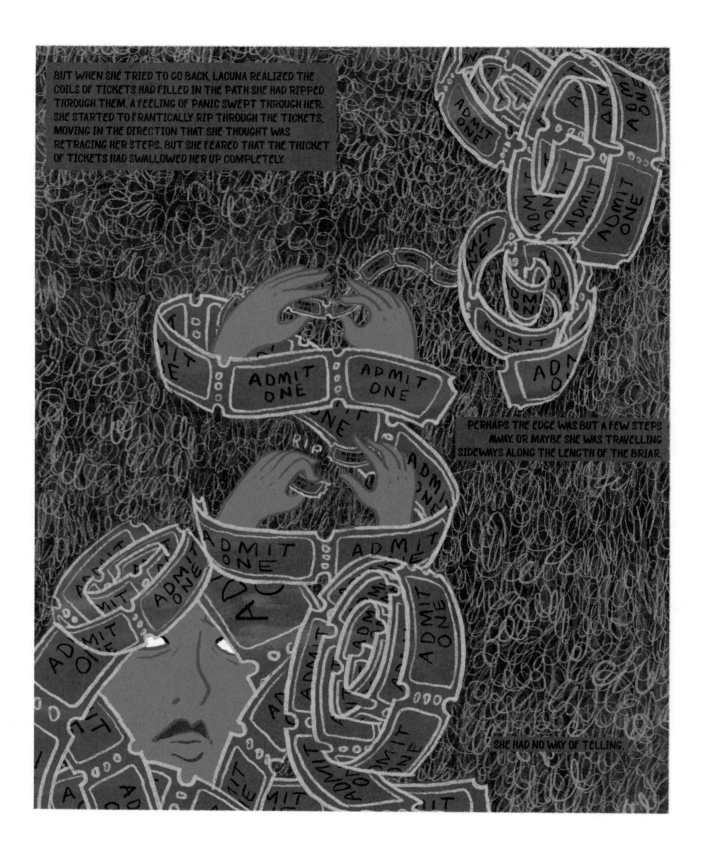

BUT WHEN SHE TRIED TO GO BACK, LACUNA REALIZED THE COILS OF TICKETS HAD FILLED IN THE PATH SHE HAD RIPPED THROUGH THEM. A FEELING OF PANIC SWEPT THROUGH HER. SHE STARTED TO FRANTICALLY RIP THROUGH THE TICKETS, MOVING IN THE DIRECTION THAT SHE THOUGHT WAS RETRACING HER STEPS. BUT SHE FEARED THAT THE THICKET OF TICKETS HAD SWALLOWED HER UP COMPLETELY.

PERHAPS THE EDGE WAS BUT A FEW STEPS AWAY. OR MAYBE SHE WAS TRAVELLING SIDEWAYS ALONG THE LENGTH OF THE BRIAR.

SHE HAD NO WAY OF TELLING.

28

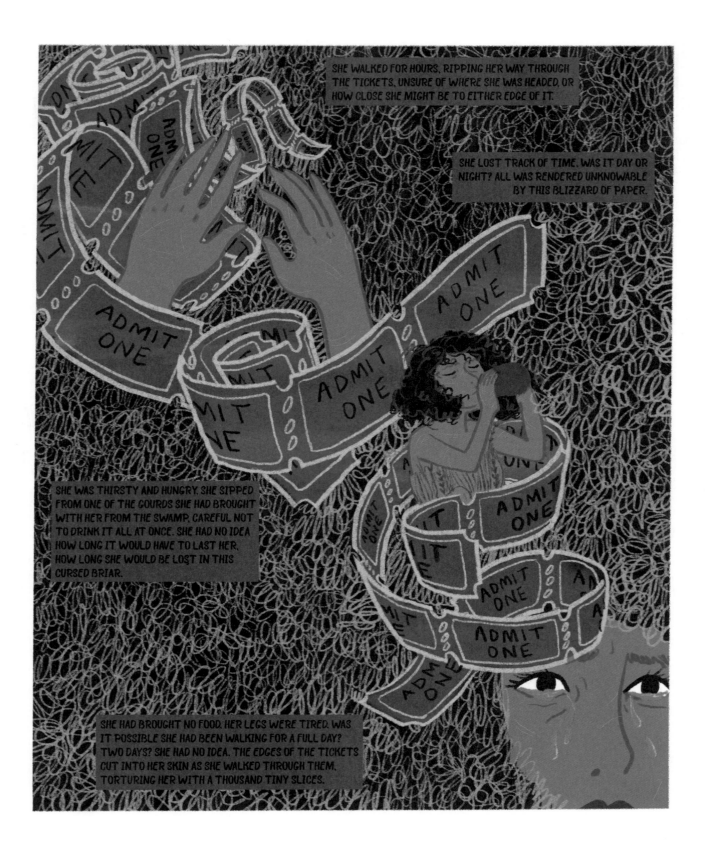

SHE WALKED FOR HOURS, RIPPING HER WAY THROUGH THE TICKETS, UNSURE OF WHERE SHE WAS HEADED, OR HOW CLOSE SHE MIGHT BE TO EITHER EDGE OF IT.

SHE LOST TRACK OF TIME. WAS IT DAY OR NIGHT? ALL WAS RENDERED UNKNOWABLE BY THIS BLIZZARD OF PAPER.

SHE WAS THIRSTY AND HUNGRY. SHE SIPPED FROM ONE OF THE GOURDS SHE HAD BROUGHT WITH HER FROM THE SWAMP, CAREFUL NOT TO DRINK IT ALL AT ONCE. SHE HAD NO IDEA HOW LONG IT WOULD HAVE TO LAST HER, HOW LONG SHE WOULD BE LOST IN THIS CURSED BRIAR.

SHE HAD BROUGHT NO FOOD. HER LEGS WERE TIRED. WAS IT POSSIBLE SHE HAD BEEN WALKING FOR A FULL DAY? TWO DAYS? SHE HAD NO IDEA. THE EDGES OF THE TICKETS CUT INTO HER SKIN AS SHE WALKED THROUGH THEM, TORTURING HER WITH A THOUSAND TINY SLICES.

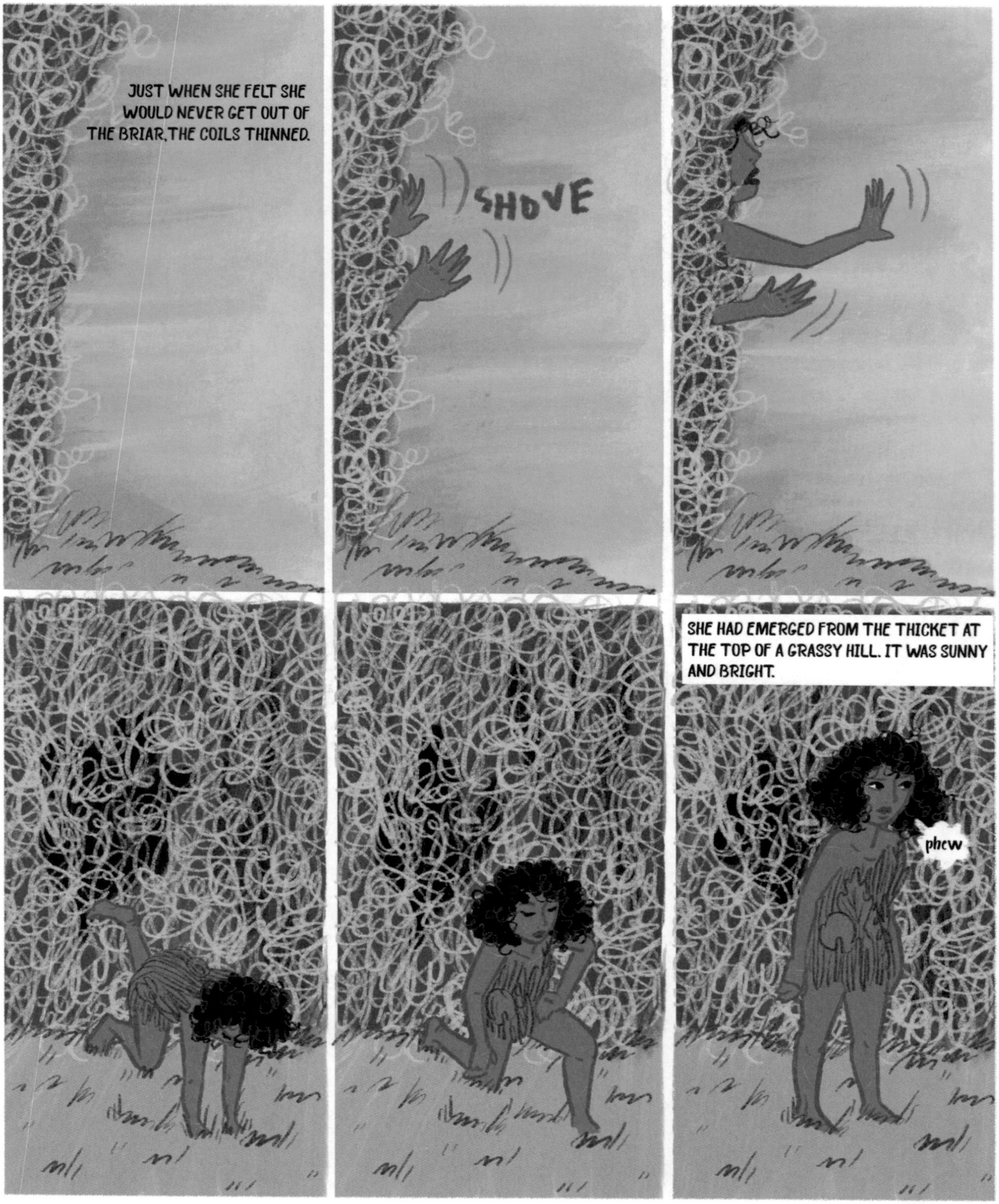
JUST WHEN SHE FELT SHE WOULD NEVER GET OUT OF THE BRIAR, THE COILS THINNED.
SHOVE
SHE HAD EMERGED FROM THE THICKET AT THE TOP OF A GRASSY HILL. IT WAS SUNNY AND BRIGHT.
phew

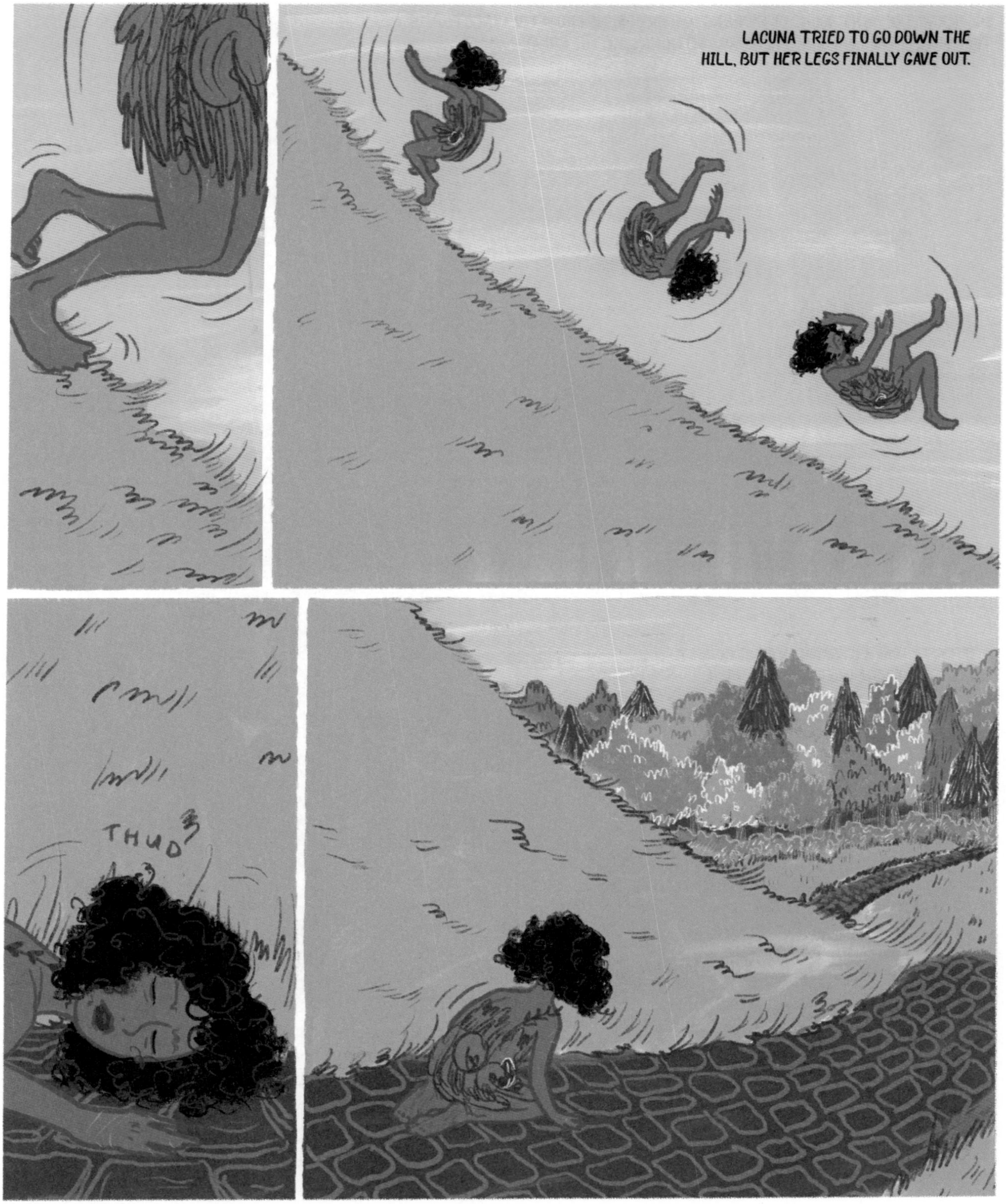
LACUNA TRIED TO GO DOWN THE HILL, BUT HER LEGS FINALLY GAVE OUT.
THUD

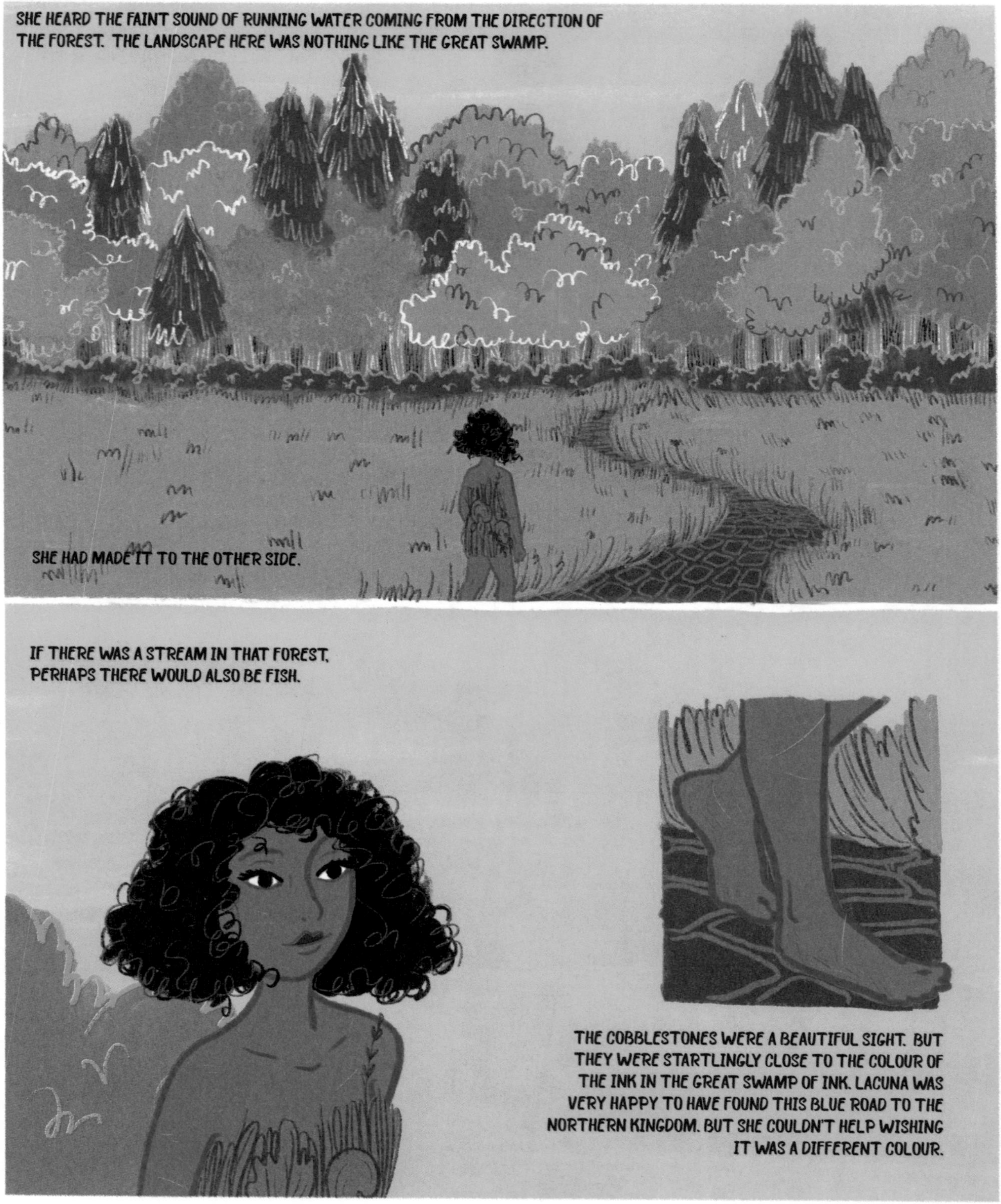
SHE HEARD THE FAINT SOUND OF RUNNING WATER COMING FROM THE DIRECTION OF THE FOREST. THE LANDSCAPE HERE WAS NOTHING LIKE THE GREAT SWAMP.
SHE HAD MADE IT TO THE OTHER SIDE.
IF THERE WAS A STREAM IN THAT FOREST, PERHAPS THERE WOULD ALSO BE FISH.
THE COBBLESTONES WERE A BEAUTIFUL SIGHT. BUT THEY WERE STARTLINGLY CLOSE TO THE COLOUR OF THE INK IN THE GREAT SWAMP OF INK. LACUNA WAS VERY HAPPY TO HAVE FOUND THIS BLUE ROAD TO THE NORTHERN KINGDOM. BUT SHE COULDN'T HELP WISHING IT WAS A DIFFERENT COLOUR.

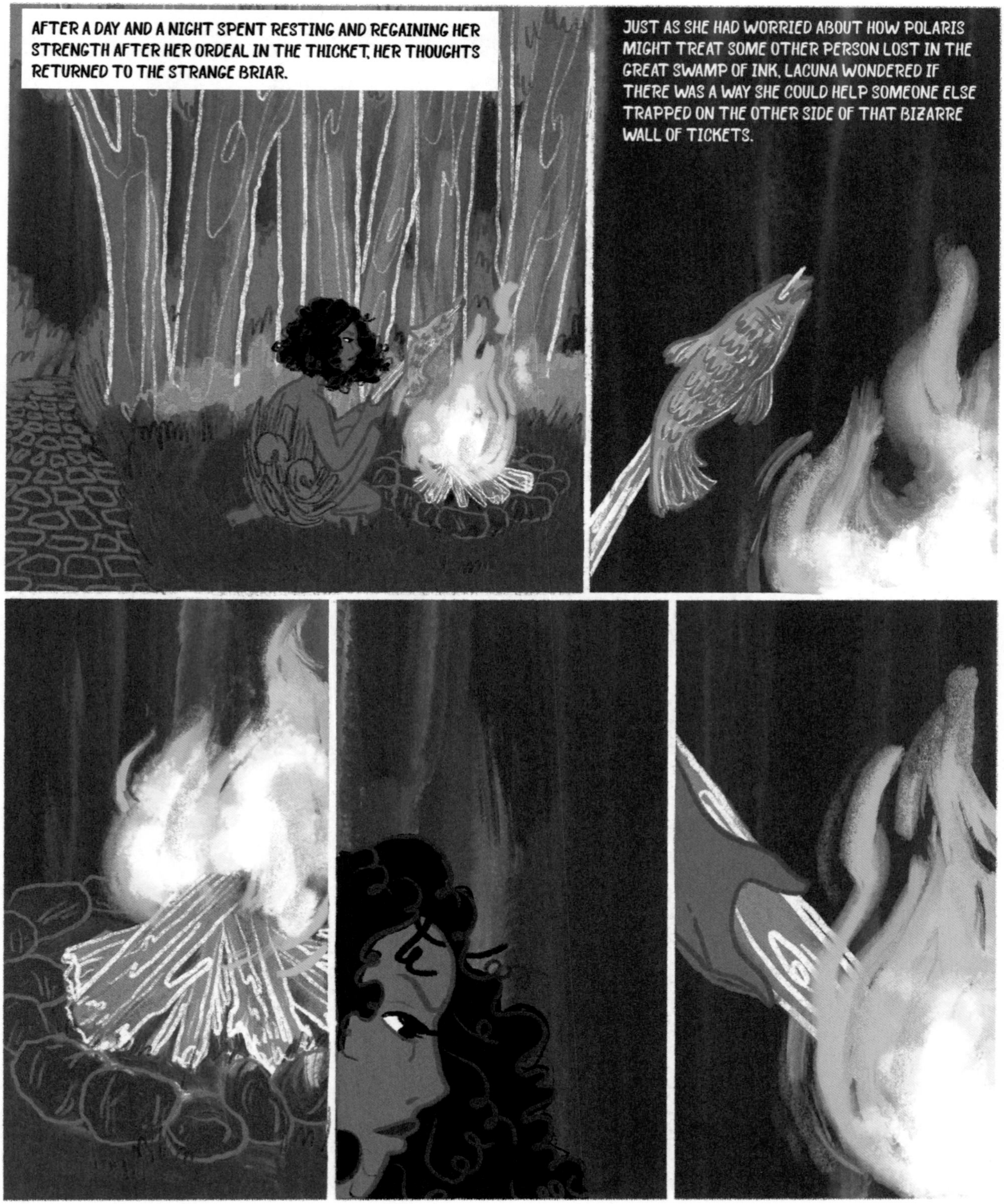
AFTER A DAY AND A NIGHT SPENT RESTING AND REGAINING HER STRENGTH AFTER HER ORDEAL IN THE THICKET, HER THOUGHTS RETURNED TO THE STRANGE BRIAR.
JUST AS SHE HAD WORRIED ABOUT HOW POLARIS MIGHT TREAT SOME OTHER PERSON LOST IN THE GREAT SWAMP OF INK, LACUNA WONDERED IF THERE WAS A WAY SHE COULD HELP SOMEONE ELSE TRAPPED ON THE OTHER SIDE OF THAT BIZARRE WALL OF TICKETS.

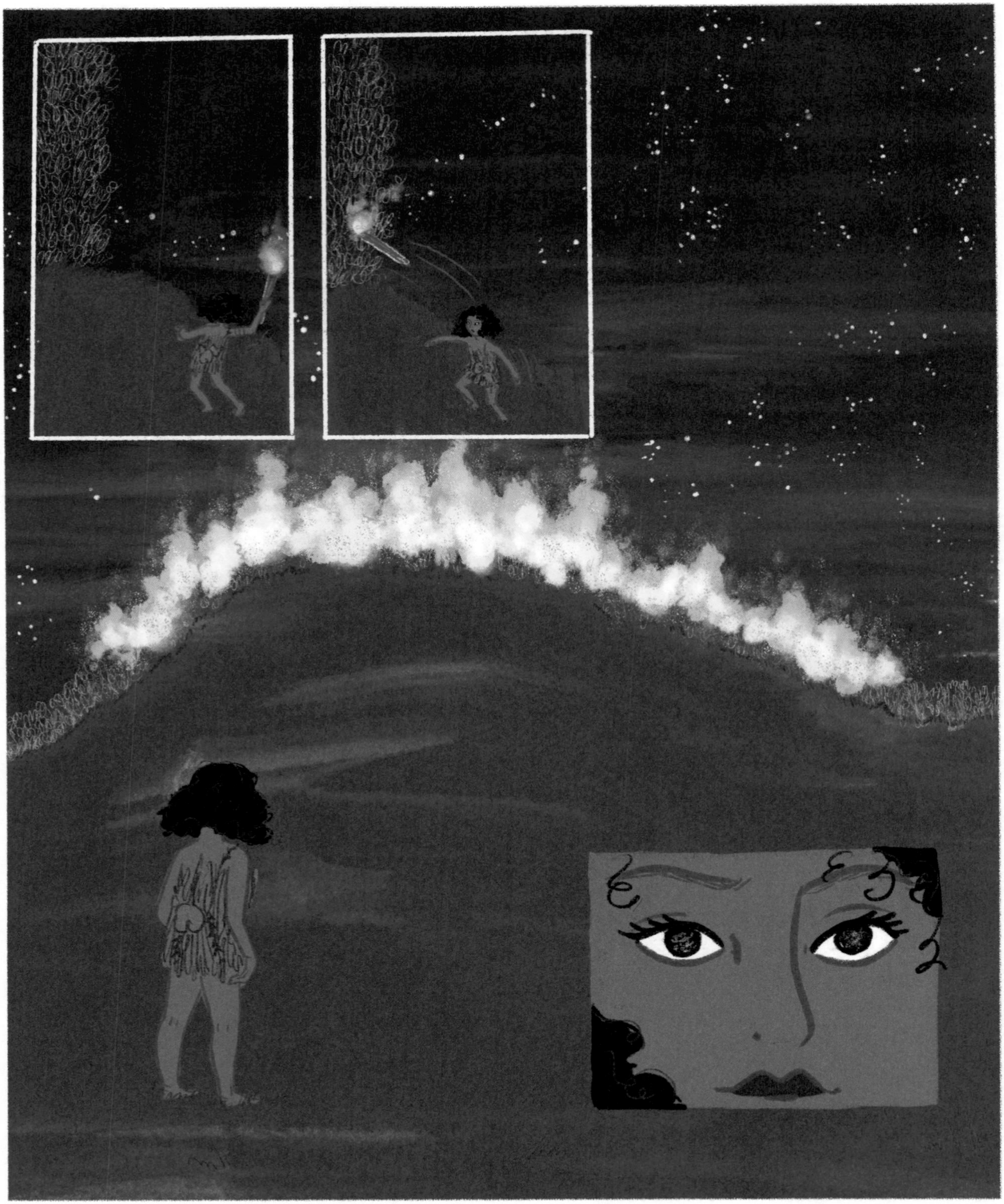

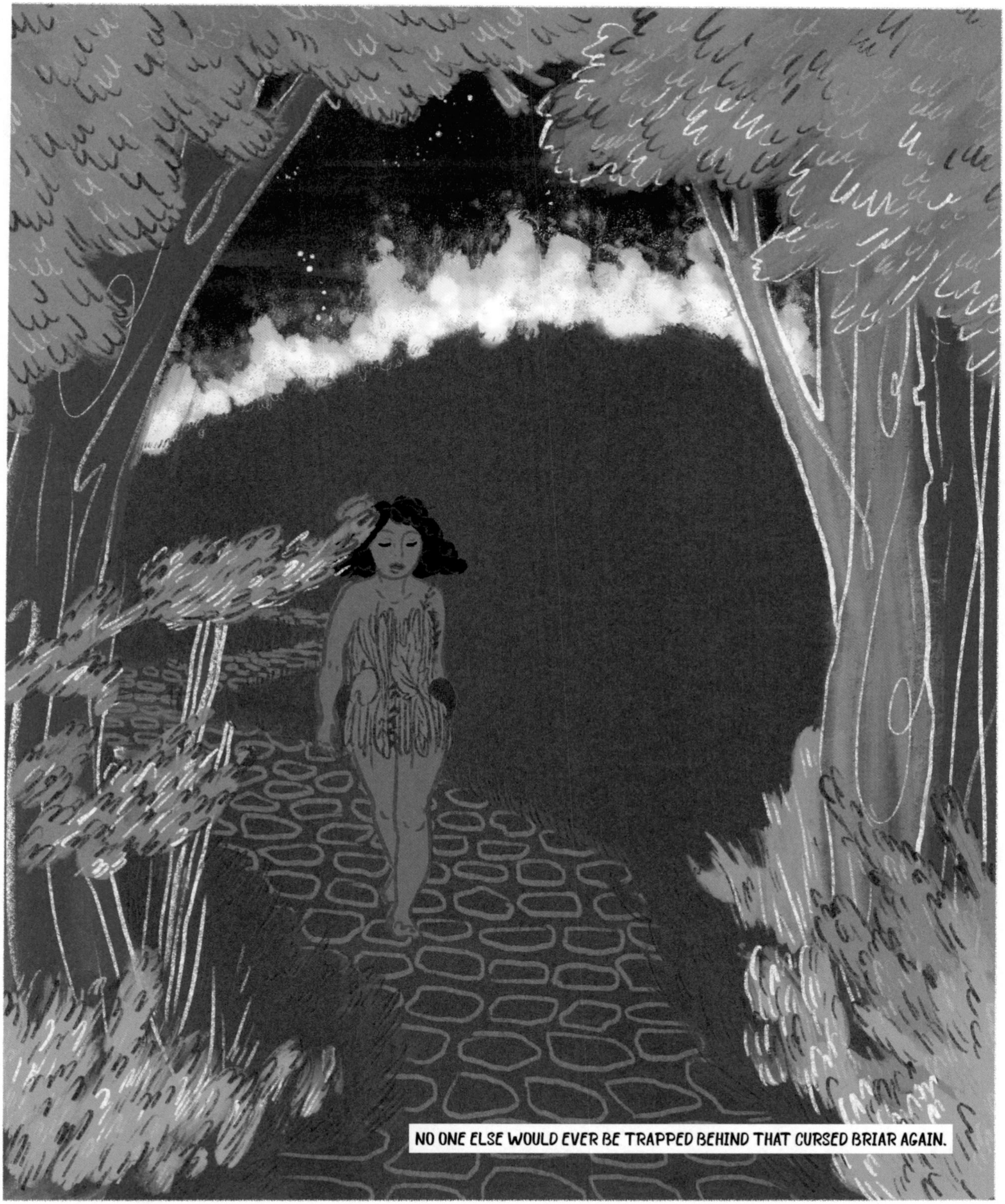
NO ONE ELSE WOULD EVER BE TRAPPED BEHIND THAT CURSED BRIAR AGAIN.

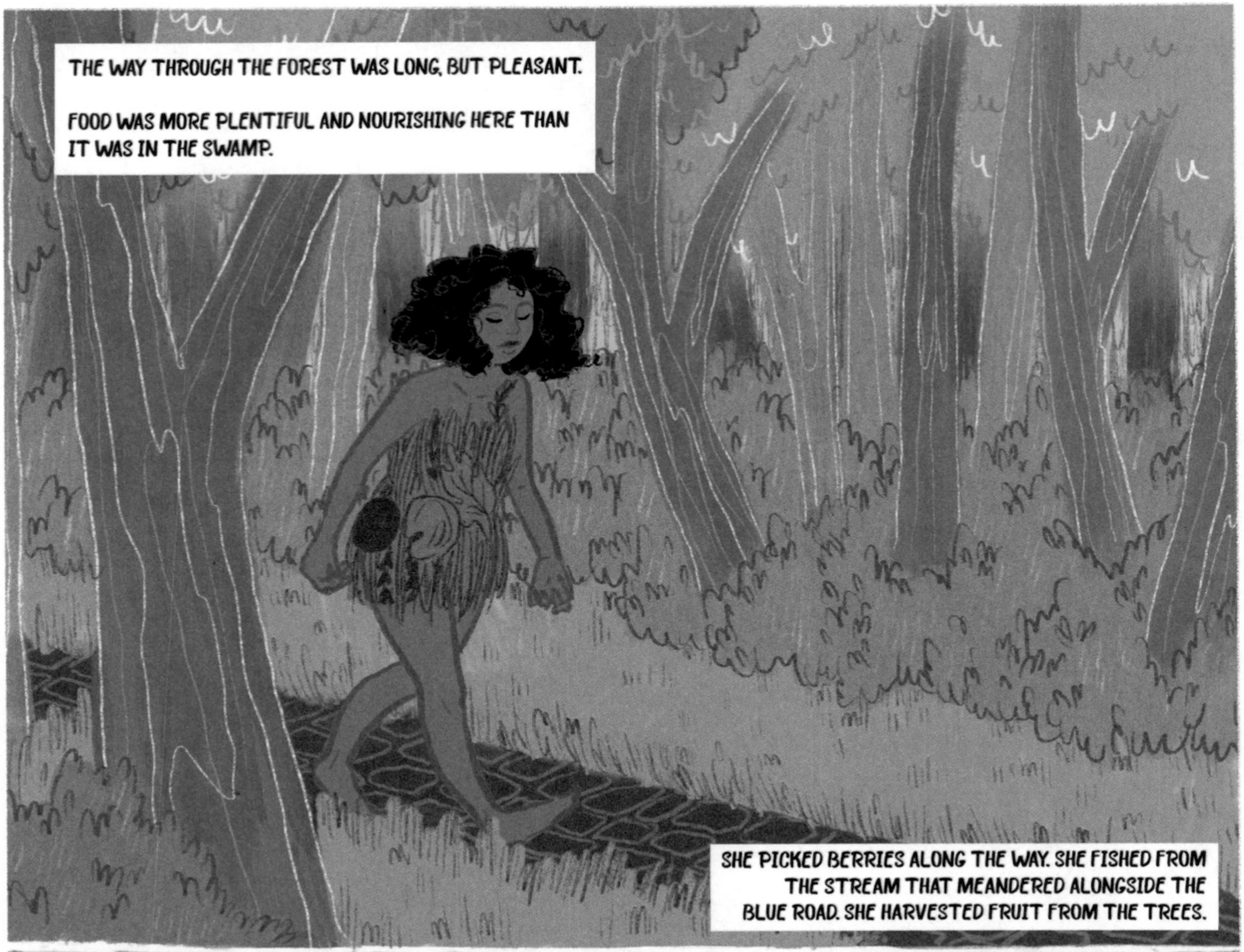
THE WAY THROUGH THE FOREST WAS LONG, BUT PLEASANT.
FOOD WAS MORE PLENTIFUL AND NOURISHING HERE THAN IT WAS IN THE SWAMP.
SHE PICKED BERRIES ALONG THE WAY. SHE FISHED FROM THE STREAM THAT MEANDERED ALONGSIDE THE BLUE ROAD. SHE HARVESTED FRUIT FROM THE TREES.

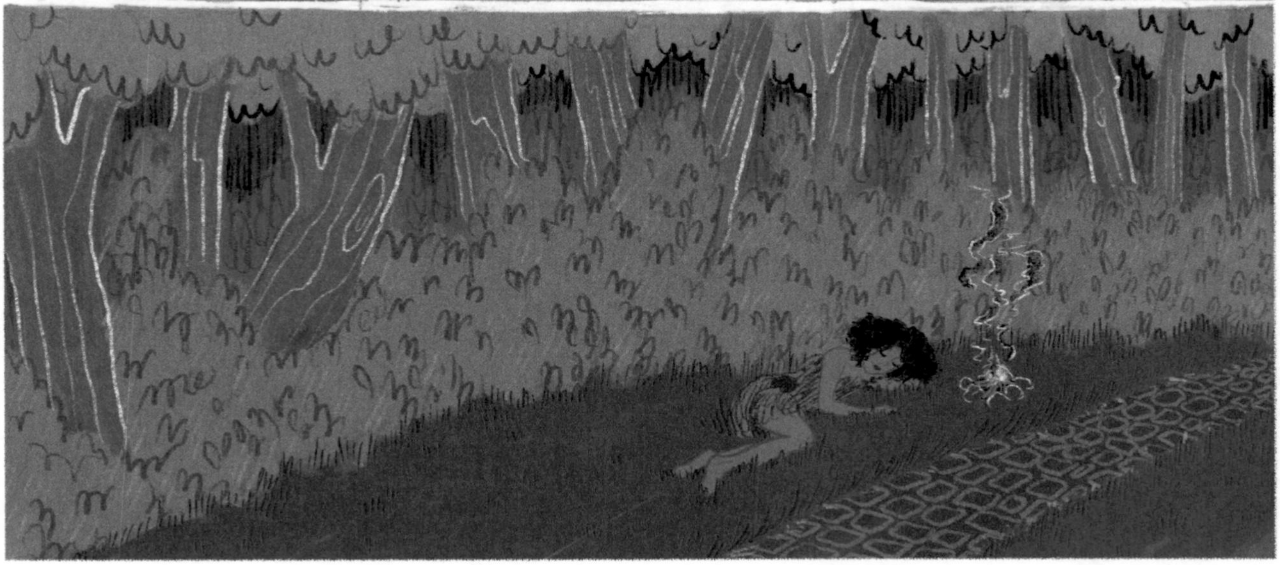

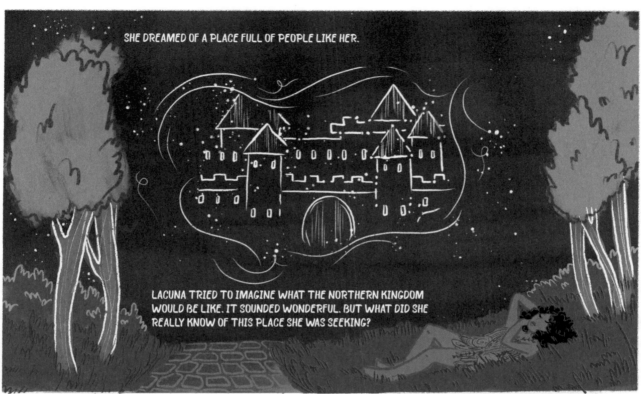

SHE DREAMED OF A PLACE FULL OF PEOPLE LIKE HER.

LACUNA TRIED TO IMAGINE WHAT THE NORTHERN KINGDOM WOULD BE LIKE. IT SOUNDED WONDERFUL. BUT WHAT DID SHE REALLY KNOW OF THIS PLACE SHE WAS SEEKING?

THE WATER IN THE STREAM WAS CLEAN AND FRESH, NOTHING LIKE THE FOUL INK FROM THE SWAMP. NEVERTHELESS, SHE USED ONLY ONE GOURD FOR WATER. THE OTHER ONE SHE LEFT FULL OF INK. THE SWAMP HAD BEEN HER HOME FOR AS LONG AS SHE COULD REMEMBER. SHE WOULD NEVER HAVE TO DRINK FROM IT AGAIN. SHE CHOSE TO KEEP ONE INK-FILLED GOURD AS A REMINDER OF WHERE SHE HAD COME FROM.

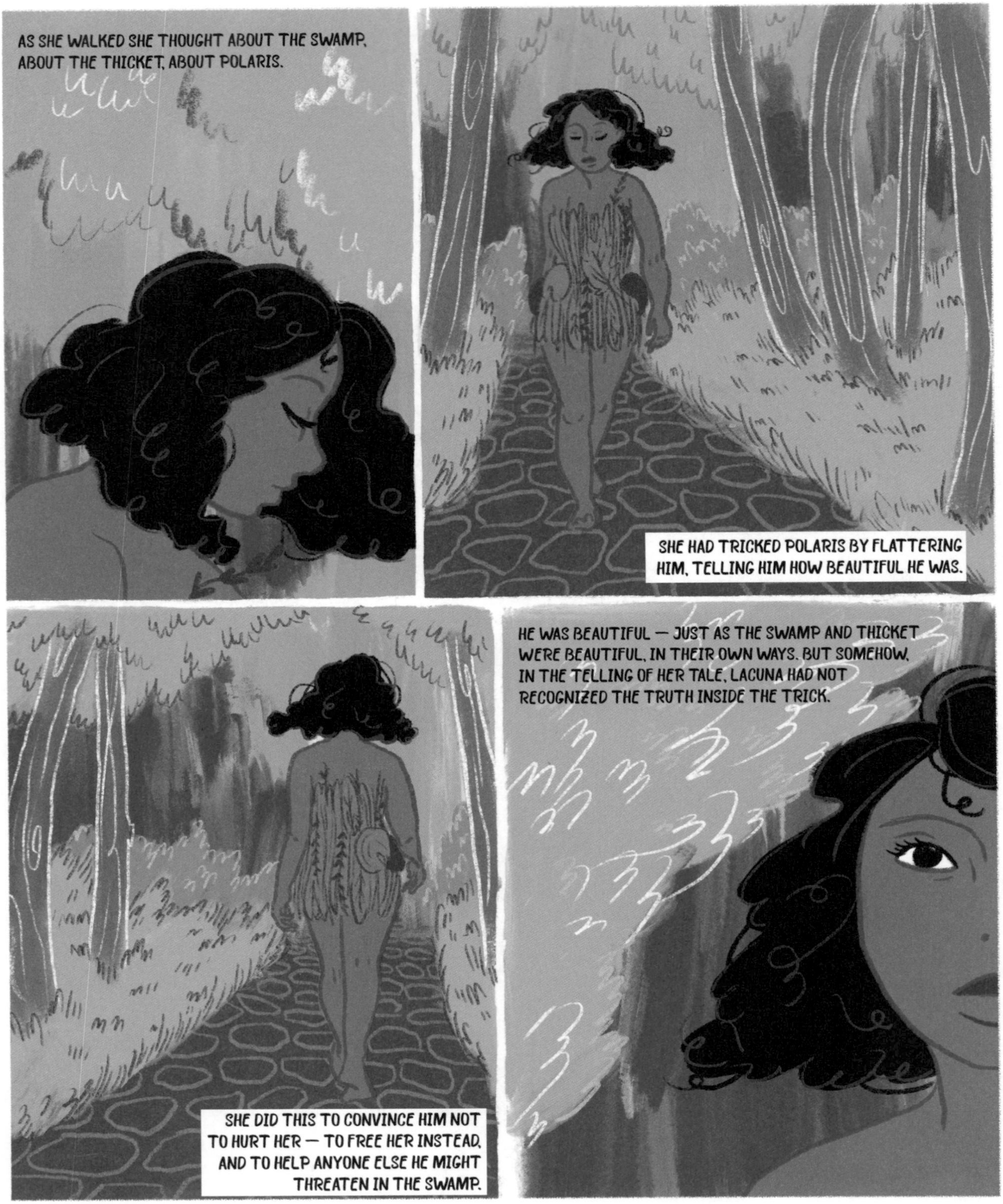
AS SHE WALKED SHE THOUGHT ABOUT THE SWAMP, ABOUT THE THICKET, ABOUT POLARIS.
SHE HAD TRICKED POLARIS BY FLATTERING HIM, TELLING HIM HOW BEAUTIFUL HE WAS.
SHE DID THIS TO CONVINCE HIM NOT TO HURT HER — TO FREE HER INSTEAD, AND TO HELP ANYONE ELSE HE MIGHT THREATEN IN THE SWAMP.
HE WAS BEAUTIFUL — JUST AS THE SWAMP AND THICKET WERE BEAUTIFUL, IN THEIR OWN WAYS. BUT SOMEHOW, IN THE TELLING OF HER TALE, LACUNA HAD NOT RECOGNIZED THE TRUTH INSIDE THE TRICK.

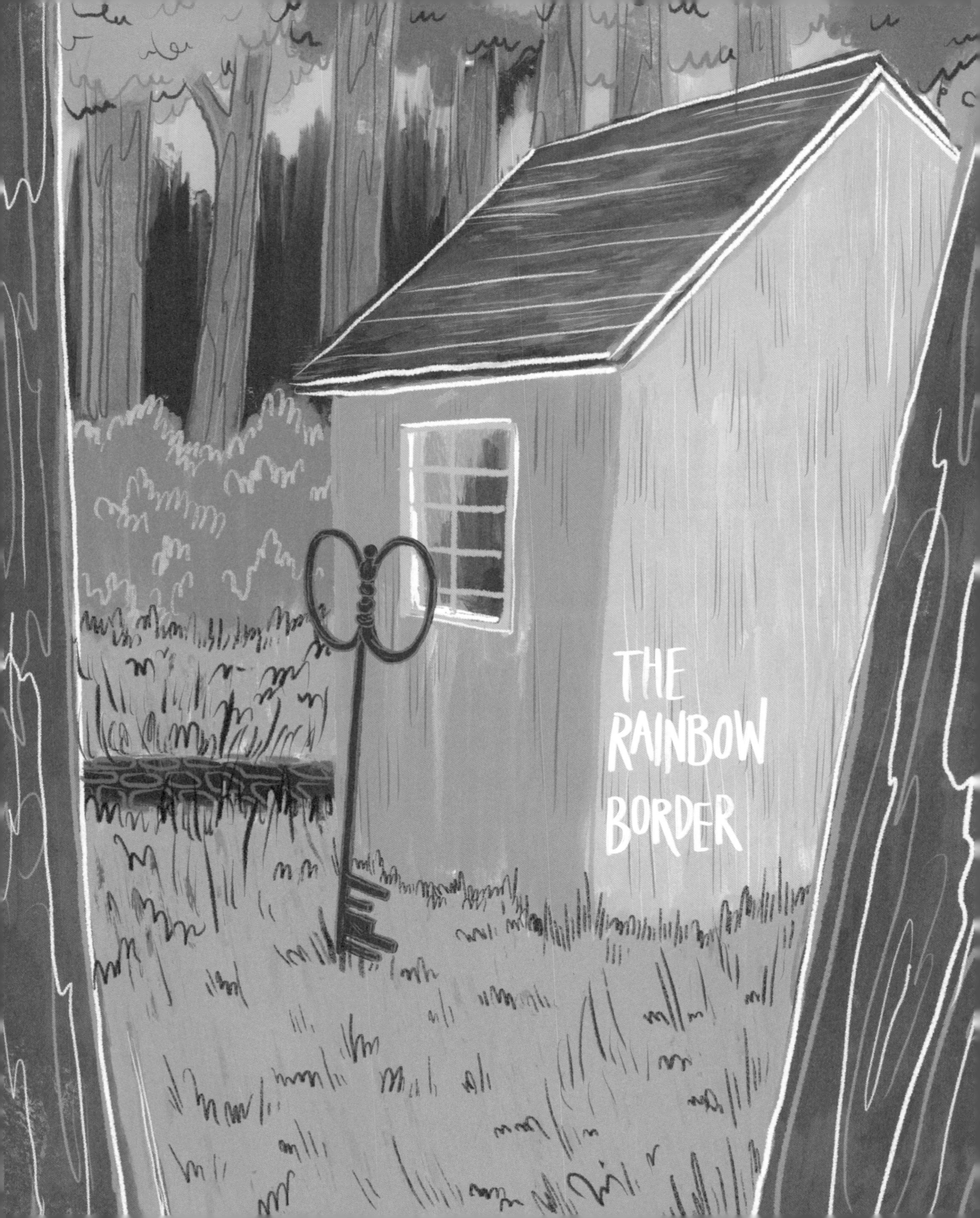
THE
RAINBOW
BORDER

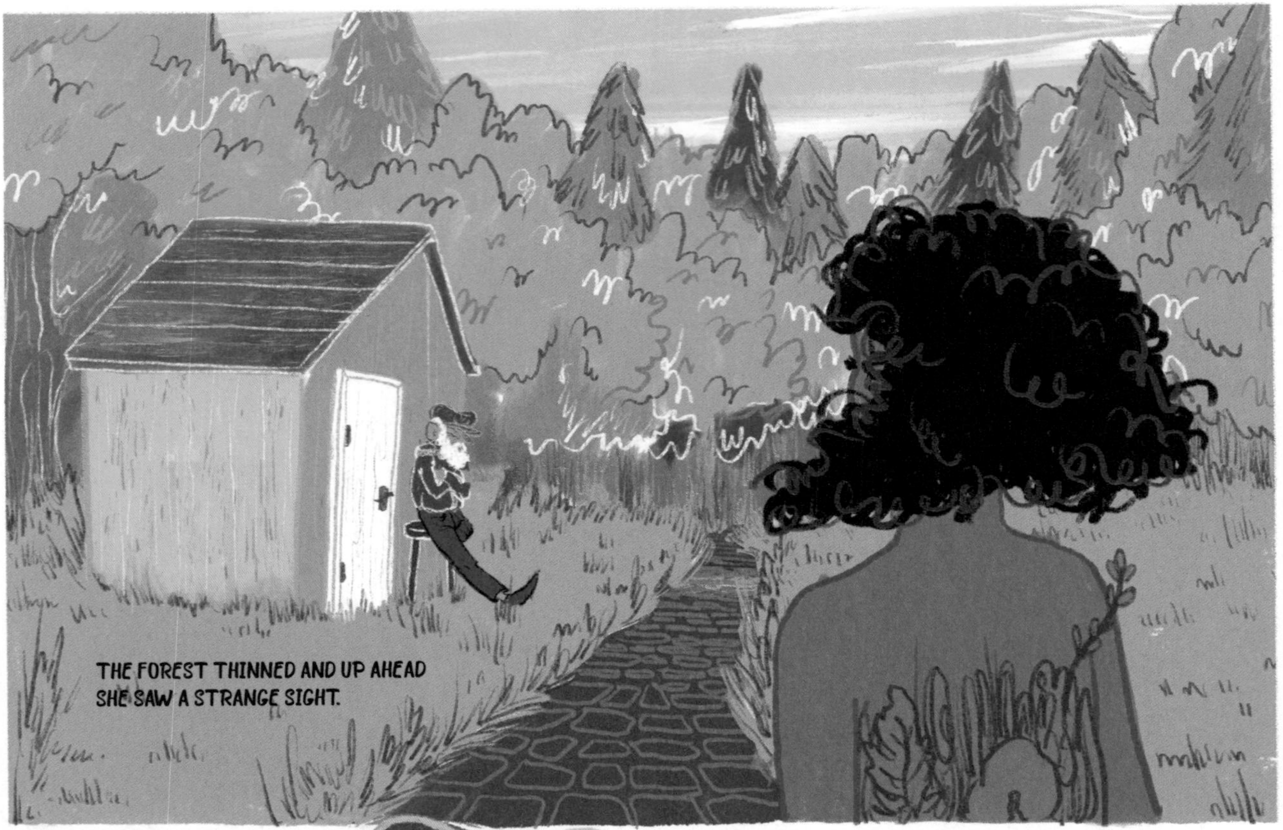
THE FOREST THINNED AND UP AHEAD SHE SAW A STRANGE SIGHT.

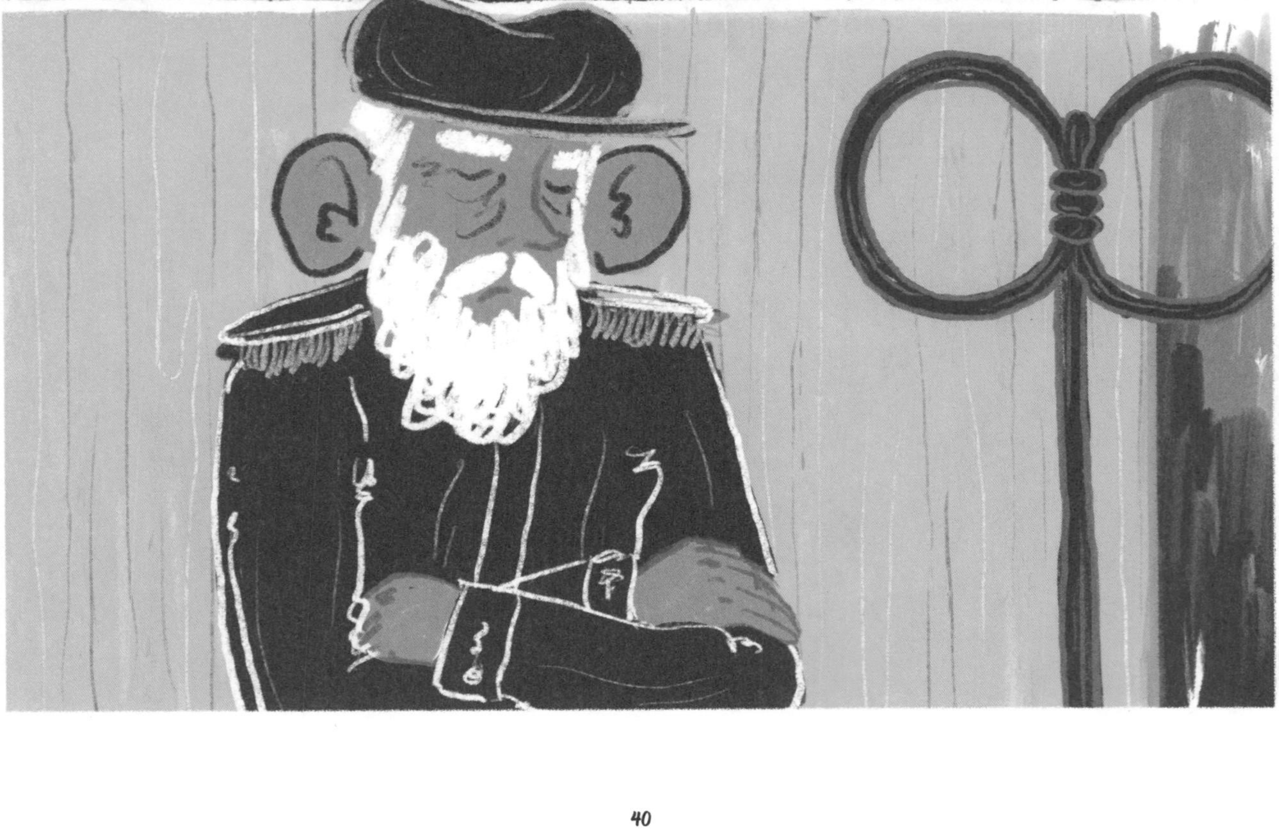

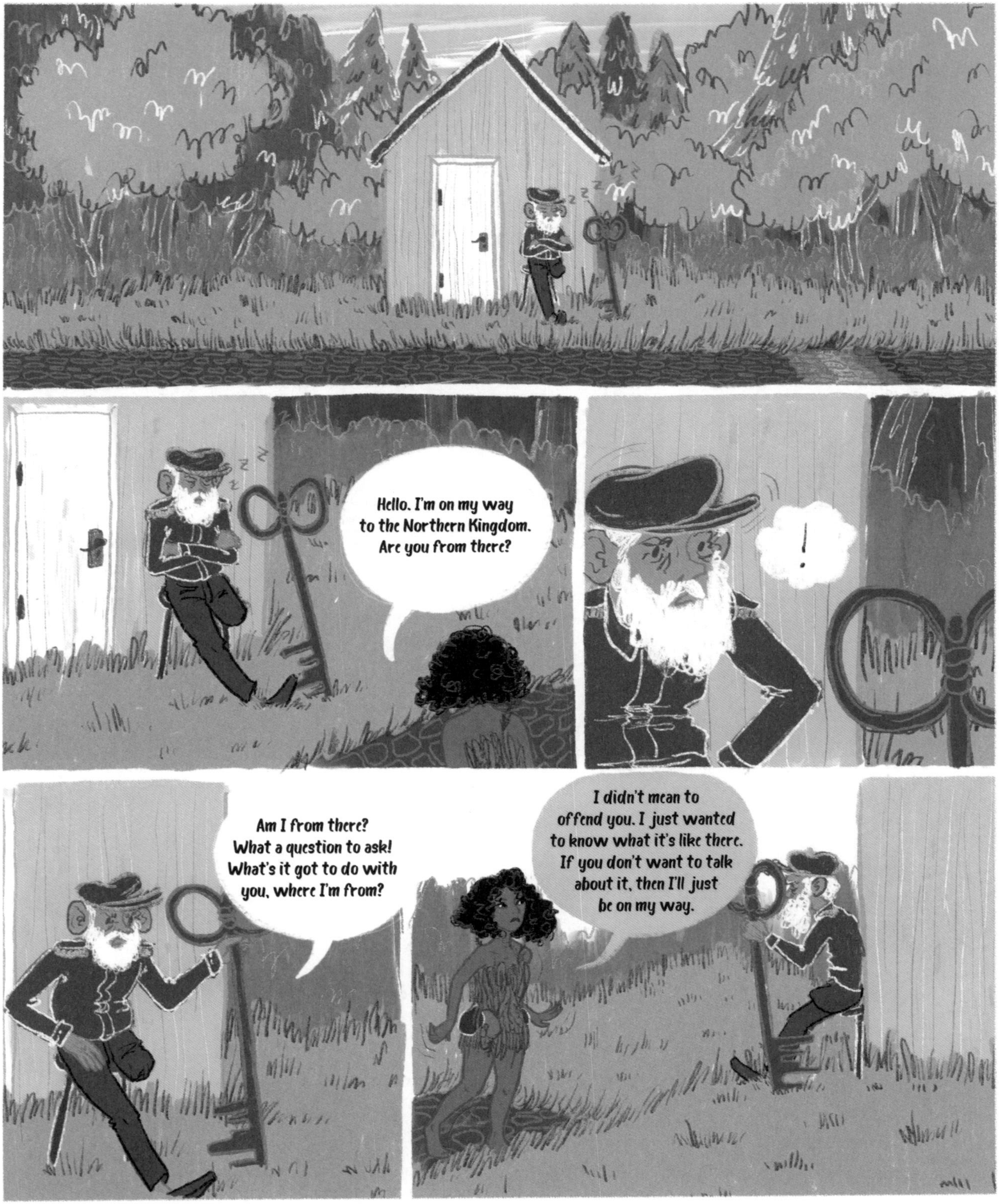
Hello. I'm on my way to the Northern Kingdom. Are you from there?
!
Am I from there? What a question to ask! What's it got to do with you, where I'm from?
I didn't mean to offend you. I just wanted to know what it's like there. If you don't want to talk about it, then I'll just be on my way.

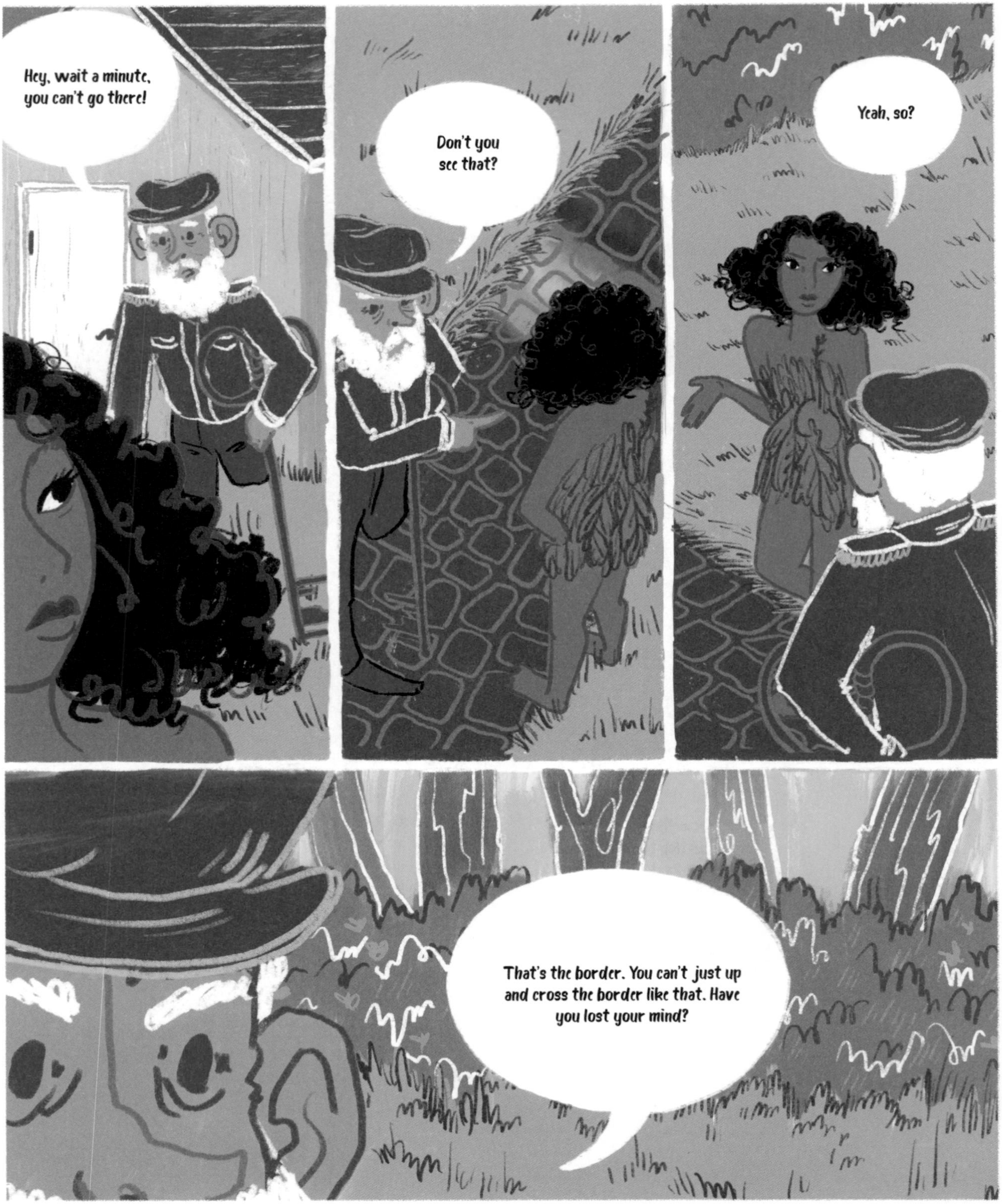
Hey, wait a minute, you can't go there!
Don't you see that?
Yeah, so?
That's the border. You can't just up and cross the border like that. Have you lost your mind?

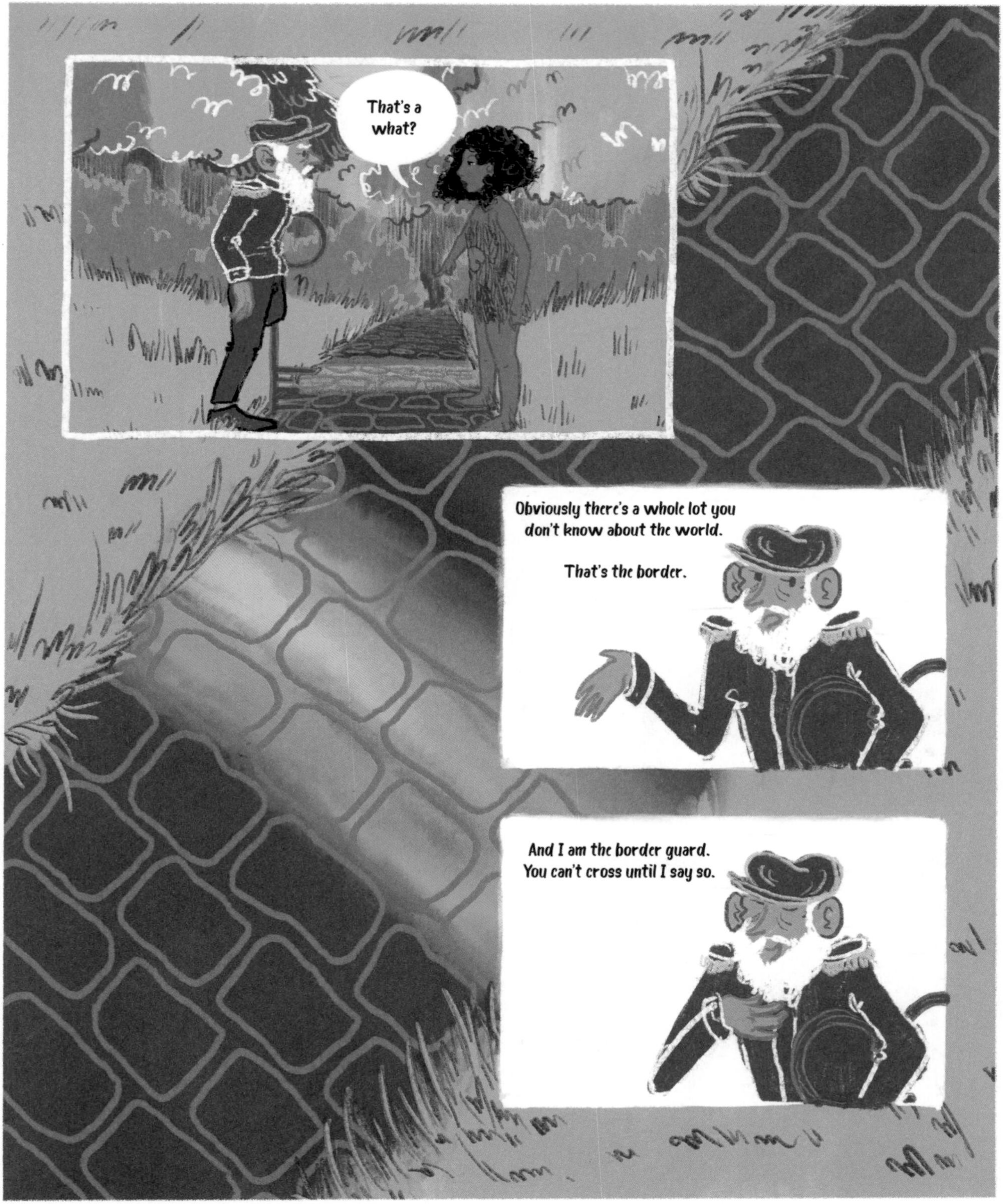
That's a what?
Obviously there's a whole lot you don't know about the world.
That's the border.
And I am the border guard. You can't cross until I say so.

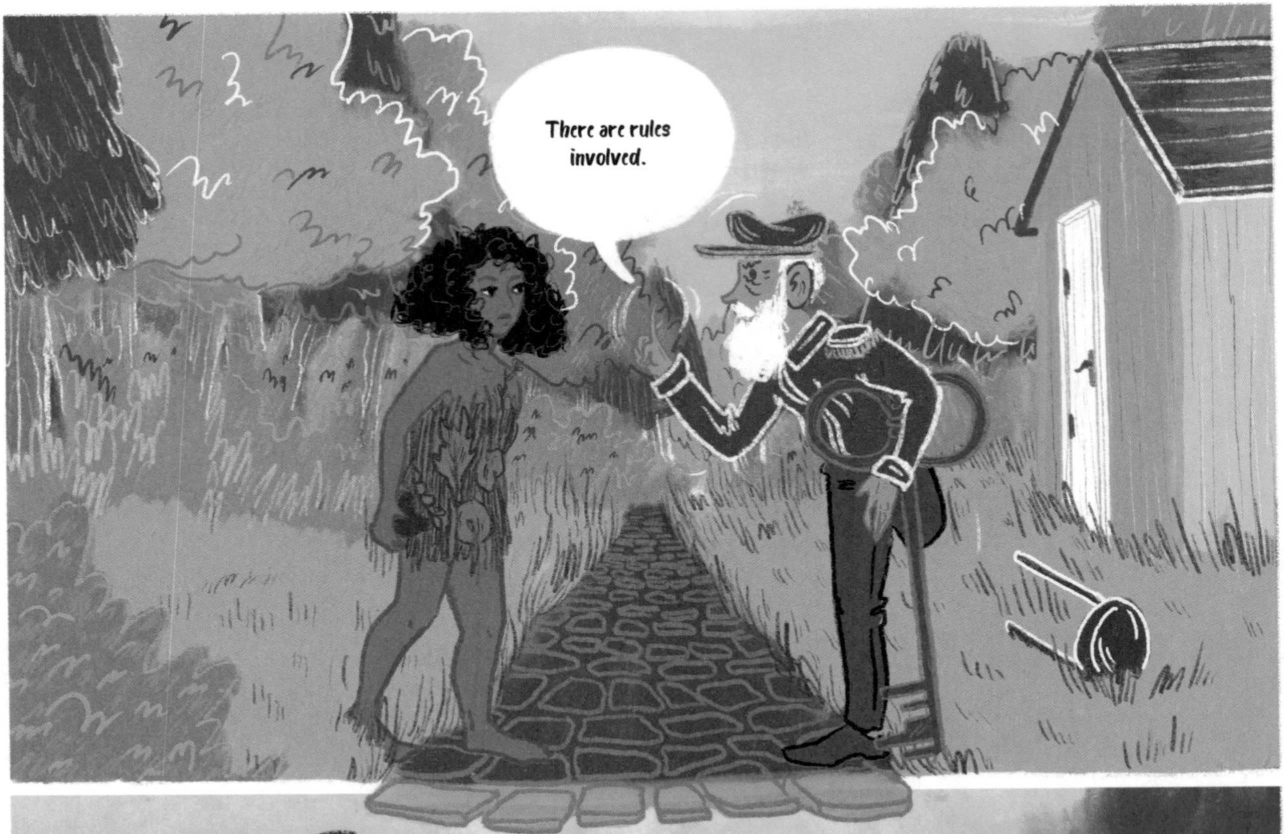
There are rules involved.

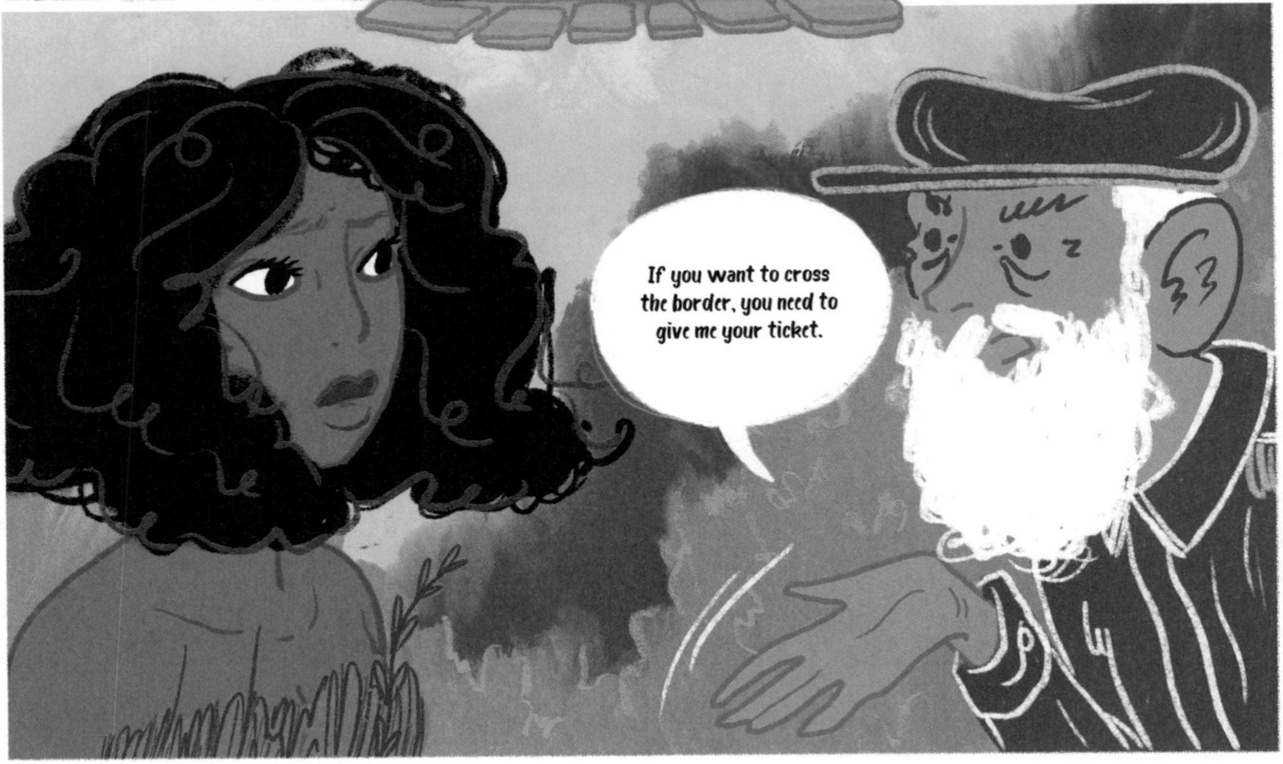
If you want to cross the border, you need to give me your ticket.

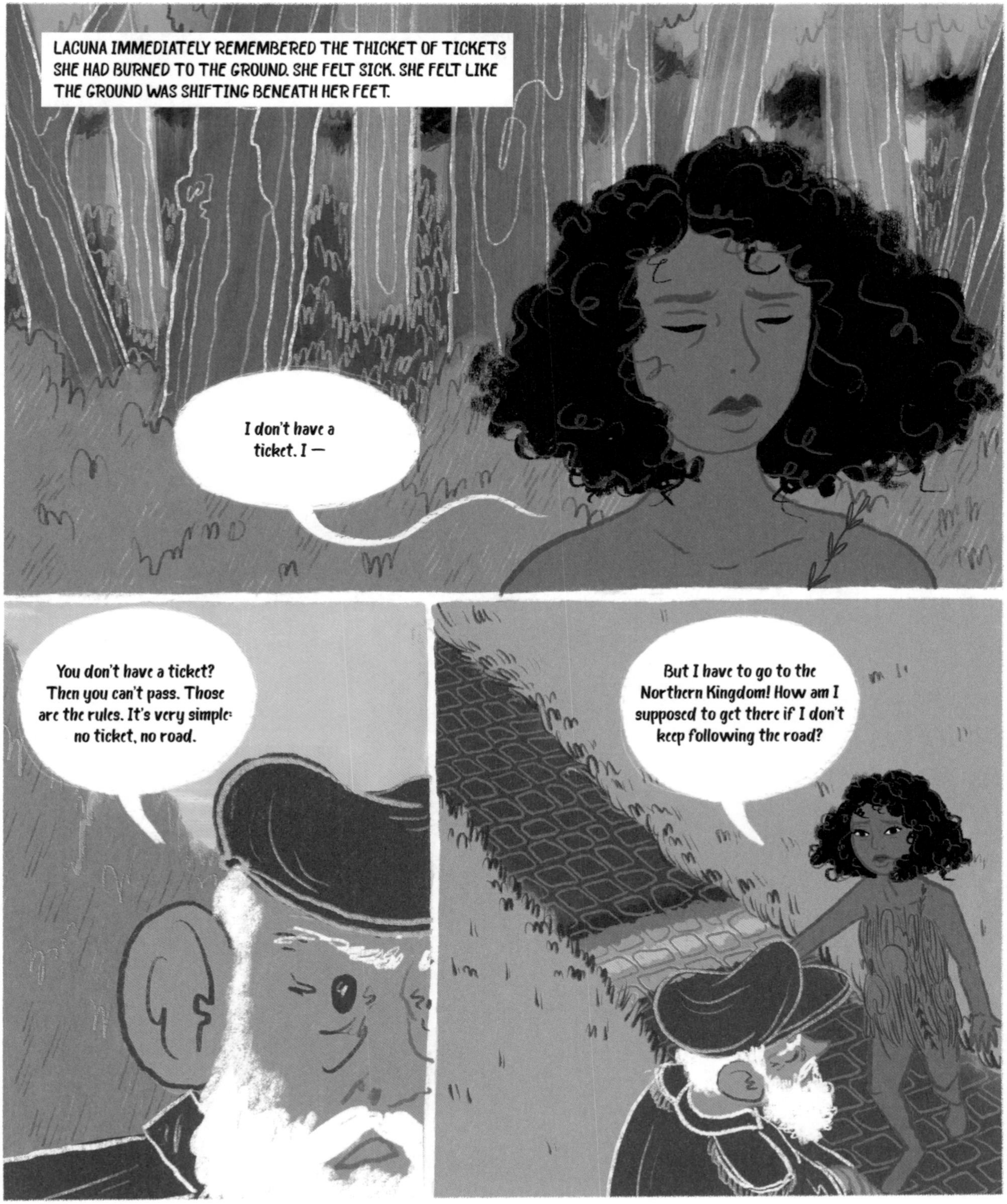
LACUNA IMMEDIATELY REMEMBERED THE THICKET OF TICKETS SHE HAD BURNED TO THE GROUND. SHE FELT SICK. SHE FELT LIKE THE GROUND WAS SHIFTING BENEATH HER FEET.
I don't have a ticket. I —
You don't have a ticket? Then you can't pass. Those are the rules. It's very simple: no ticket, no road.
But I have to go to the Northern Kingdom! How am I supposed to get there if I don't keep following the road?

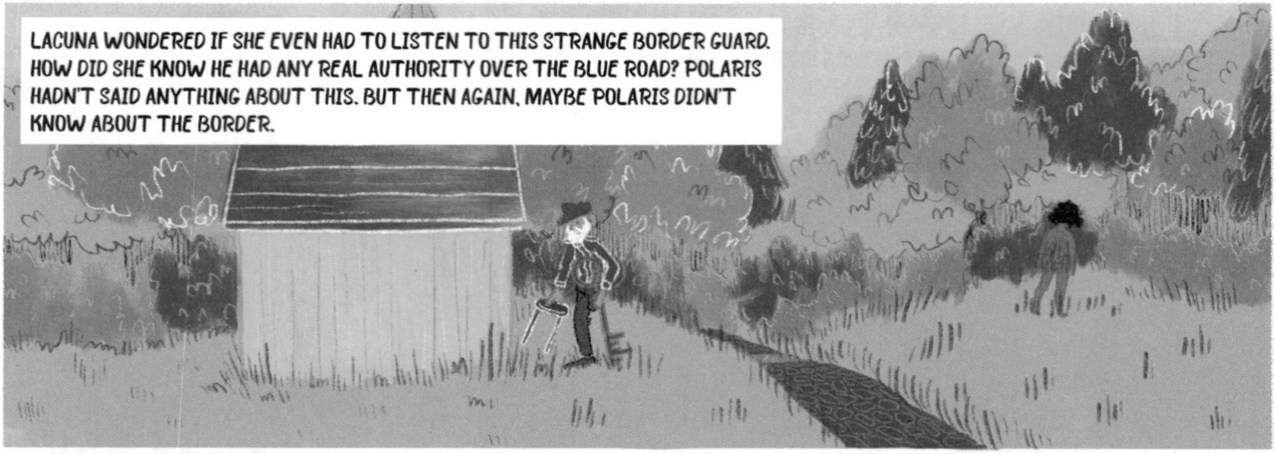
LACUNA WONDERED IF SHE EVEN HAD TO LISTEN TO THIS STRANGE BORDER GUARD. HOW DID SHE KNOW HE HAD ANY REAL AUTHORITY OVER THE BLUE ROAD? POLARIS HADN'T SAID ANYTHING ABOUT THIS. BUT THEN AGAIN, MAYBE POLARIS DIDN'T KNOW ABOUT THE BORDER.

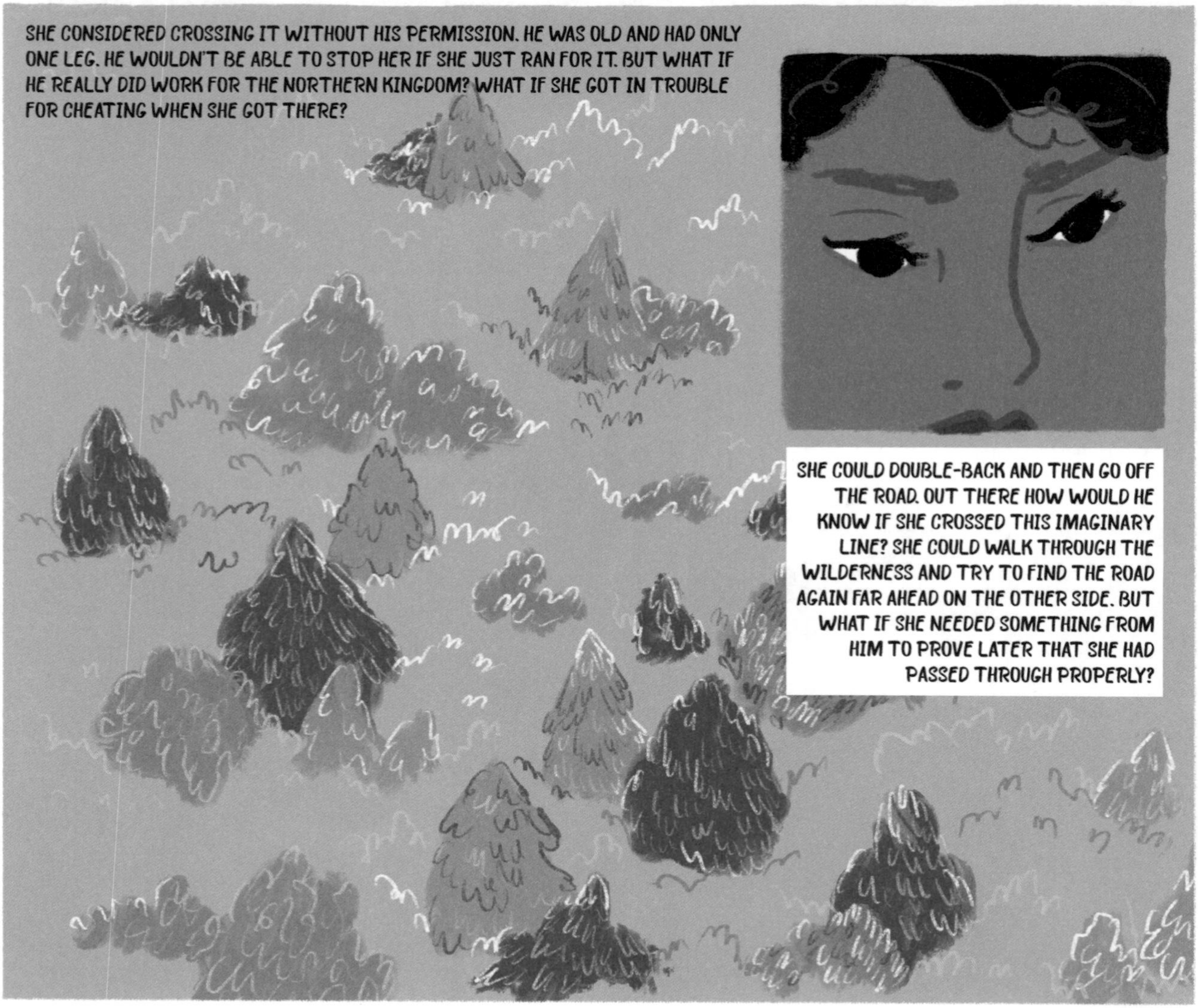
SHE CONSIDERED CROSSING IT WITHOUT HIS PERMISSION. HE WAS OLD AND HAD ONLY ONE LEG. HE WOULDN'T BE ABLE TO STOP HER IF SHE JUST RAN FOR IT. BUT WHAT IF HE REALLY DID WORK FOR THE NORTHERN KINGDOM? WHAT IF SHE GOT IN TROUBLE FOR CHEATING WHEN SHE GOT THERE?
SHE COULD DOUBLE-BACK AND THEN GO OFF THE ROAD. OUT THERE HOW WOULD HE KNOW IF SHE CROSSED THIS IMAGINARY LINE? SHE COULD WALK THROUGH THE WILDERNESS AND TRY TO FIND THE ROAD AGAIN FAR AHEAD ON THE OTHER SIDE. BUT WHAT IF SHE NEEDED SOMETHING FROM HIM TO PROVE LATER THAT SHE HAD PASSED THROUGH PROPERLY?

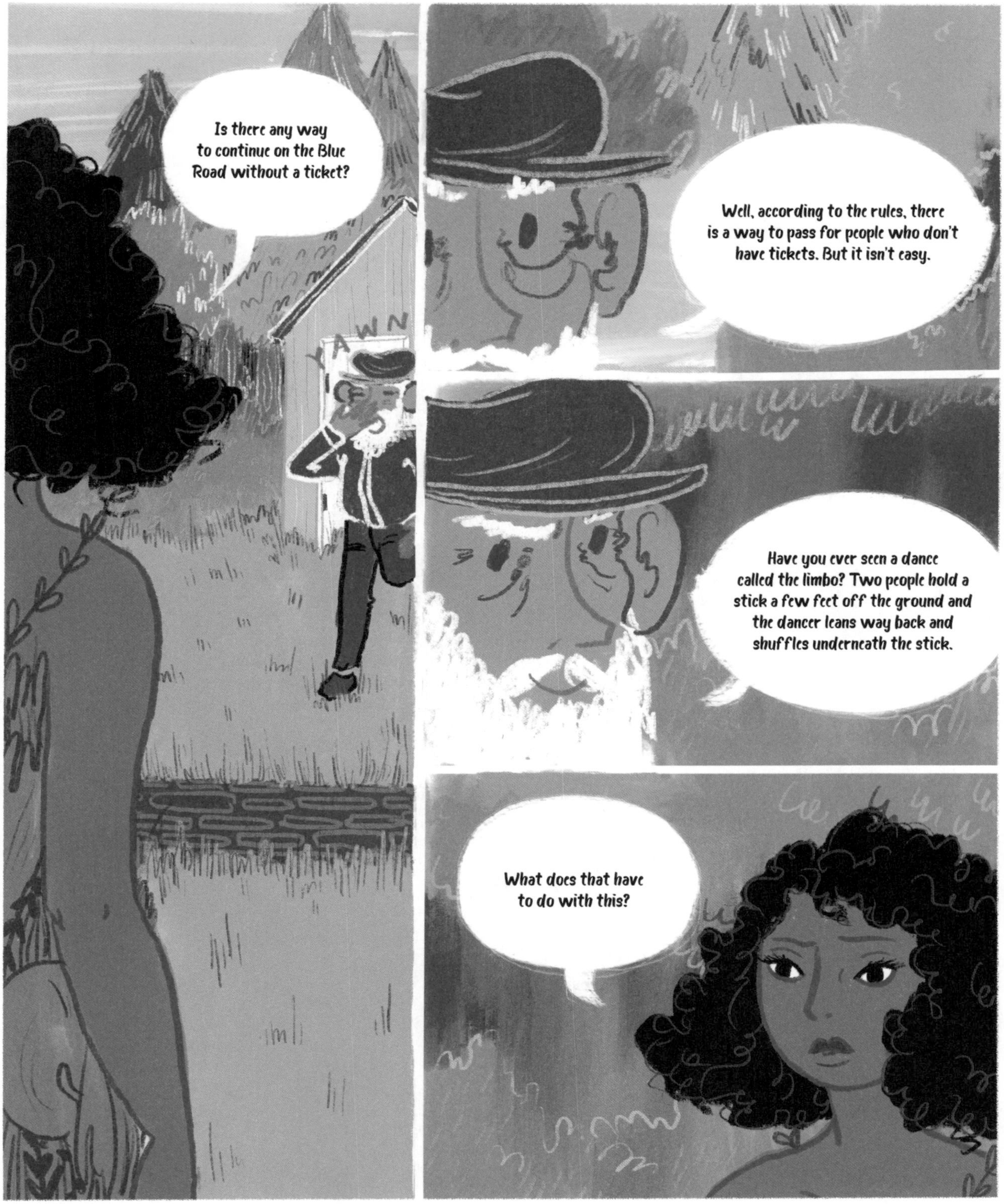
Is there any way to continue on the Blue Road without a ticket?
YAWN
Well, according to the rules, there is a way to pass for people who don't have tickets. But it isn't easy.
Have you ever seen a dance called the limbo? Two people hold a stick a few feet off the ground and the dancer leans way back and shuffles underneath the stick.
What does that have to do with this?

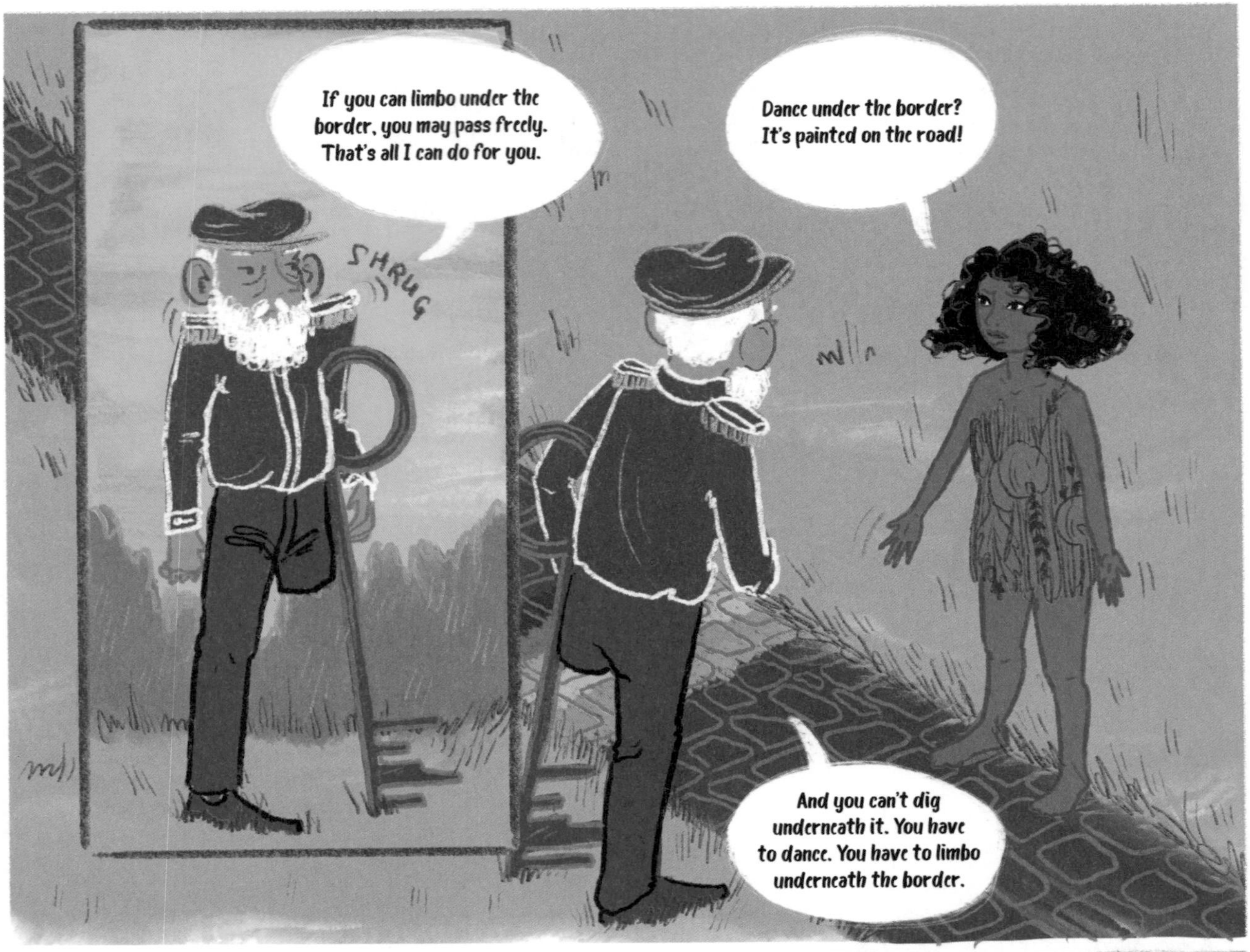
If you can limbo under the border, you may pass freely. That's all I can do for you.
SHRUG
Dance under the border? It's painted on the road!
And you can't dig underneath it. You have to dance. You have to limbo underneath the border.

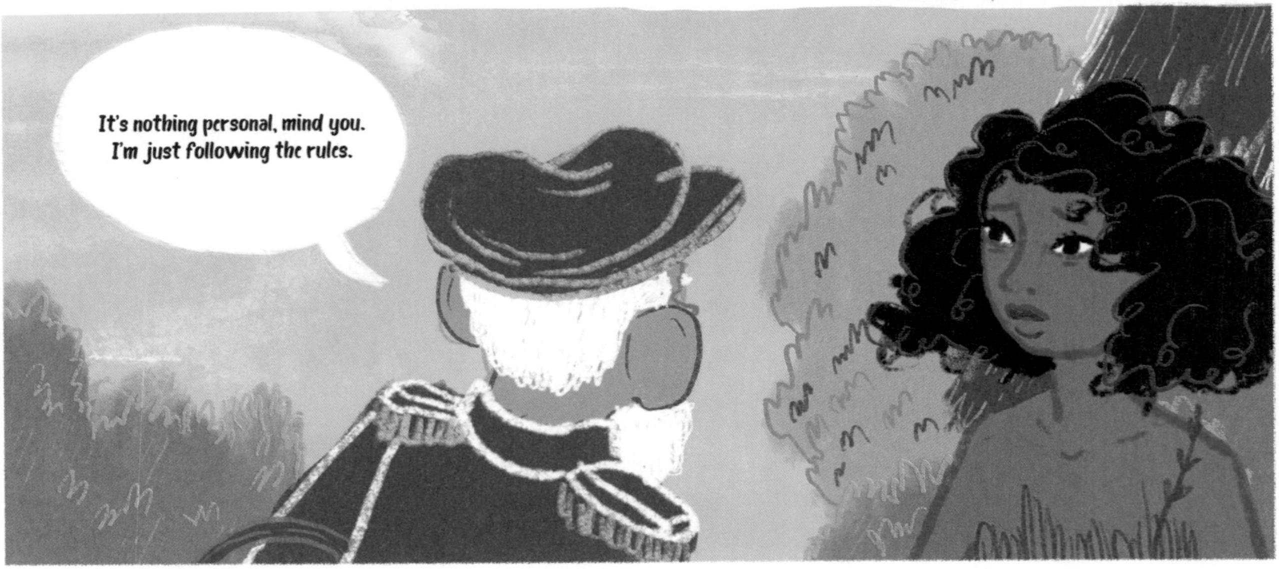
It's nothing personal, mind you. I'm just following the rules.

LACUNA WAS DEVASTATED. BUT SHE KNEW SHE NEEDED TO REMAIN CALM AND THINK OF A WAY OUT OF THIS SITUATION.

SHE CAREFULLY CONSIDERED THE CIRCUMSTANCES. LACUNA KNEW THAT NO ONE COULD LIMBO BENEATH A PAINTED BORDER. SHE THOUGHT AND THOUGHT, BUT COULD SEE NO WAY OUT OF HER PREDICAMENT.

THERE WAS NOTHING ELSE TO DO BUT SET UP A CAMP BESIDE THE BORDER GUARD'S BOOTH AND WAIT UNTIL AN IDEA CAME TO HER.

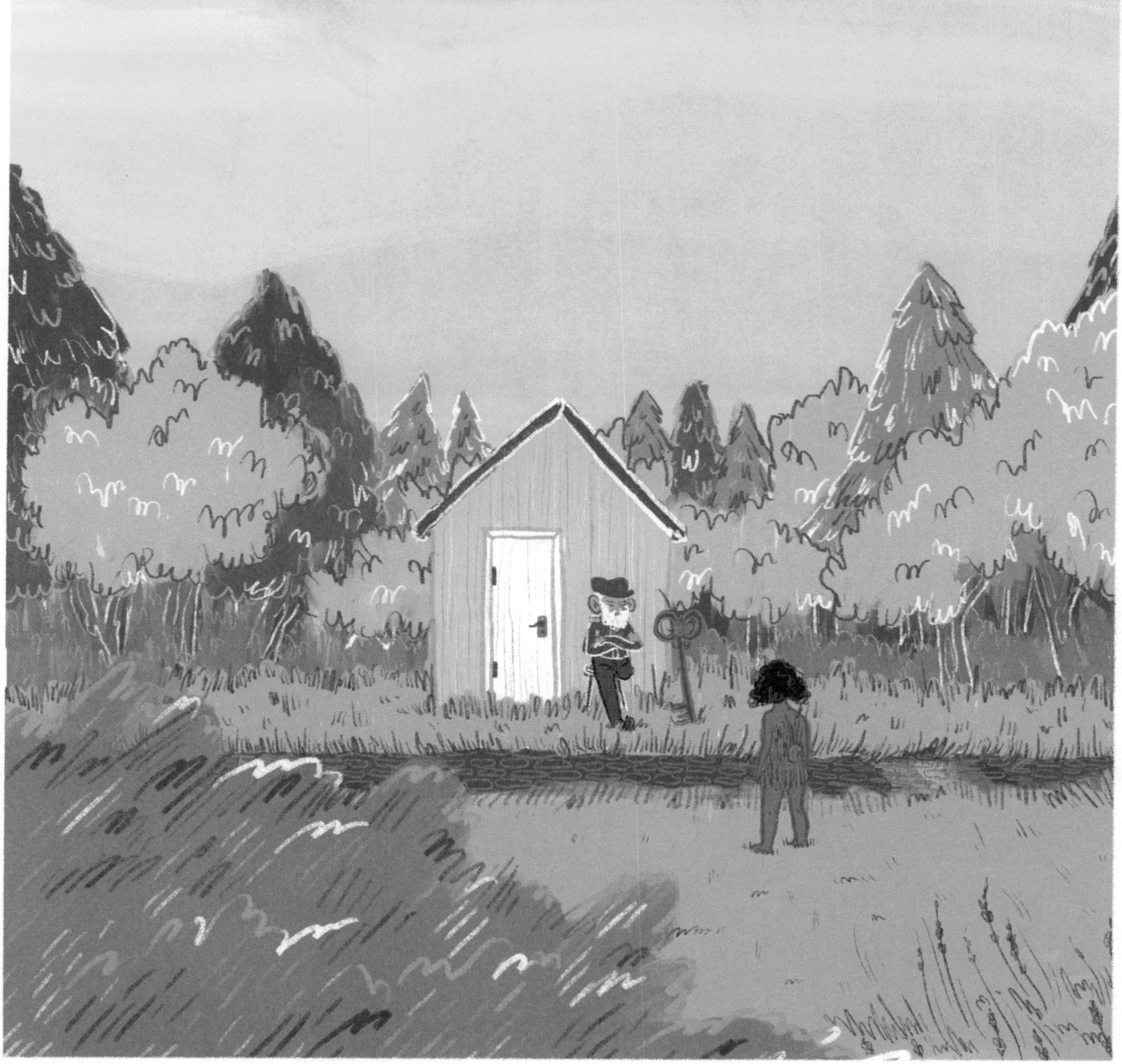

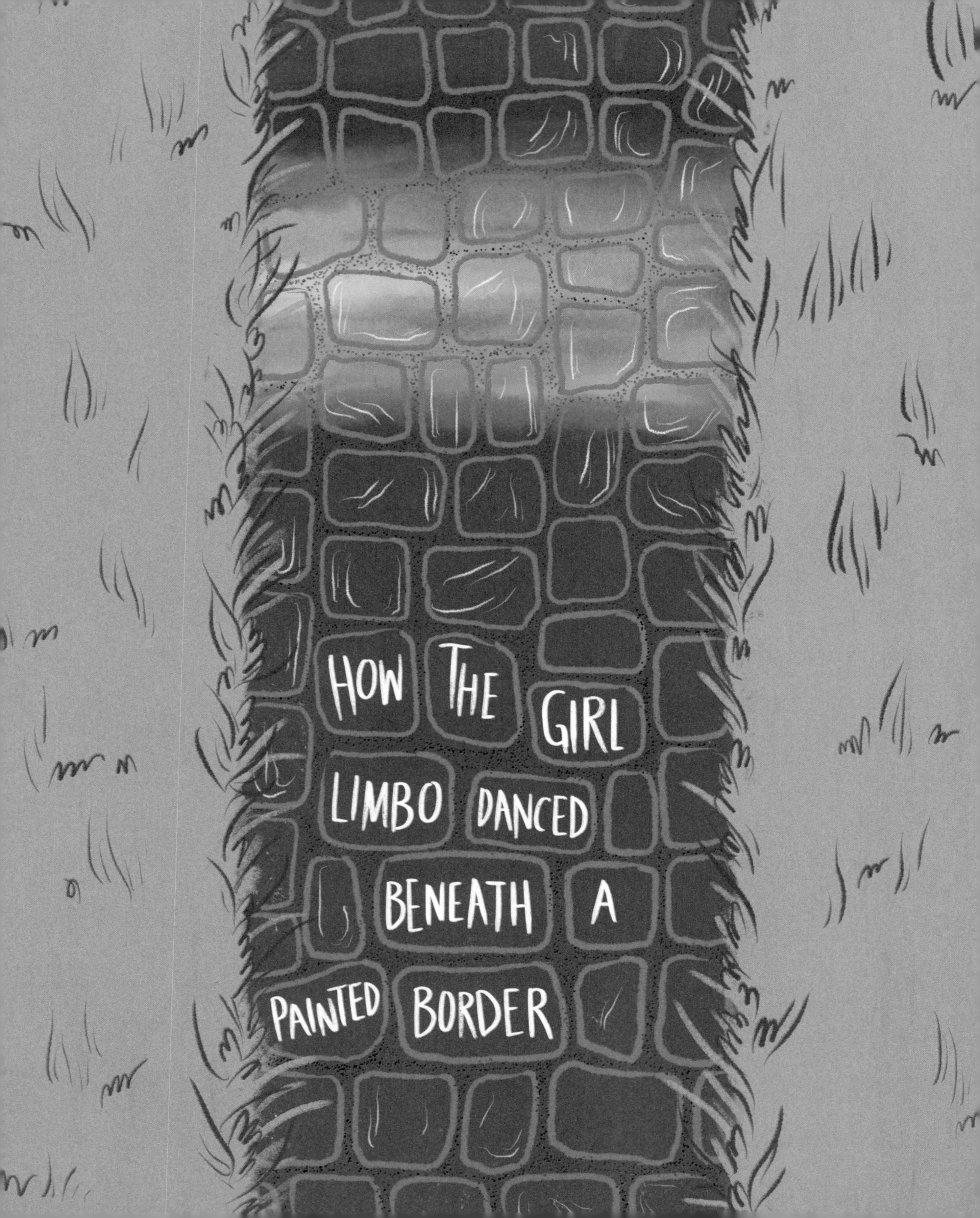
HOW THE GIRL LIMBO DANCED BENEATH A PAINTED BORDER

FOR DAYS, LACUNA CAMPED BESIDE THE BORDER GUARD'S BOOTH. THEY PASSED THE TIME BY PLAYING CARDS.

ONE DAY, WHILE THEY WERE PLAYING, SHE NOTICED A TINY BIRD FLYING LOW TO THE GROUND. IT WAS HEADING NORTH TOWARD THE BORDER.

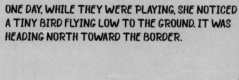

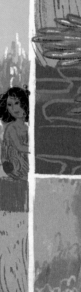

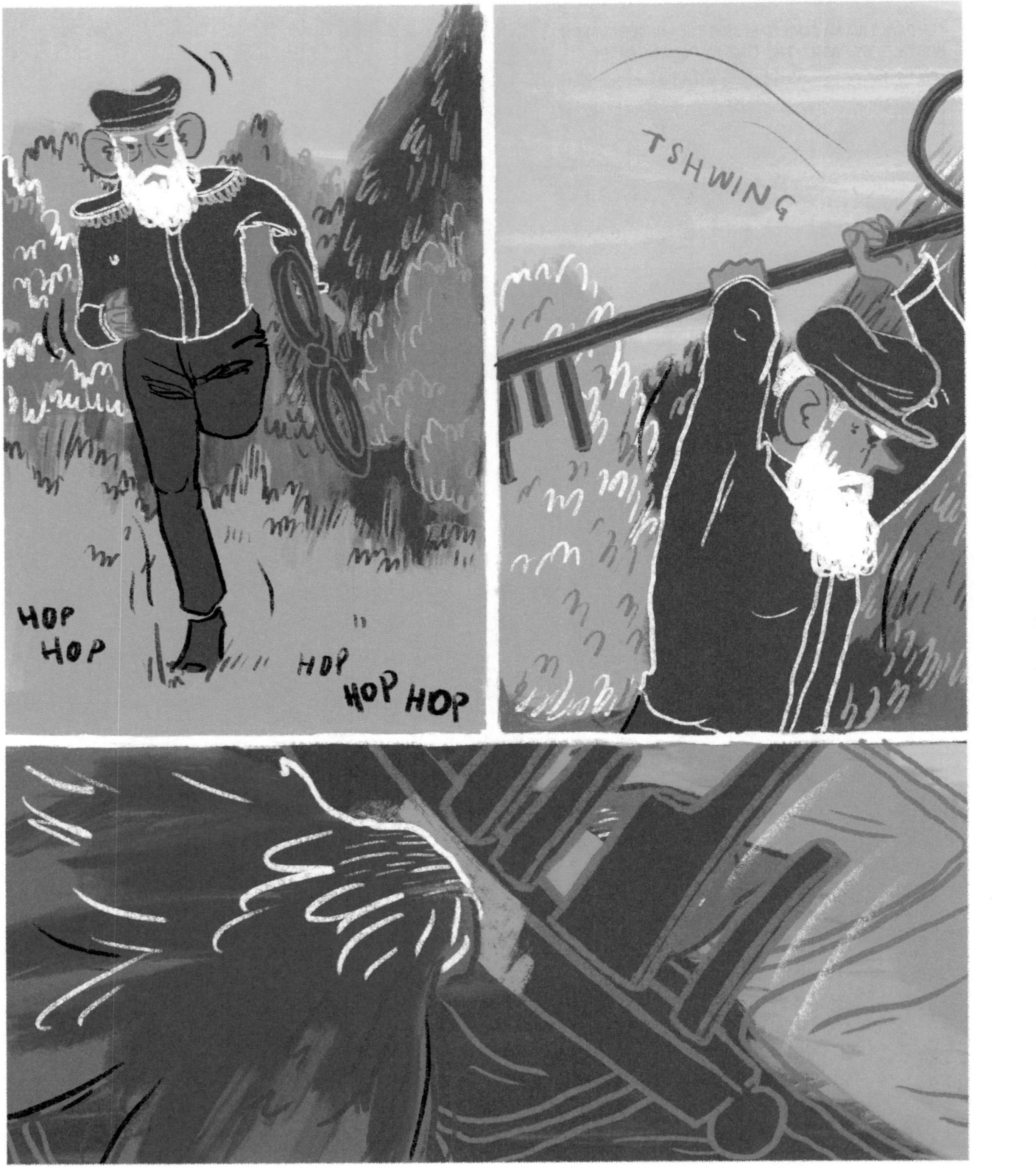
HOP
HOP
HOP
HOP HOP
TSHWING

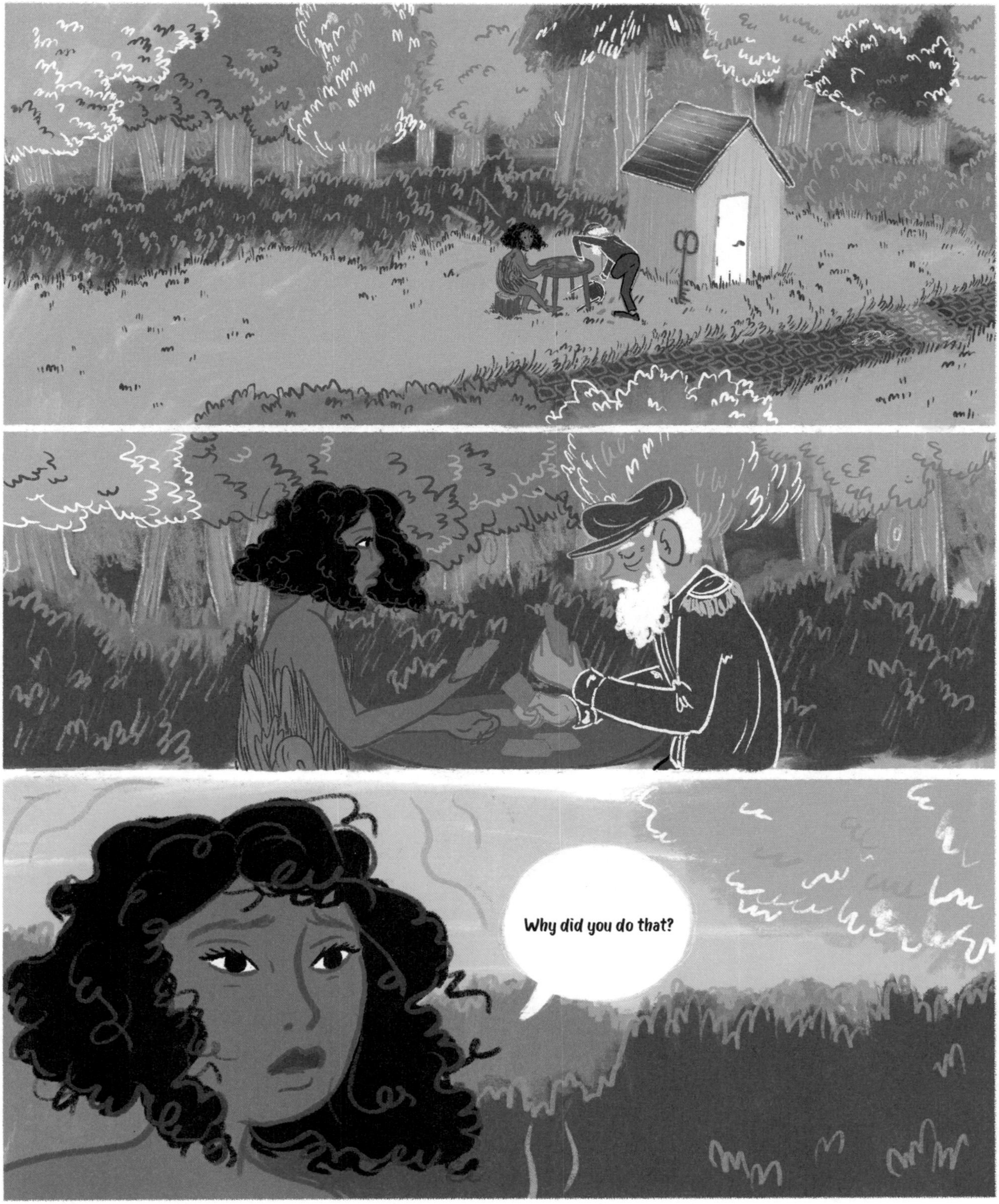
Why did you do that?

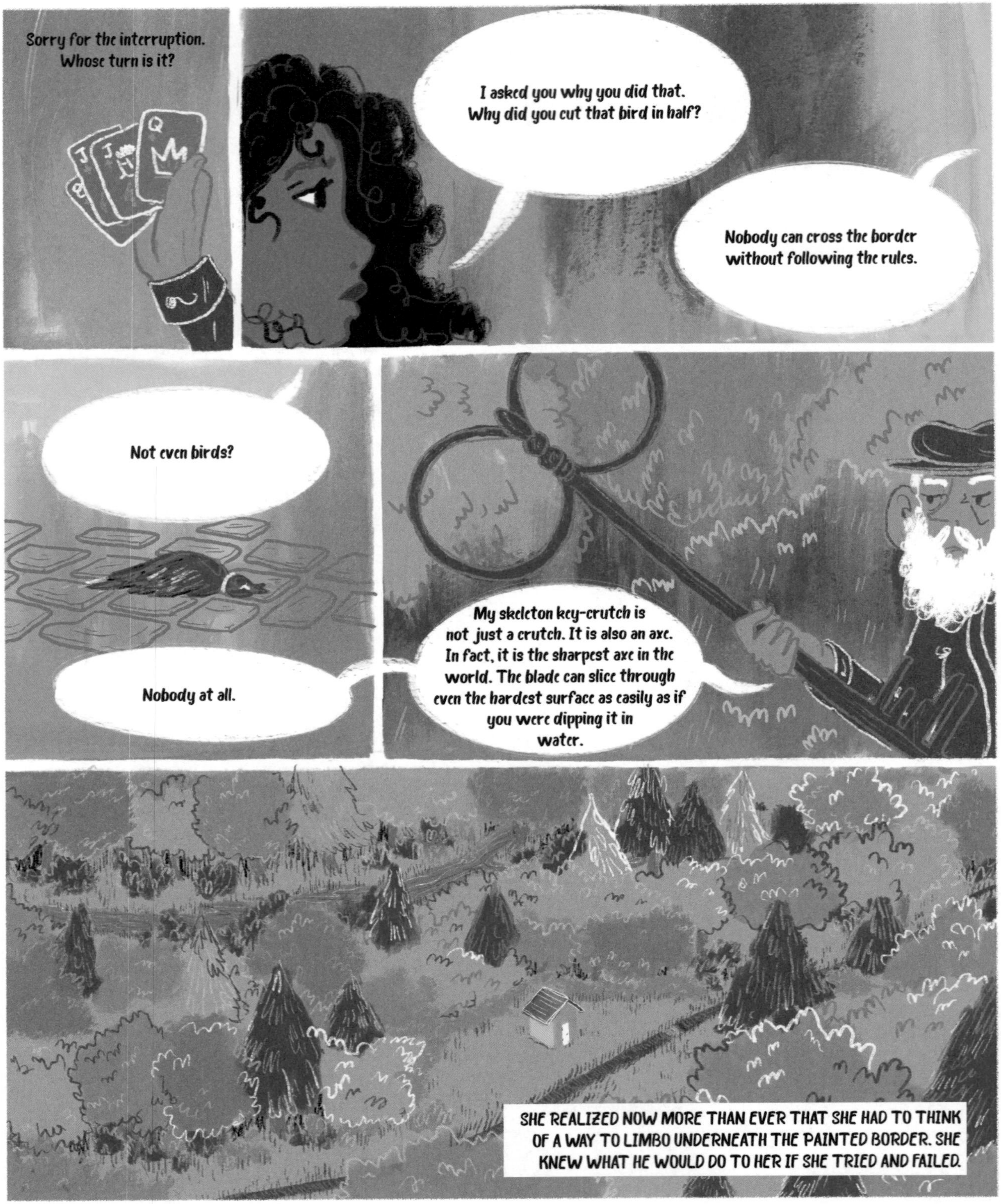
Sorry for the interruption. Whose turn is it?
I asked you why you did that. Why did you cut that bird in half?
Nobody can cross the border without following the rules.
Not even birds?
Nobody at all.
My skeleton key-crutch is not just a crutch. It is also an axe. In fact, it is the sharpest axe in the world. The blade can slice through even the hardest surface as easily as if you were dipping it in water.
SHE REALIZED NOW MORE THAN EVER THAT SHE HAD TO THINK OF A WAY TO LIMBO UNDERNEATH THE PAINTED BORDER. SHE KNEW WHAT HE WOULD DO TO HER IF SHE TRIED AND FAILED.

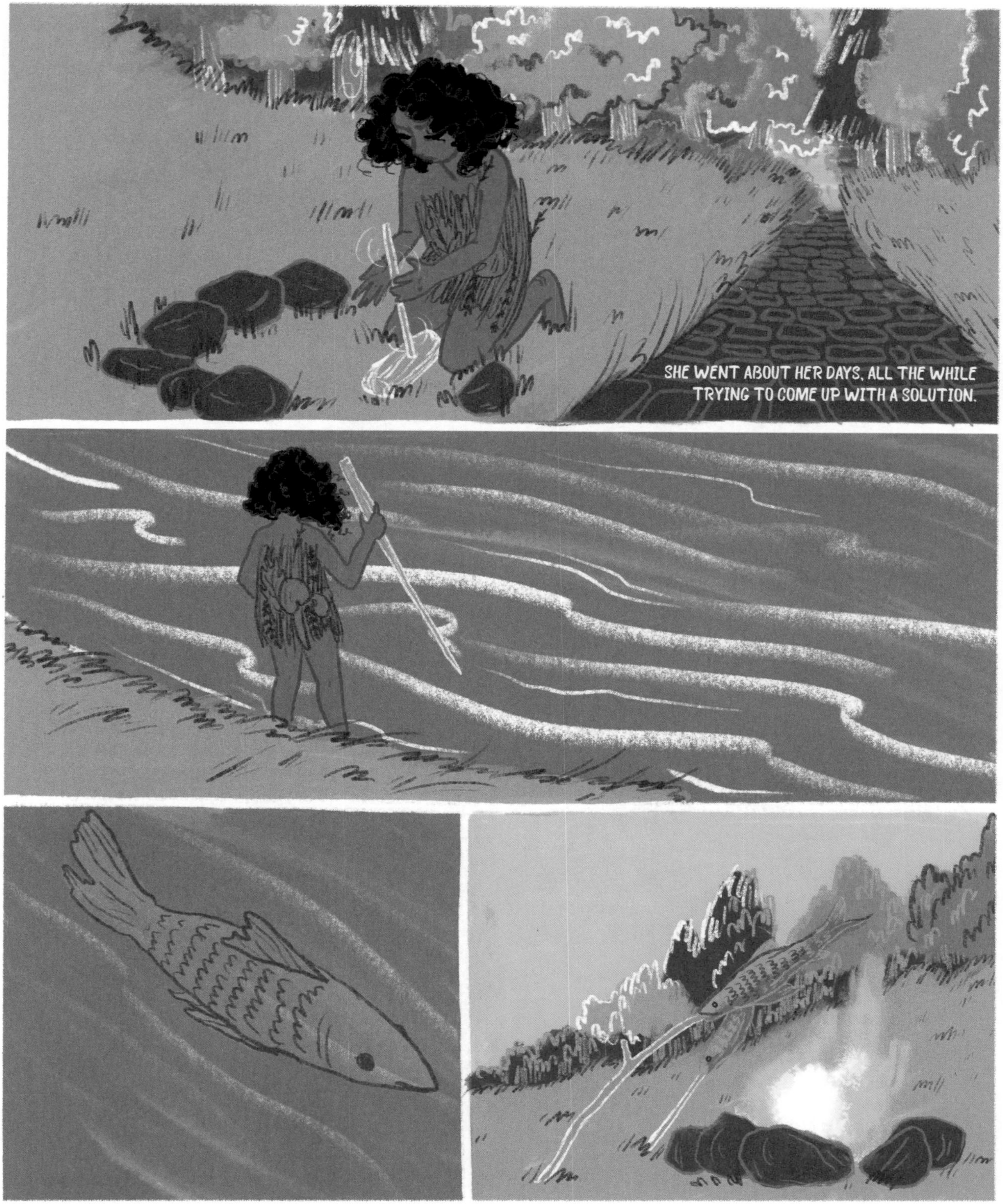
SHE WENT ABOUT HER DAYS, ALL THE WHILE TRYING TO COME UP WITH A SOLUTION.

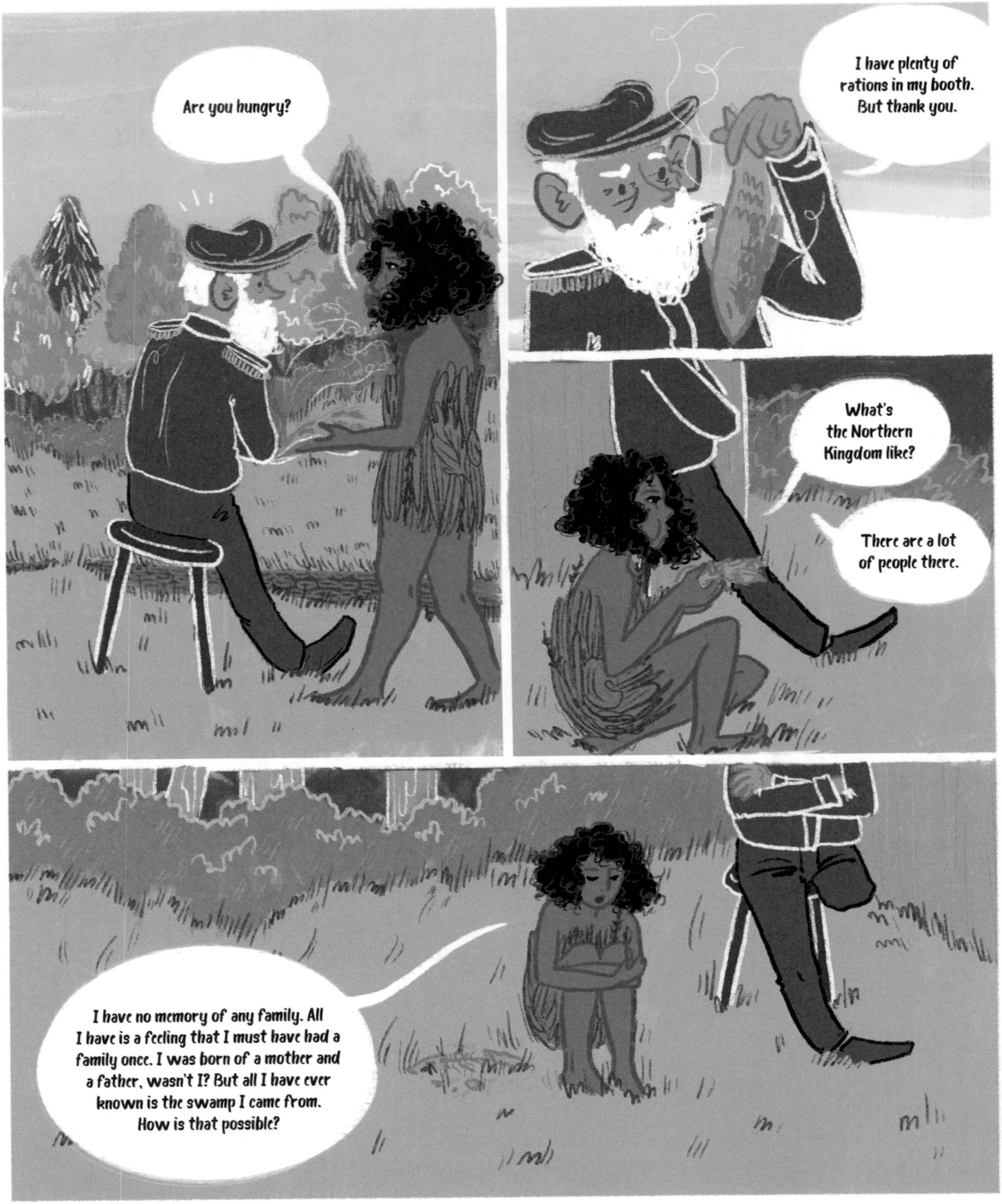
Are you hungry?
I have plenty of rations in my booth. But thank you.
What's the Northern Kingdom like?
There are a lot of people there.
I have no memory of any family. All I have is a feeling that I must have had a family once. I was born of a mother and a father, wasn't I? But all I have ever known is the swamp I came from. How is that possible?

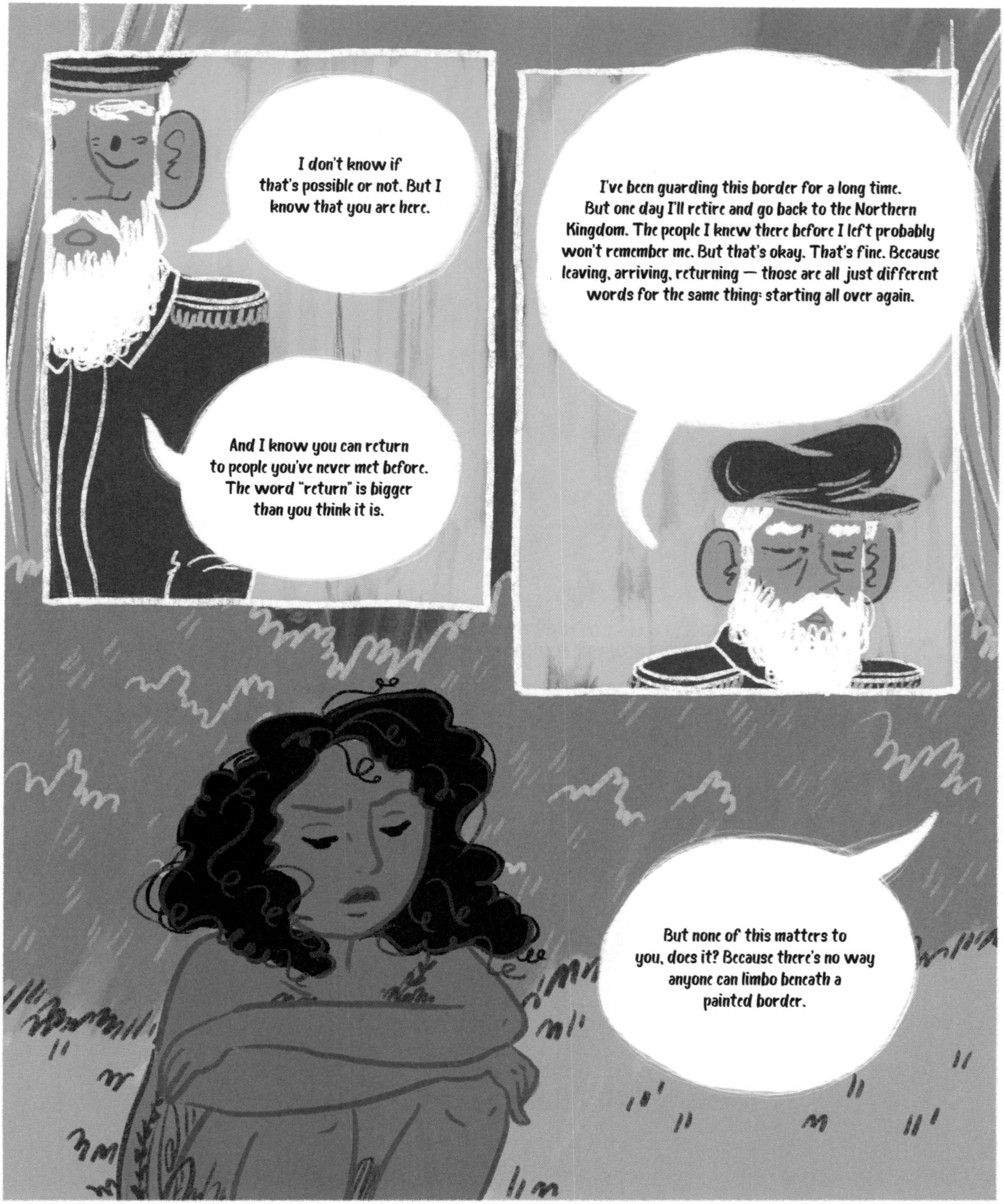
I don't know if that's possible or not. But I know that you are here.
And I know you can return to people you've never met before. The word "return" is bigger than you think it is.
I've been guarding this border for a long time. But one day I'll retire and go back to the Northern Kingdom. The people I knew there before I left probably won't remember me. But that's okay. That's fine. Because leaving, arriving, returning — those are all just different words for the same thing: starting all over again.
But none of this matters to you, does it? Because there's no way anyone can limbo beneath a painted border.

MONTHS PASSED WHILE LACUNA STAYED BY THE BORDER GUARD'S SHACK. THERE WAS NOWHERE ELSE FOR HER TO GO.

TIME WENT ON.

SEASONS CHANGED.

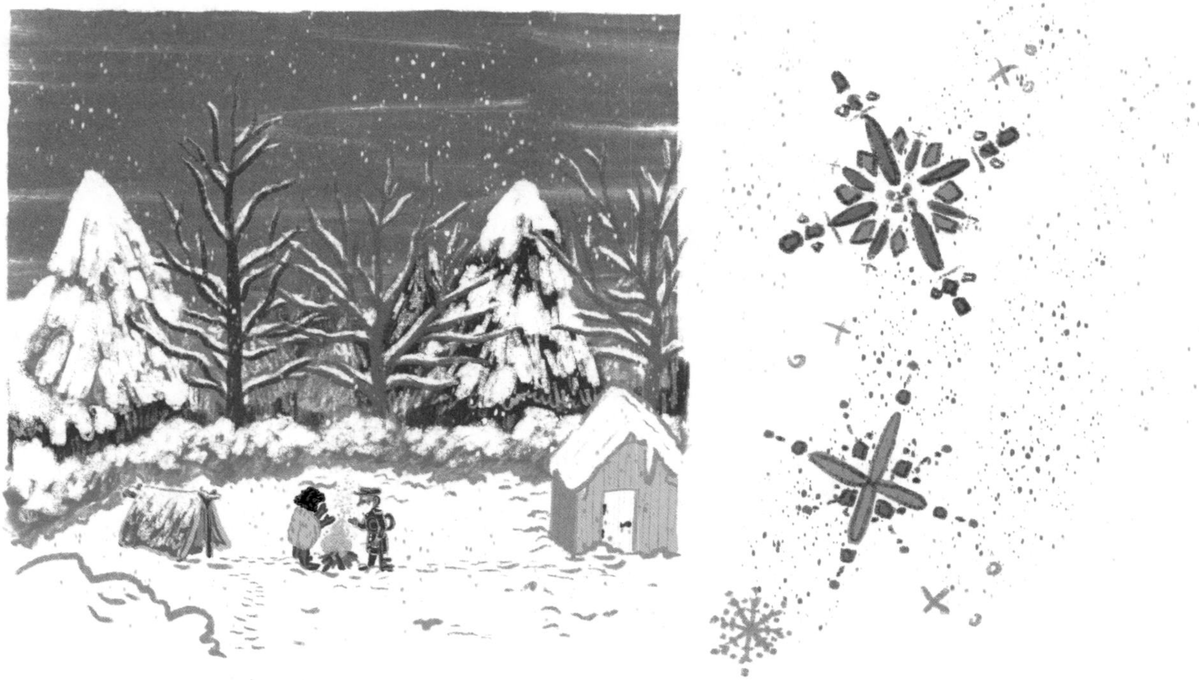

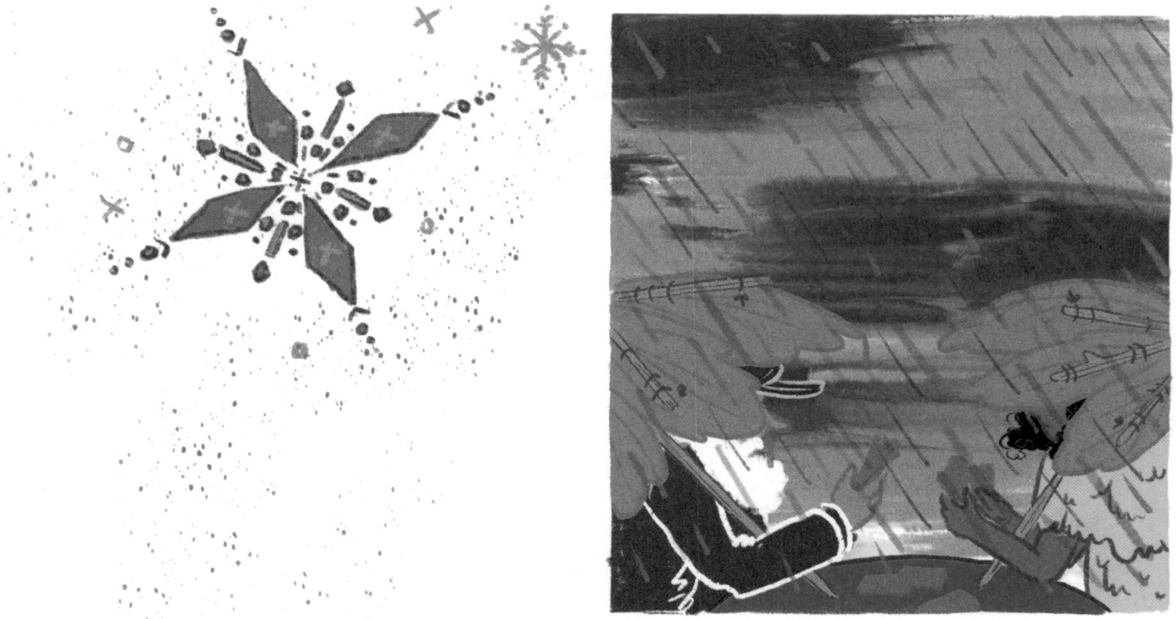

SHE WAITED FOR AN ANSWER TO ARRIVE.

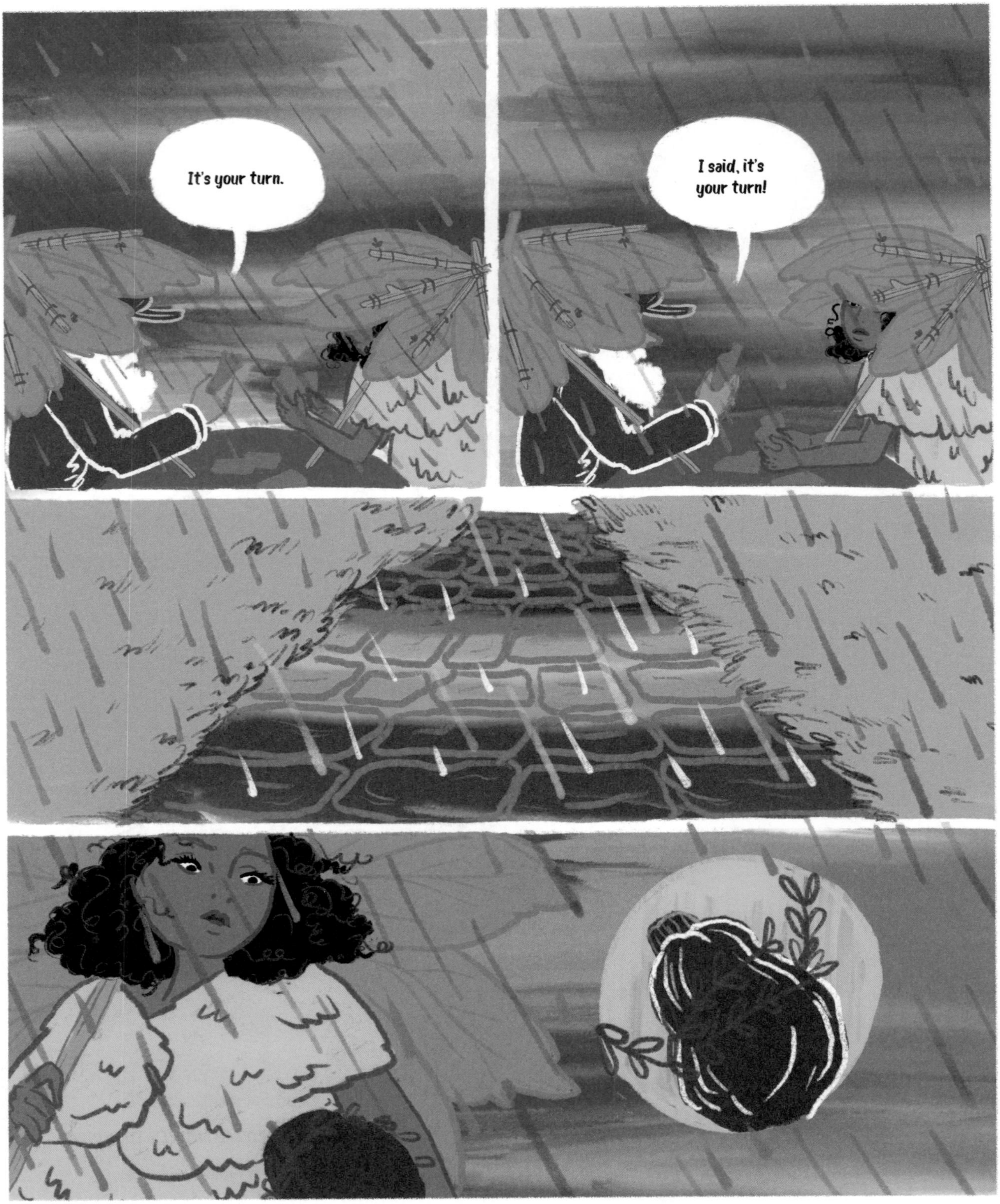
It's your turn.
I said, it's your turn!

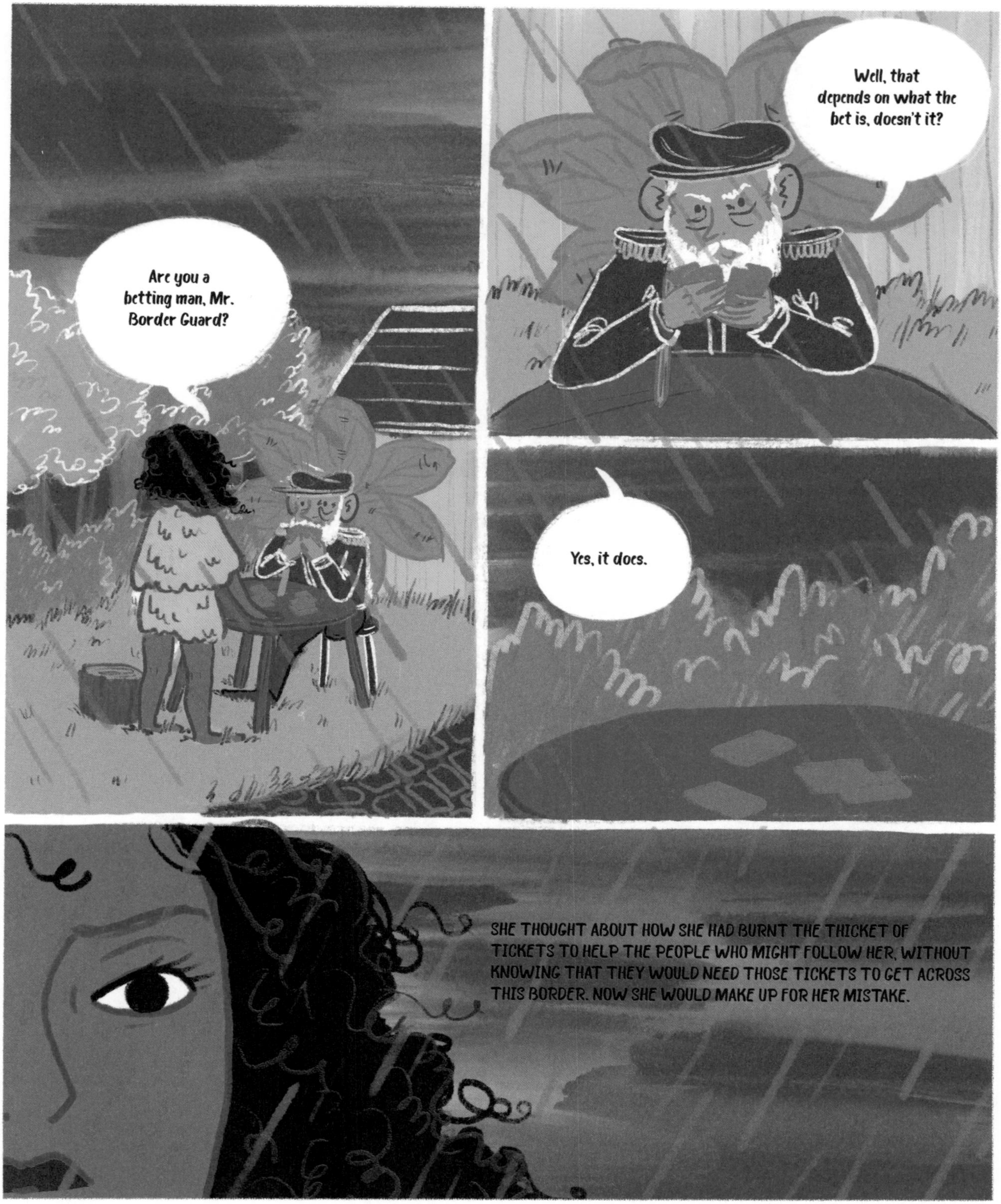
Are you a betting man, Mr. Border Guard?
Well, that depends on what the bet is, doesn't it?
Yes, it does.
SHE THOUGHT ABOUT HOW SHE HAD BURNT THE THICKET OF TICKETS TO HELP THE PEOPLE WHO MIGHT FOLLOW HER, WITHOUT KNOWING THAT THEY WOULD NEED THOSE TICKETS TO GET ACROSS THIS BORDER. NOW SHE WOULD MAKE UP FOR HER MISTAKE.

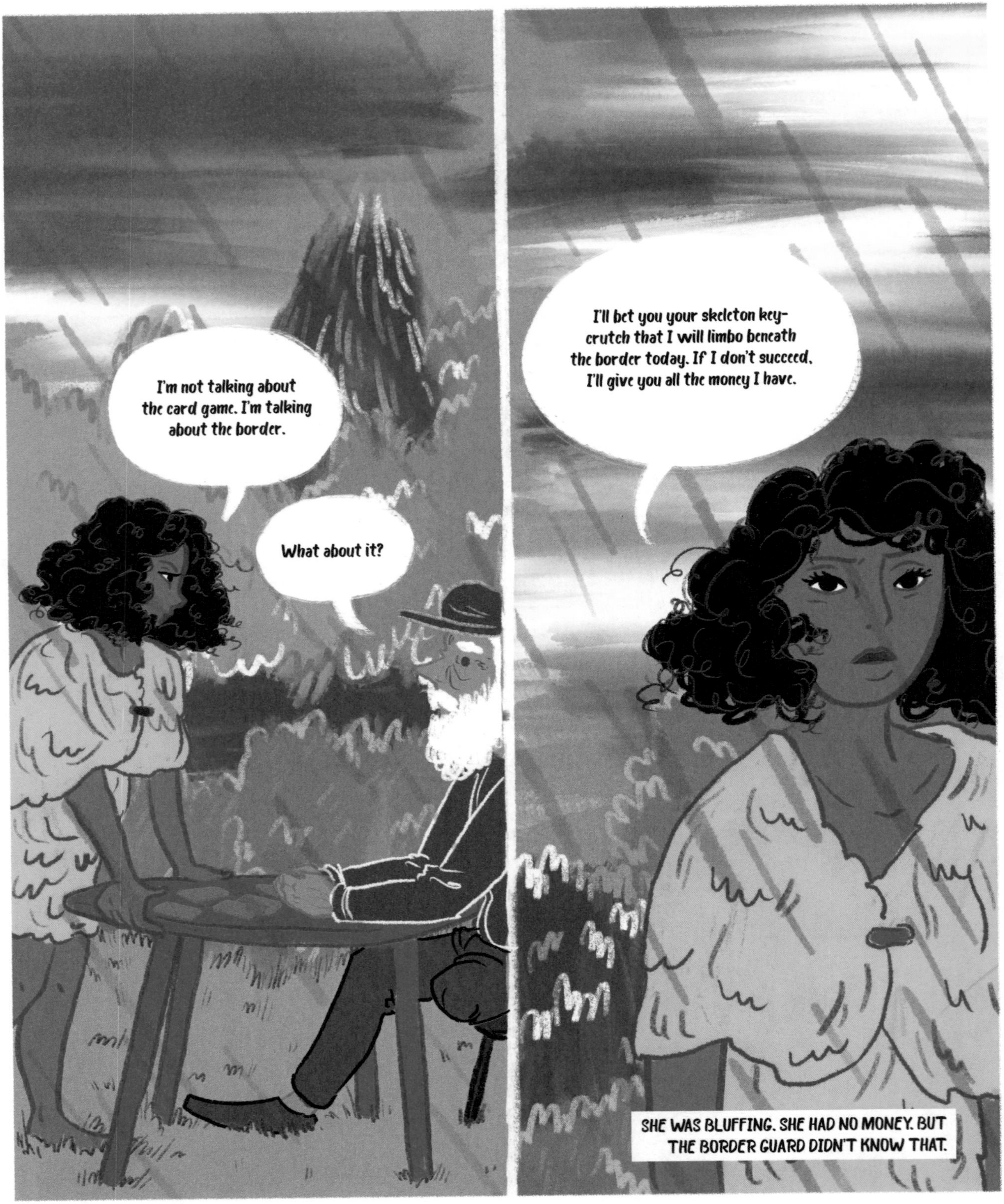
I'm not talking about the card game. I'm talking about the border.
What about it?
I'll bet you your skeleton key-crutch that I will limbo beneath the border today. If I don't succeed, I'll give you all the money I have.
SHE WAS BLUFFING. SHE HAD NO MONEY. BUT THE BORDER GUARD DIDN'T KNOW THAT.

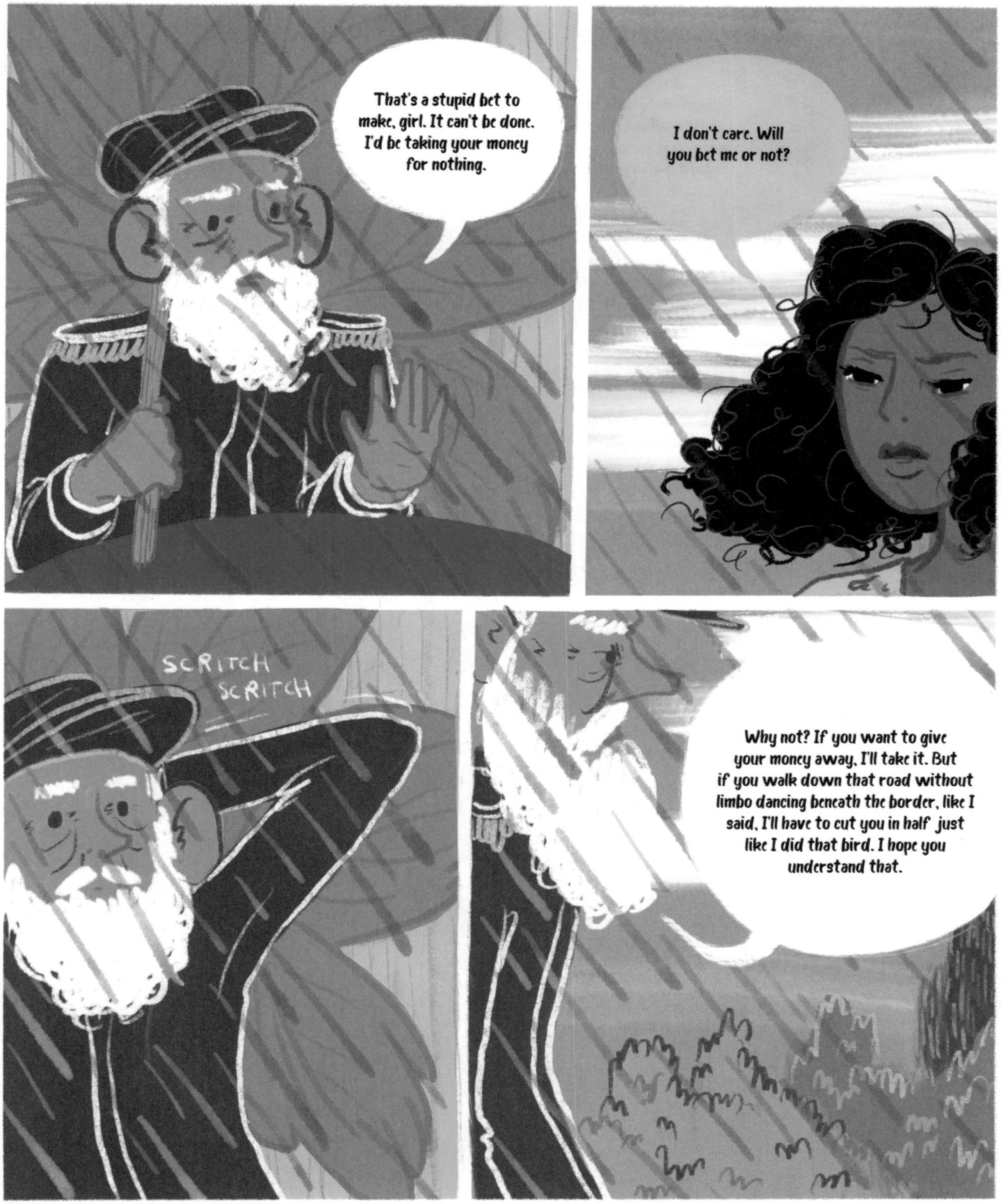
That's a stupid bet to make, girl. It can't be done. I'd be taking your money for nothing.
I don't care. Will you bet me or not?
SCRITCH SCRITCH
Why not? If you want to give your money away, I'll take it. But if you walk down that road without limbo dancing beneath the border, like I said, I'll have to cut you in half just like I did that bird. I hope you understand that.

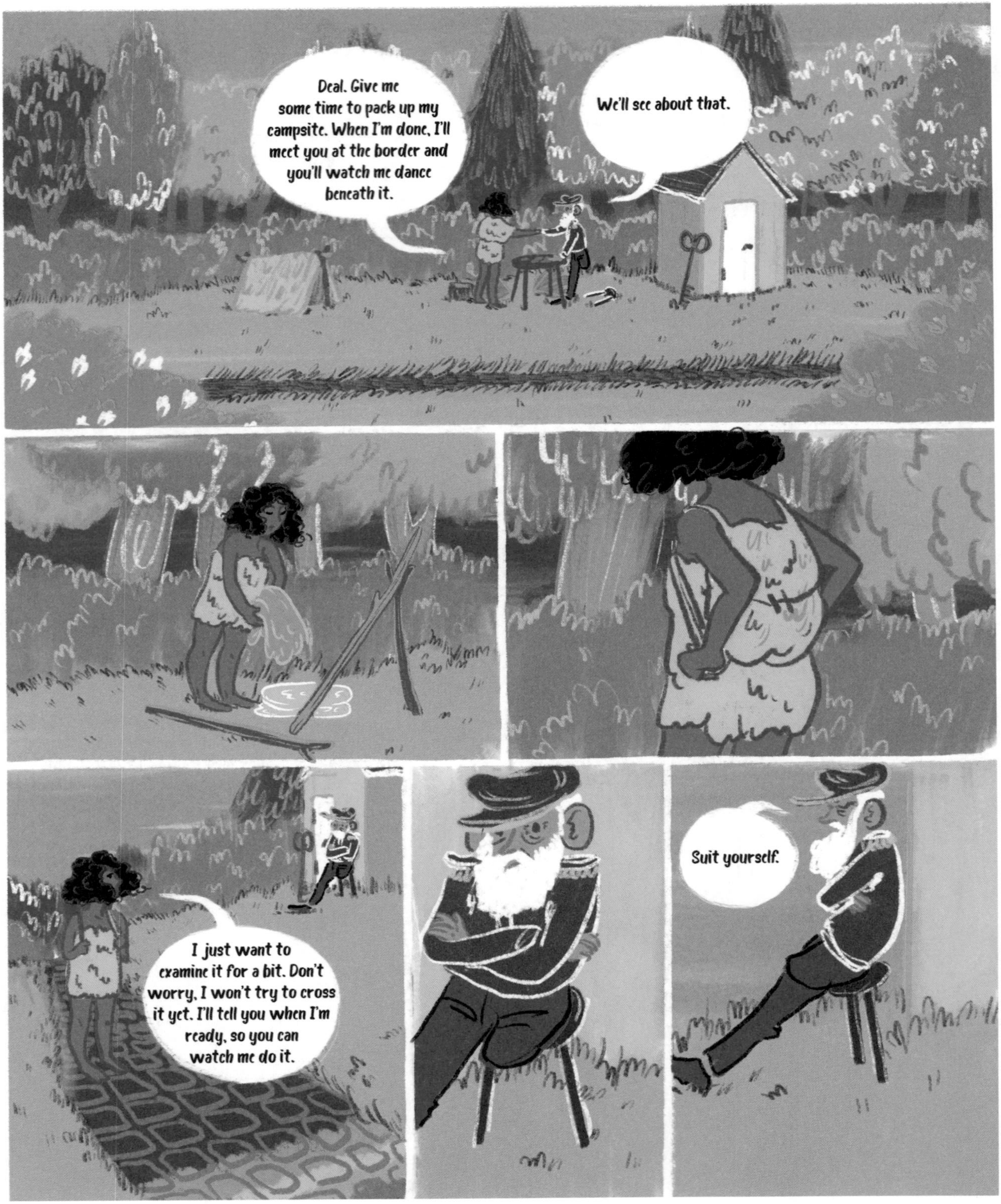
Deal. Give me some time to pack up my campsite. When I'm done, I'll meet you at the border and you'll watch me dance beneath it.
We'll see about that.
I just want to examine it for a bit. Don't worry, I won't try to cross it yet. I'll tell you when I'm ready, so you can watch me do it.
Suit yourself.

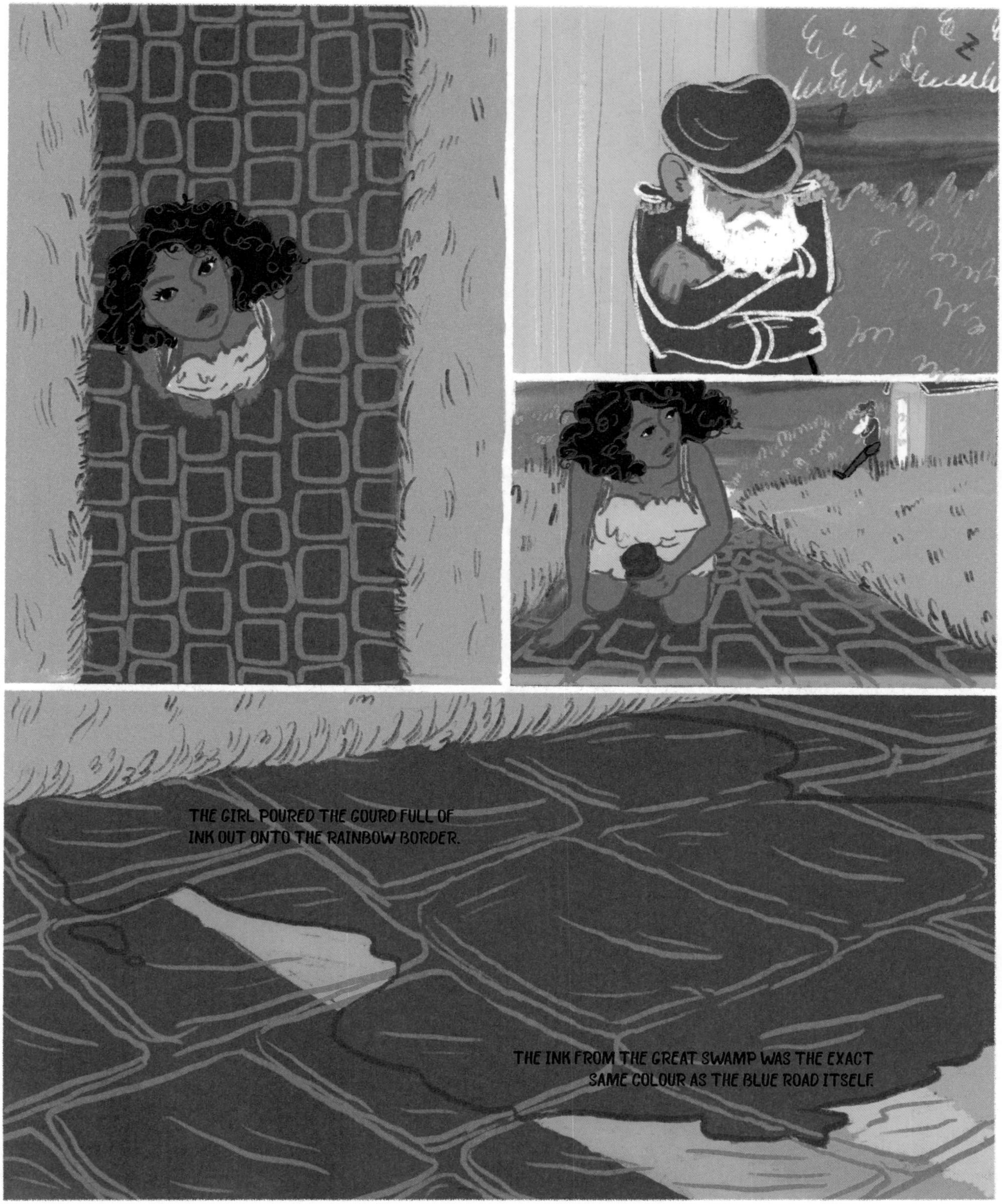
Z Z
Z
THE GIRL POURED THE GOURD FULL OF INK OUT ONTO THE RAINBOW BORDER.
THE INK FROM THE GREAT SWAMP WAS THE EXACT SAME COLOUR AS THE BLUE ROAD ITSELF.

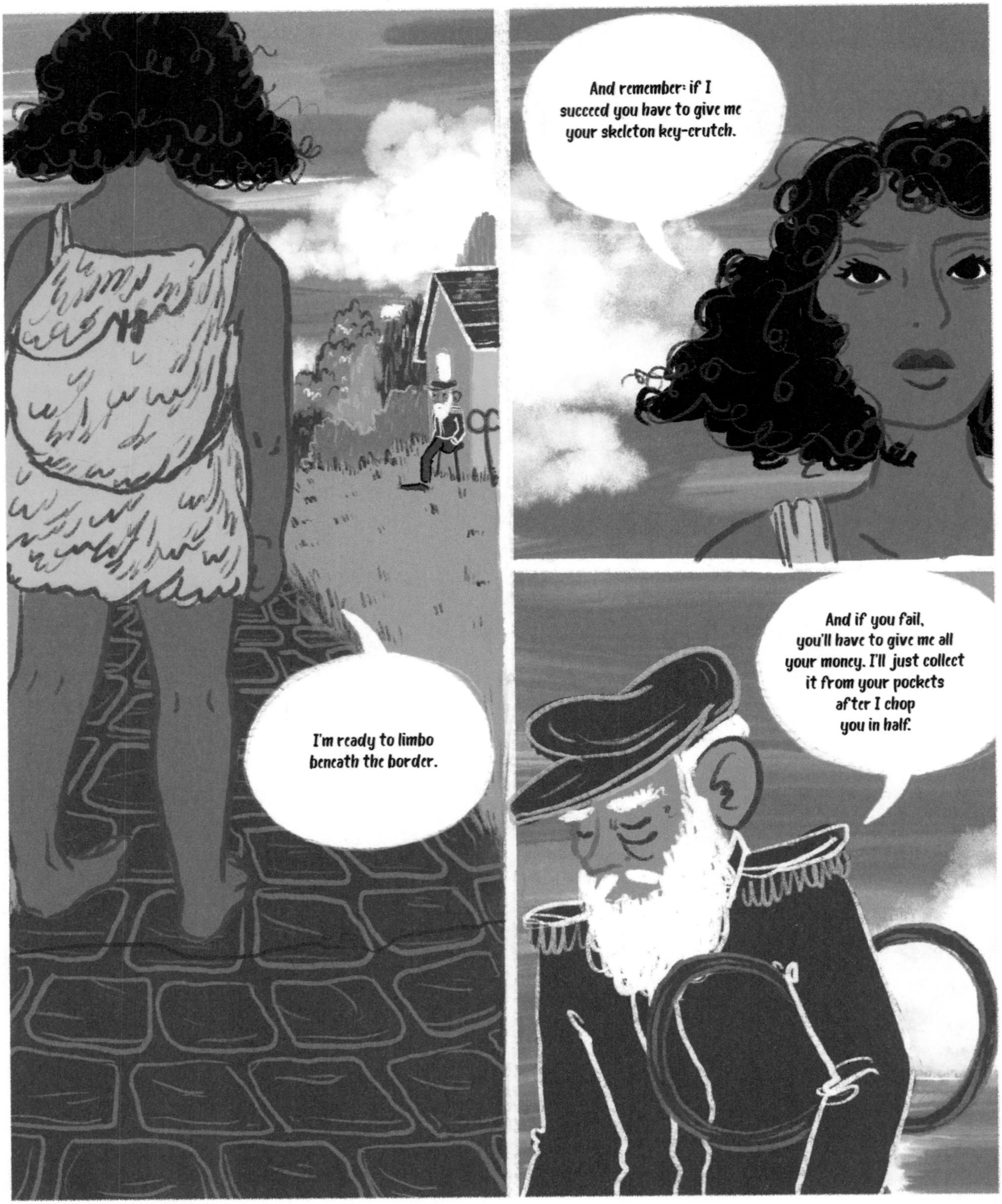
I'm ready to limbo beneath the border.
And remember: if I succeed you have to give me your skeleton key-crutch.
And if you fail, you'll have to give me all your money. I'll just collect it from your pockets after I chop you in half.

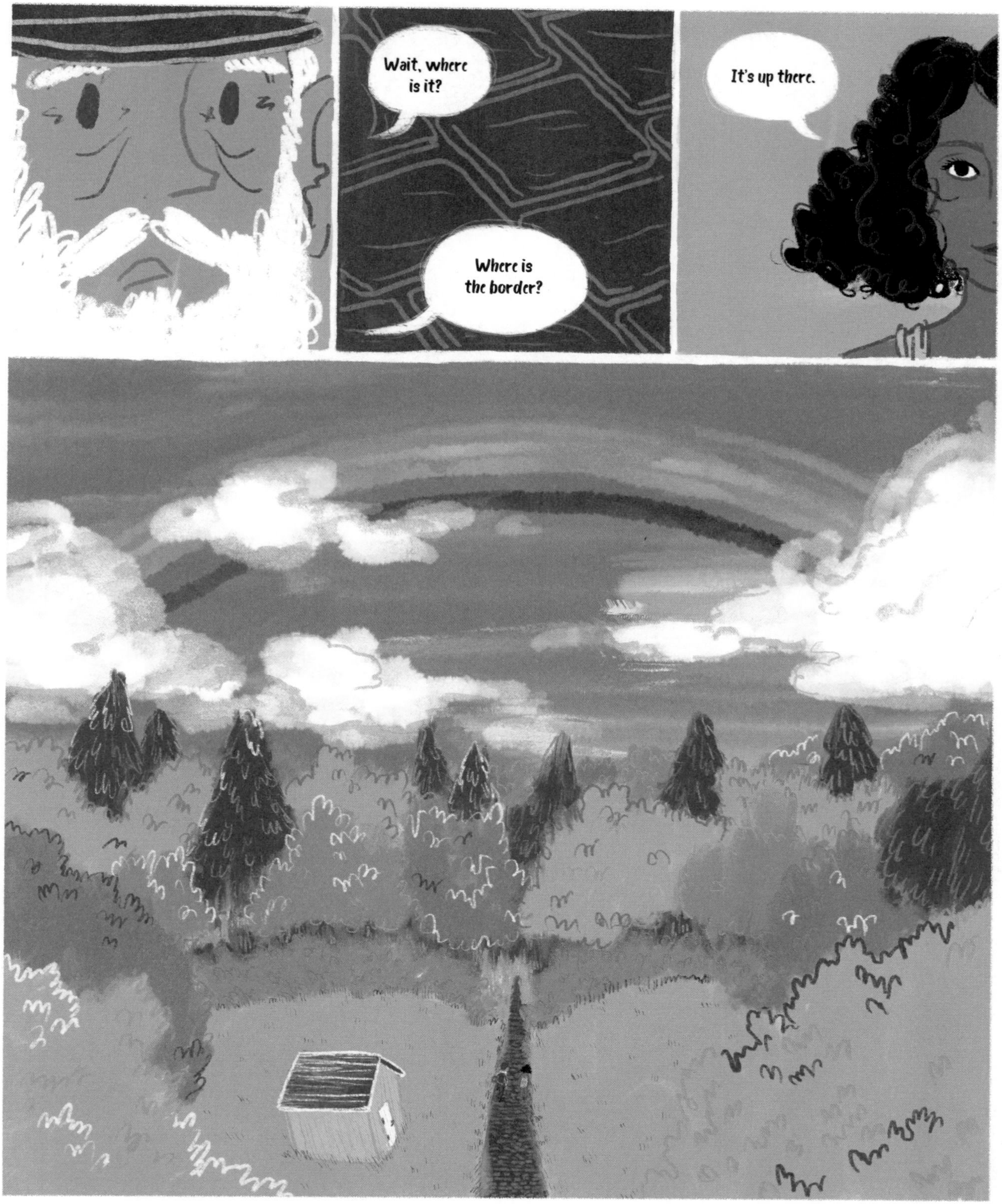
Wait, where is it?
Where is the border?
It's up there.

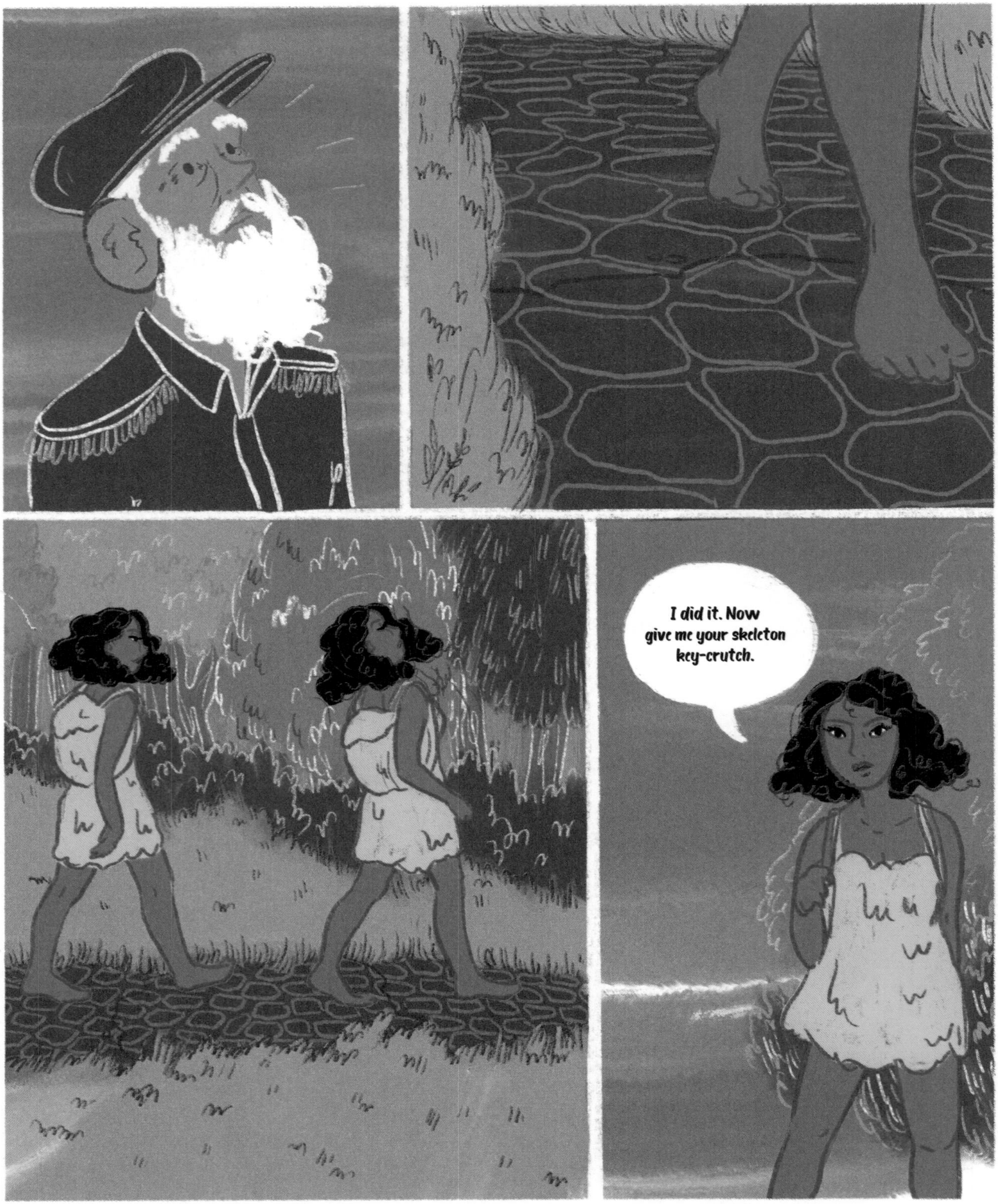
I did it. Now give me your skeleton key-crutch.

THE BORDER GUARD COULD SAY NOTHING. WITHOUT HIS SKELETON KEY-CRUTCH, HE WOULD NO LONGER BE ABLE TO PROPERLY DEFEND THE BORDER.

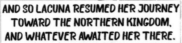

We made a deal. Give me the crutch.

Just like you said yourself: I'm just following the rules.

AND SO LACUNA RESUMED HER JOURNEY TOWARD THE NORTHERN KINGDOM, AND WHATEVER AWAITED HER THERE.

SCRATCH SCRATCH

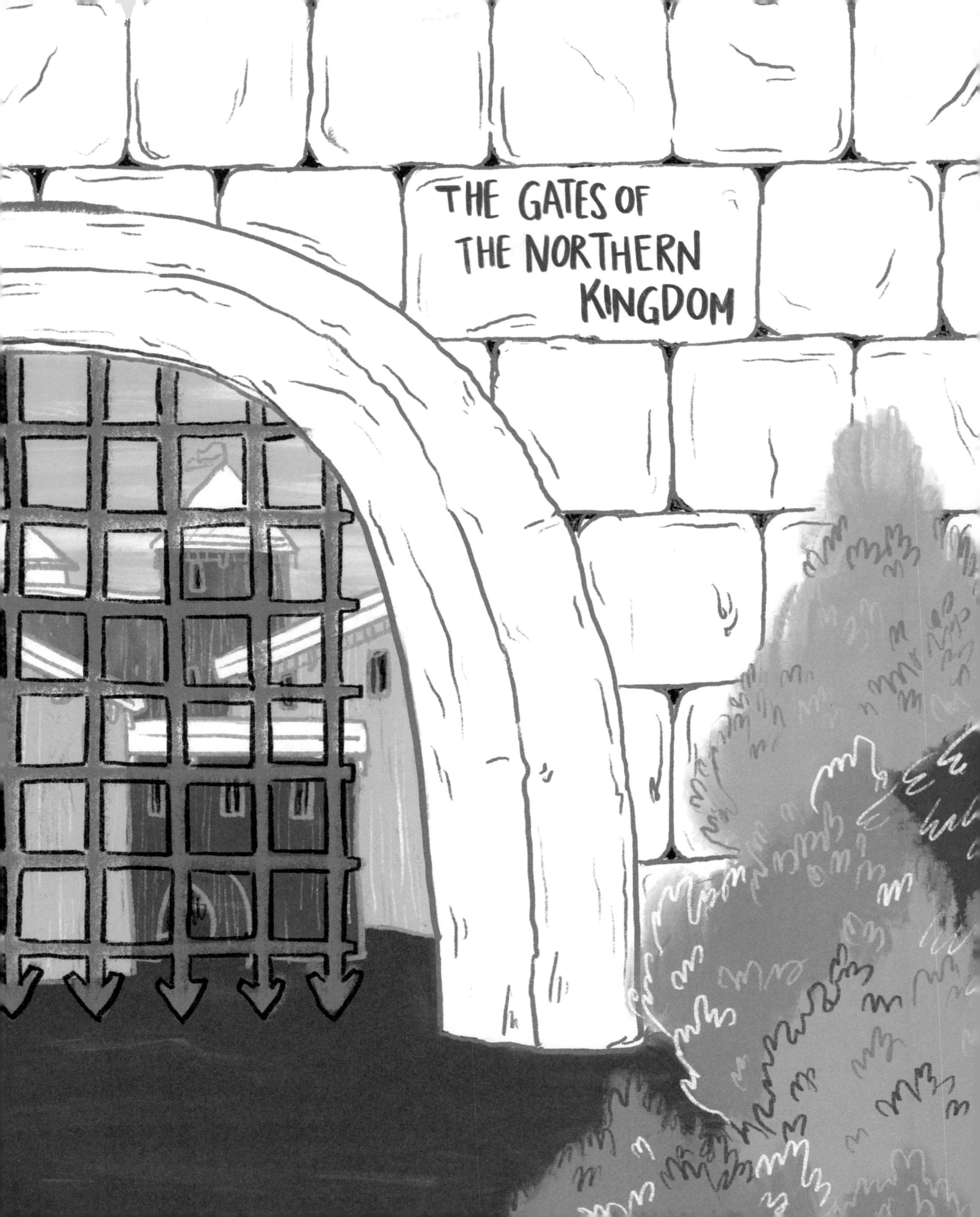
THE GATES OF
THE NORTHERN
KINGDOM

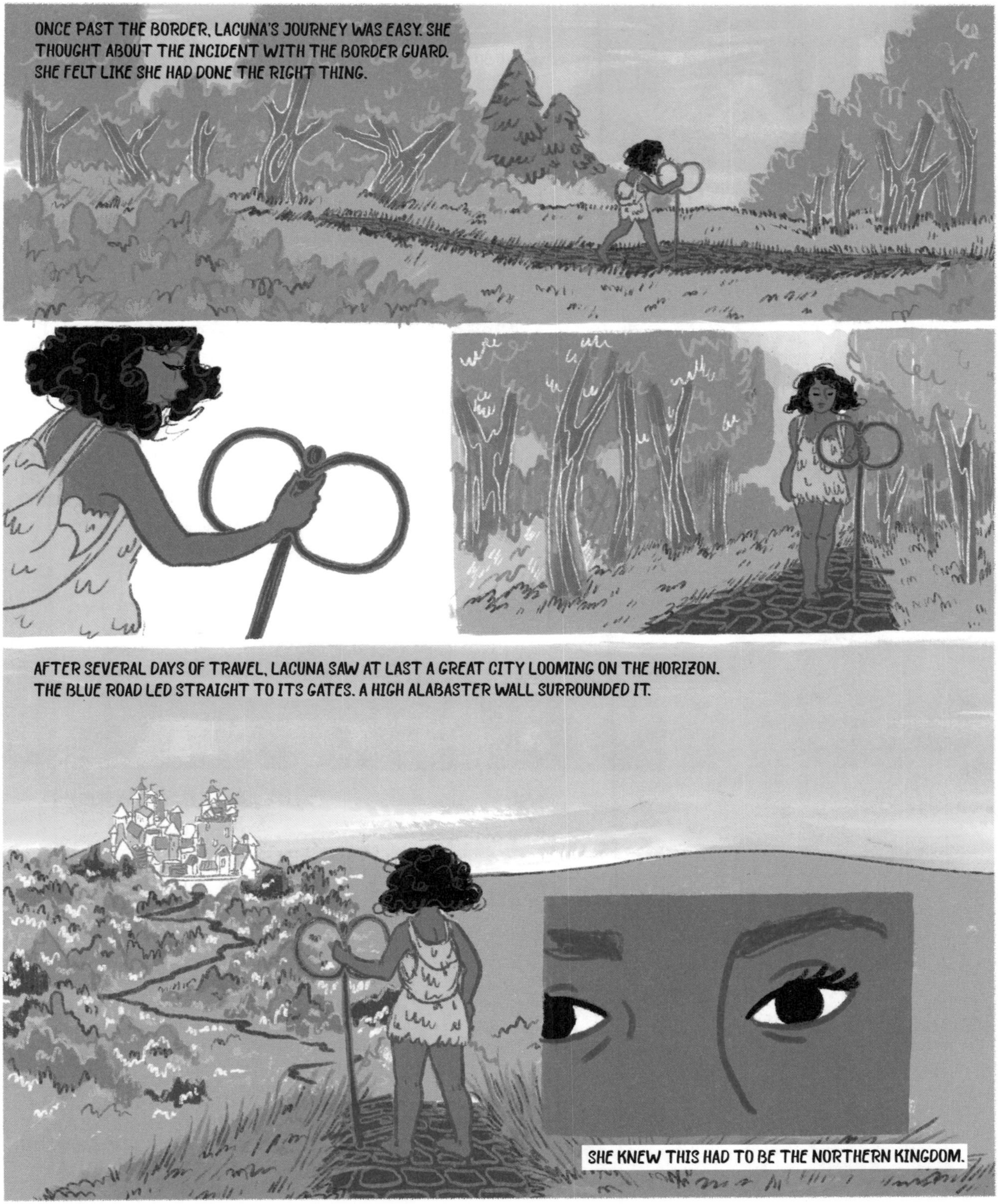
ONCE PAST THE BORDER, LACUNA'S JOURNEY WAS EASY. SHE THOUGHT ABOUT THE INCIDENT WITH THE BORDER GUARD. SHE FELT LIKE SHE HAD DONE THE RIGHT THING.
AFTER SEVERAL DAYS OF TRAVEL, LACUNA SAW AT LAST A GREAT CITY LOOMING ON THE HORIZON. THE BLUE ROAD LED STRAIGHT TO ITS GATES. A HIGH ALABASTER WALL SURROUNDED IT.
SHE KNEW THIS HAD TO BE THE NORTHERN KINGDOM.

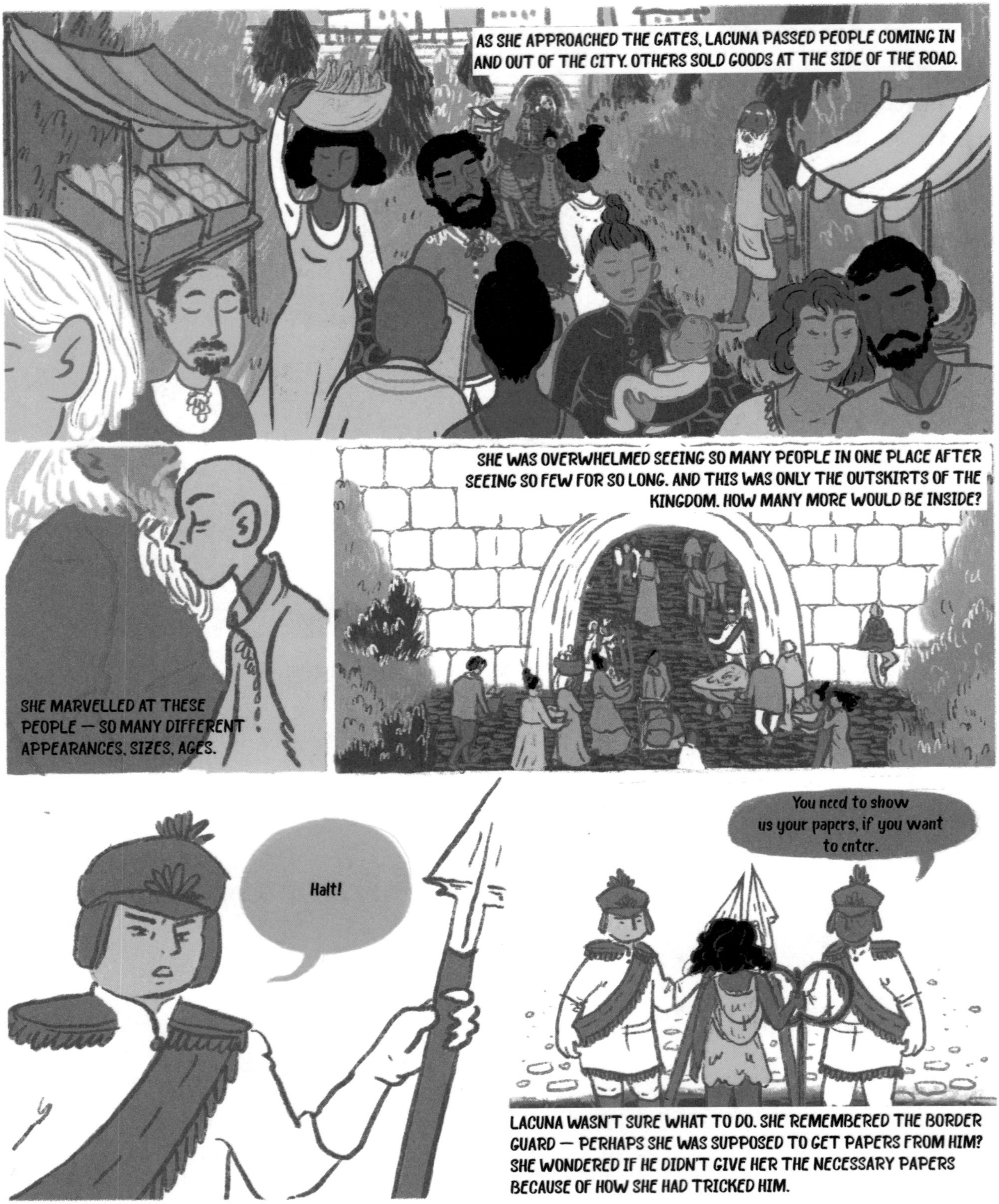
AS SHE APPROACHED THE GATES, LACUNA PASSED PEOPLE COMING IN AND OUT OF THE CITY. OTHERS SOLD GOODS AT THE SIDE OF THE ROAD.
SHE MARVELLED AT THESE PEOPLE — SO MANY DIFFERENT APPEARANCES, SIZES, AGES.
SHE WAS OVERWHELMED SEEING SO MANY PEOPLE IN ONE PLACE AFTER SEEING SO FEW FOR SO LONG. AND THIS WAS ONLY THE OUTSKIRTS OF THE KINGDOM. HOW MANY MORE WOULD BE INSIDE?
Halt!
You need to show us your papers, if you want to enter.
LACUNA WASN'T SURE WHAT TO DO. SHE REMEMBERED THE BORDER GUARD — PERHAPS SHE WAS SUPPOSED TO GET PAPERS FROM HIM? SHE WONDERED IF HE DIDN'T GIVE HER THE NECESSARY PAPERS BECAUSE OF HOW SHE HAD TRICKED HIM.

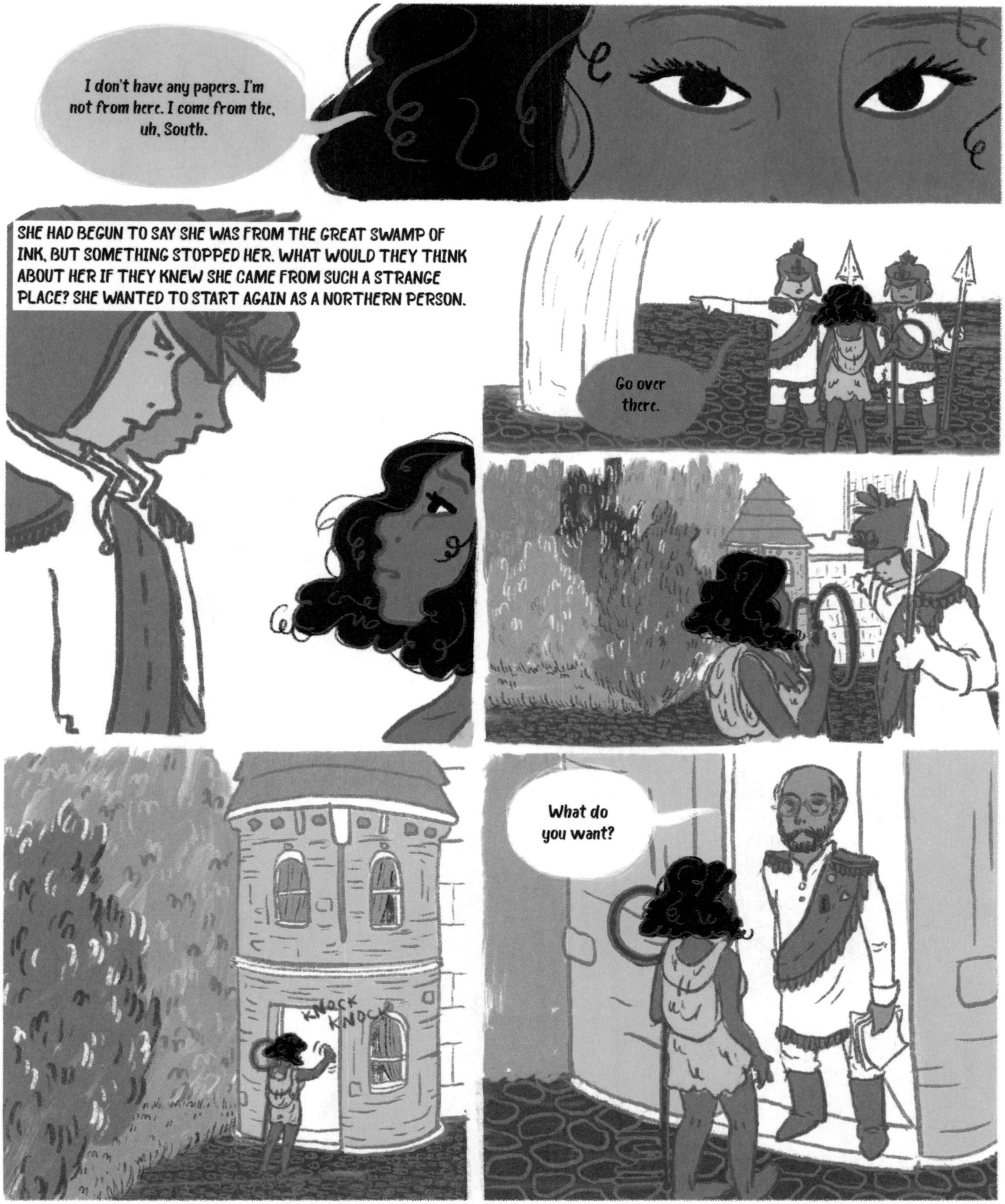
I don't have any papers. I'm not from here. I come from the, uh, South.
SHE HAD BEGUN TO SAY SHE WAS FROM THE GREAT SWAMP OF INK, BUT SOMETHING STOPPED HER. WHAT WOULD THEY THINK ABOUT HER IF THEY KNEW SHE CAME FROM SUCH A STRANGE PLACE? SHE WANTED TO START AGAIN AS A NORTHERN PERSON.
Go over there.
KNOCK KNOCK
What do you want?

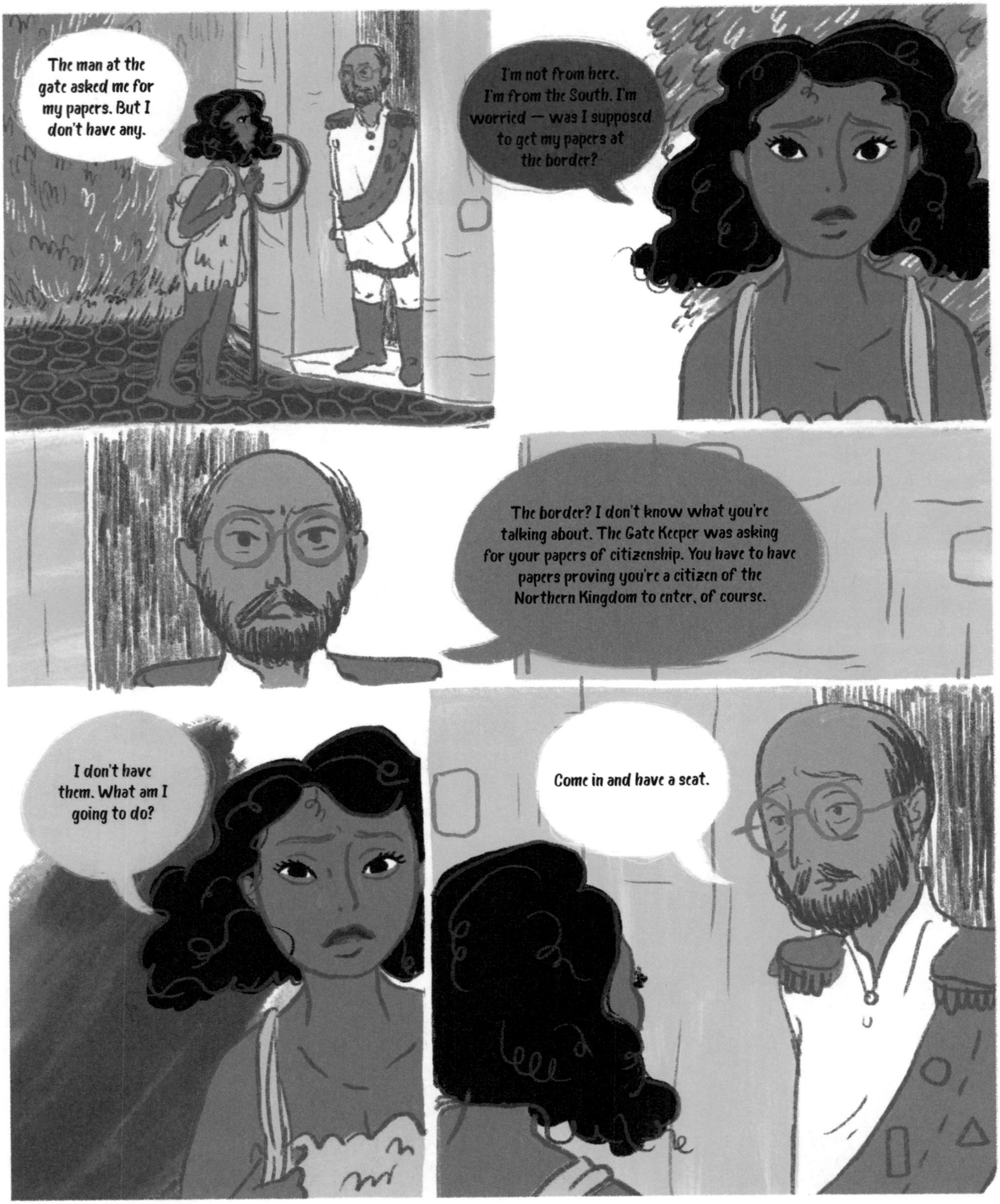
The man at the gate asked me for my papers. But I don't have any.
I'm not from here. I'm from the South. I'm worried — was I supposed to get my papers at the border?
The border? I don't know what you're talking about. The Gate Keeper was asking for your papers of citizenship. You have to have papers proving you're a citizen of the Northern Kingdom to enter, of course.
I don't have them. What am I going to do?
Come in and have a seat.

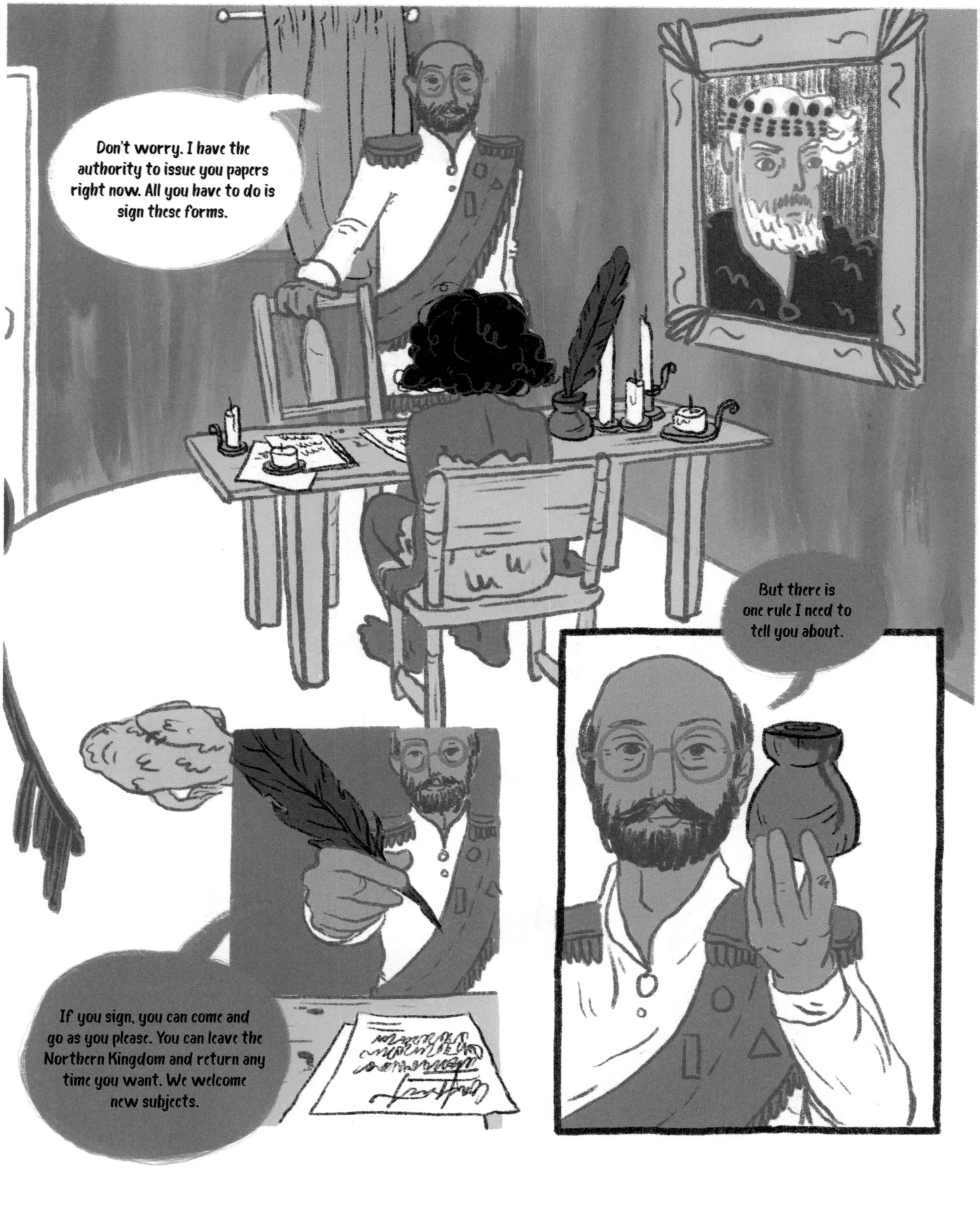
Don't worry. I have the authority to issue you papers right now. All you have to do is sign these forms.
If you sign, you can come and go as you please. You can leave the Northern Kingdom and return any time you want. We welcome new subjects.
But there is one rule I need to tell you about.

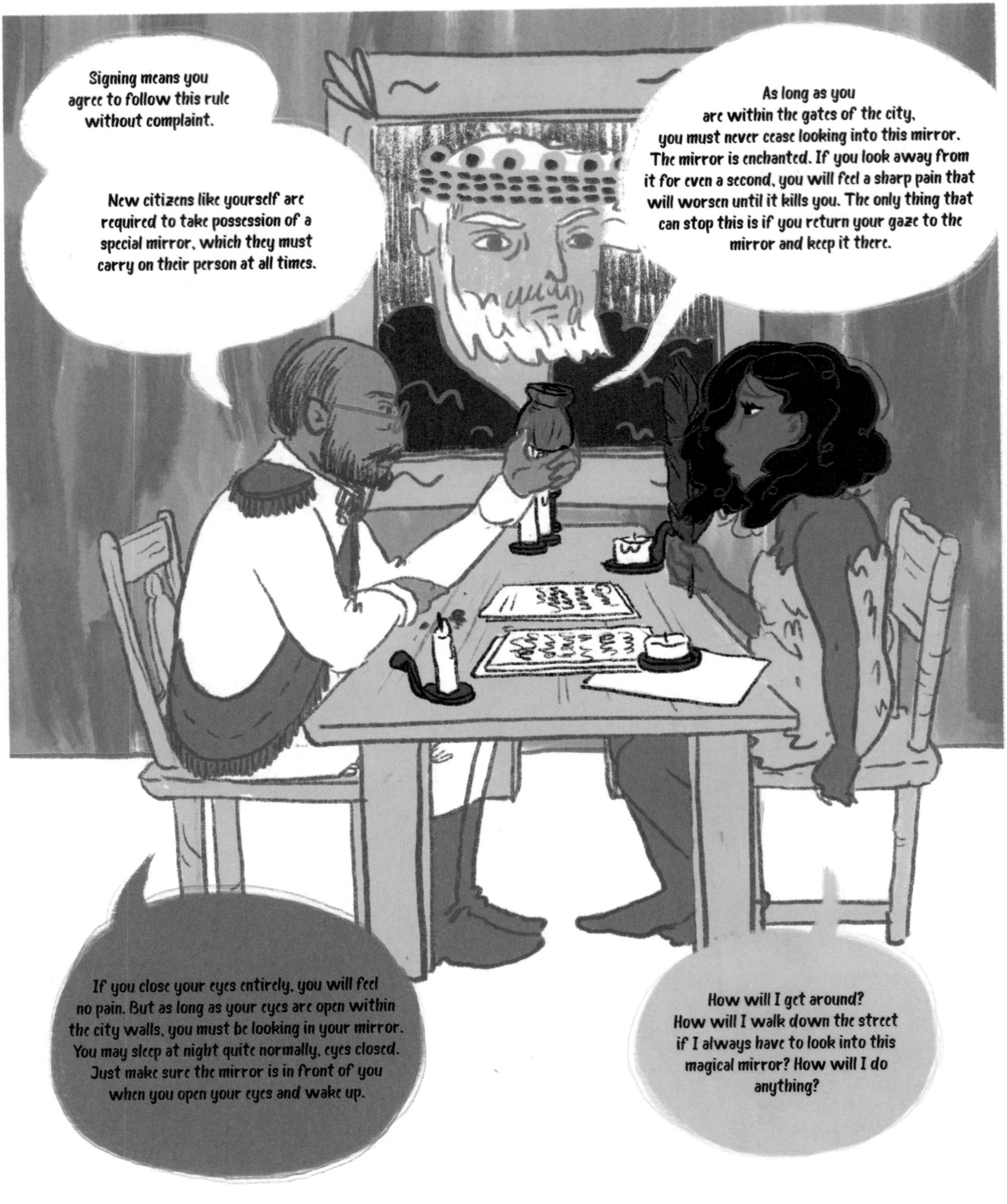
Signing means you agree to follow this rule without complaint.
New citizens like yourself are required to take possession of a special mirror, which they must carry on their person at all times.
As long as you are within the gates of the city, you must never cease looking into this mirror. The mirror is enchanted. If you look away from it for even a second, you will feel a sharp pain that will worsen until it kills you. The only thing that can stop this is if you return your gaze to the mirror and keep it there.
If you close your eyes entirely, you will feel no pain. But as long as your eyes are open within the city walls, you must be looking in your mirror. You may sleep at night quite normally, eyes closed. Just make sure the mirror is in front of you when you open your eyes and wake up.
How will I get around? How will I walk down the street if I always have to look into this magical mirror? How will I do anything?

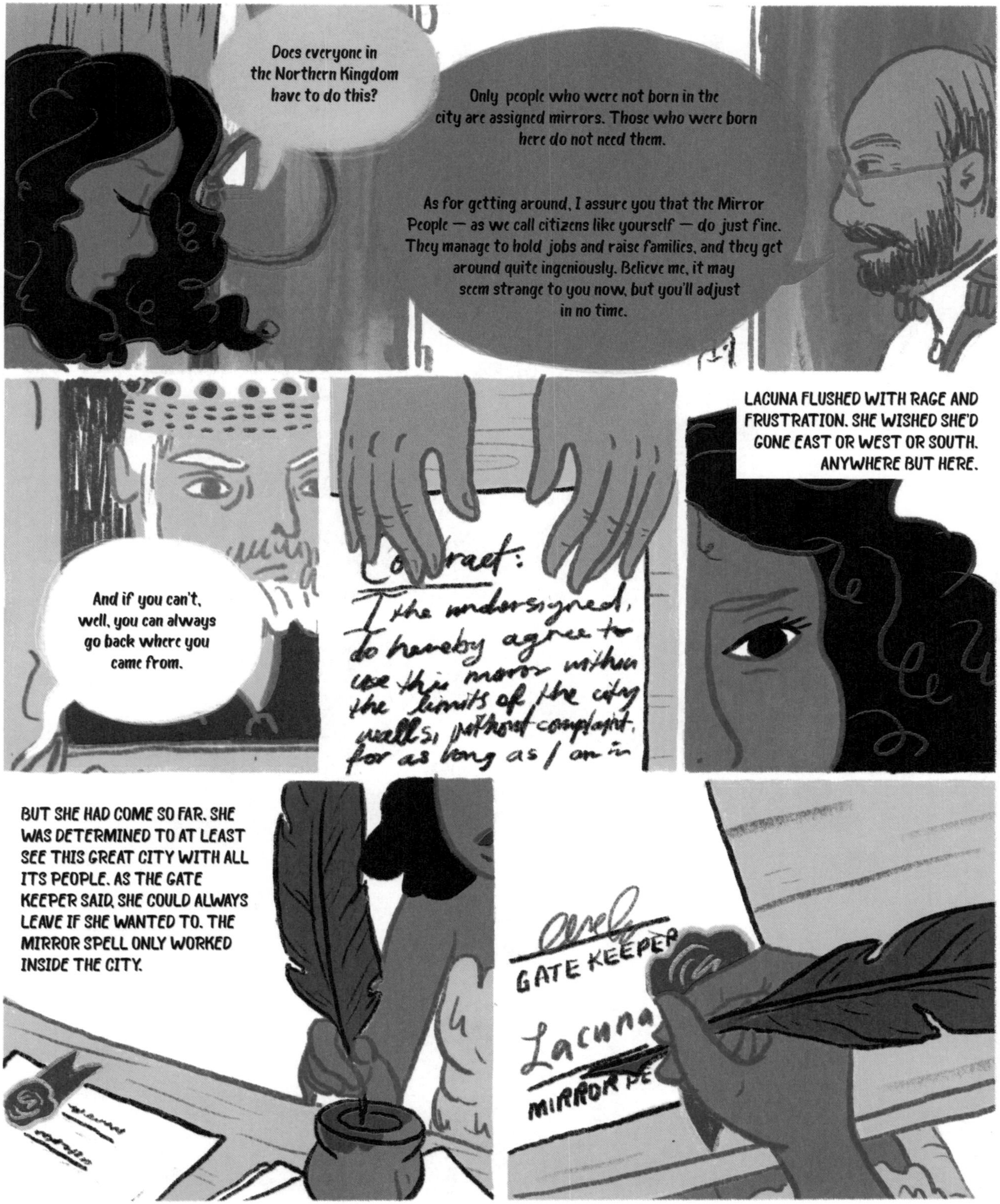
Does everyone in the Northern Kingdom have to do this?
Only people who were not born in the city are assigned mirrors. Those who were born here do not need them.
As for getting around, I assure you that the Mirror People — as we call citizens like yourself — do just fine. They manage to hold jobs and raise families, and they get around quite ingeniously. Believe me, it may seem strange to you now, but you'll adjust in no time.
And if you can't, well, you can always go back where you came from.
I the undersigned, do hereby agree to use this mirror within the limits of the city walls, without complaint, for as long as I am in
LACUNA FLUSHED WITH RAGE AND FRUSTRATION. SHE WISHED SHE'D GONE EAST OR WEST OR SOUTH. ANYWHERE BUT HERE.
BUT SHE HAD COME SO FAR. SHE WAS DETERMINED TO AT LEAST SEE THIS GREAT CITY WITH ALL ITS PEOPLE. AS THE GATE KEEPER SAID, SHE COULD ALWAYS LEAVE IF SHE WANTED TO. THE MIRROR SPELL ONLY WORKED INSIDE THE CITY.
GATE KEEPER
Lacuna

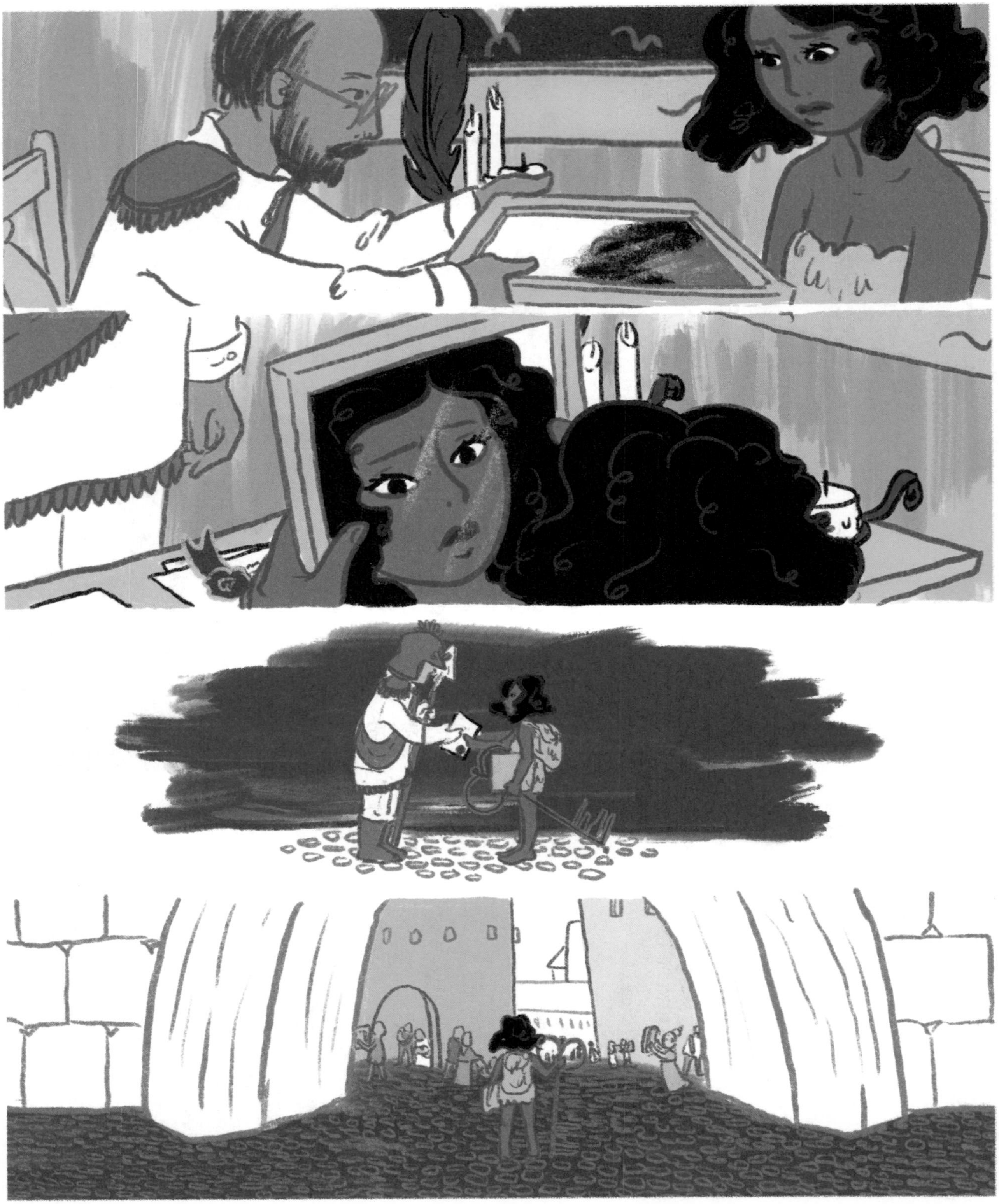

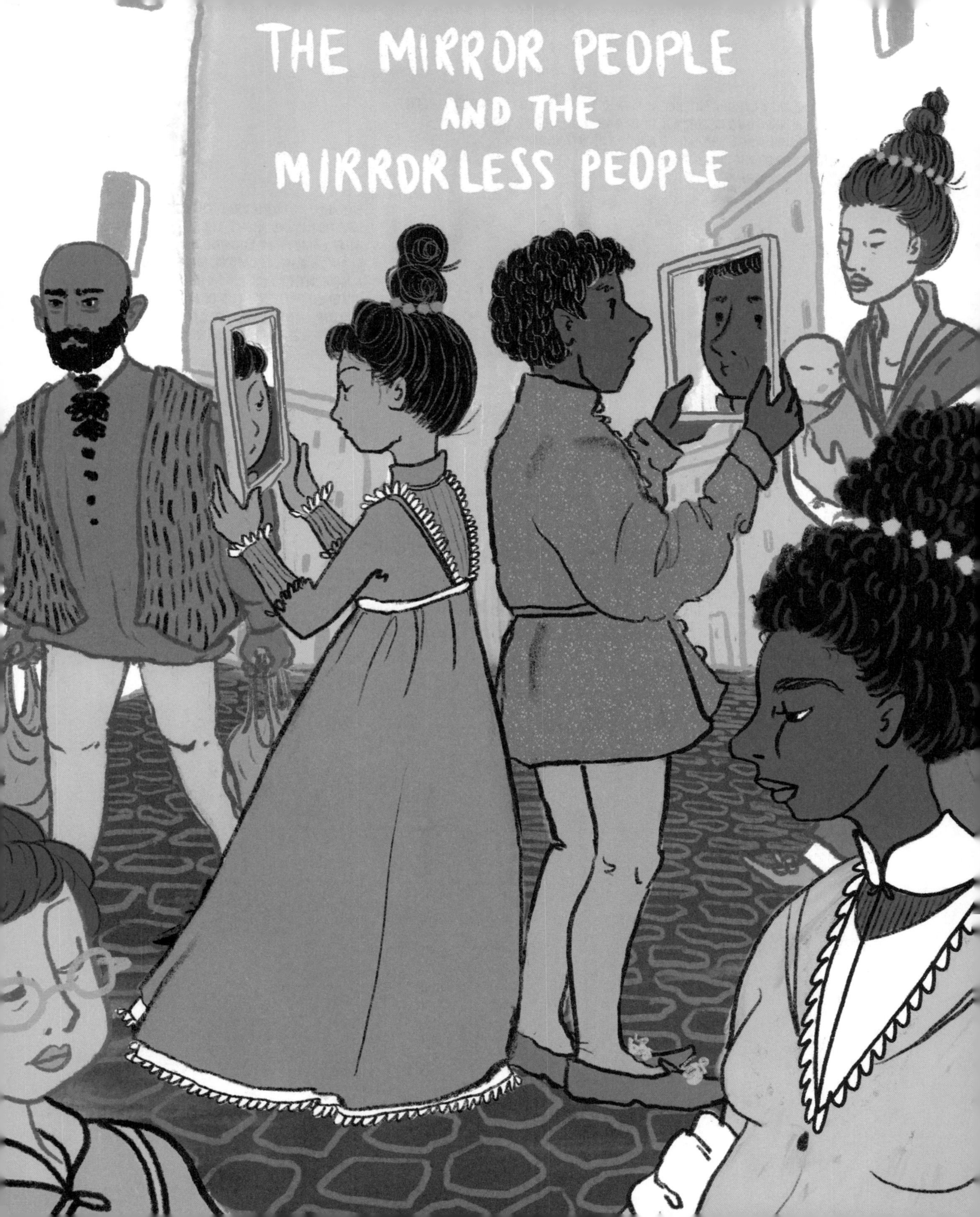
THE MIRROR PEOPLE
AND THE
MIRRORLESS PEOPLE

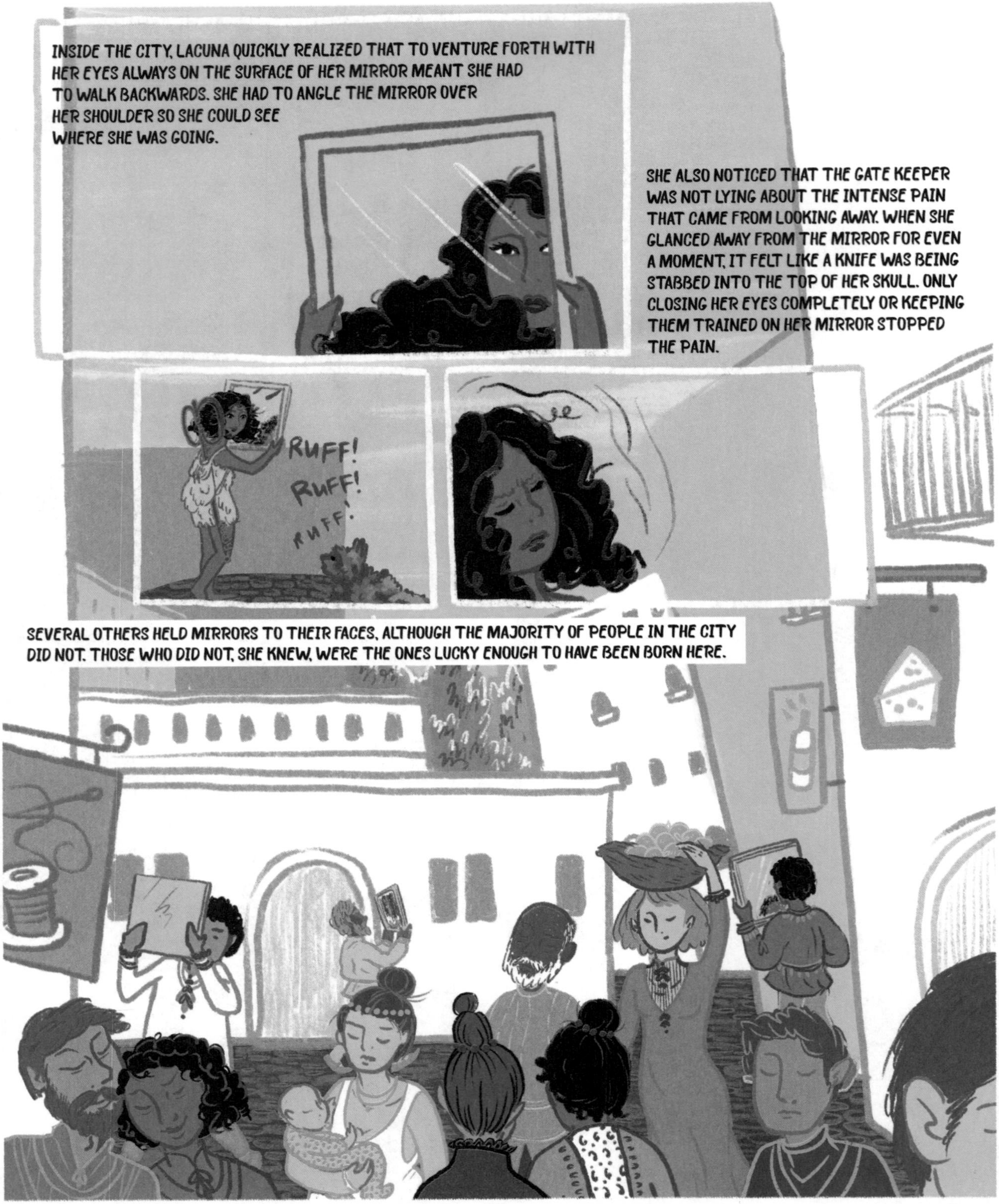
INSIDE THE CITY, LACUNA QUICKLY REALIZED THAT TO VENTURE FORTH WITH HER EYES ALWAYS ON THE SURFACE OF HER MIRROR MEANT SHE HAD TO WALK BACKWARDS. SHE HAD TO ANGLE THE MIRROR OVER HER SHOULDER SO SHE COULD SEE WHERE SHE WAS GOING.
SHE ALSO NOTICED THAT THE GATE KEEPER WAS NOT LYING ABOUT THE INTENSE PAIN THAT CAME FROM LOOKING AWAY. WHEN SHE GLANCED AWAY FROM THE MIRROR FOR EVEN A MOMENT, IT FELT LIKE A KNIFE WAS BEING STABBED INTO THE TOP OF HER SKULL. ONLY CLOSING HER EYES COMPLETELY OR KEEPING THEM TRAINED ON HER MIRROR STOPPED THE PAIN.
RUFF!
RUFF!
RUFF!
SEVERAL OTHERS HELD MIRRORS TO THEIR FACES, ALTHOUGH THE MAJORITY OF PEOPLE IN THE CITY DID NOT. THOSE WHO DID NOT, SHE KNEW, WERE THE ONES LUCKY ENOUGH TO HAVE BEEN BORN HERE.

IT LOOKED LIKE MANY OF THESE PEOPLE HAD BEEN DOING THIS FOR YEARS. THEY WERE SKILLED AT WALKING BACKWARDS, TALKING TO EACH OTHER, AND EVEN READING WORDS IN BOOKS OR NEWSPAPERS BACKWARDS. ALL BY ANGLING THEIR MIRRORS IN THE RIGHT DIRECTION.

SHE SPENT HER FIRST DAY WALKING AROUND THE CITY, TRYING TO GET USED TO NAVIGATING THE STREETS THIS WAY.

LACUNA STARTED LOOKING FOR A PLACE TO STAY, AND FOR WORK.

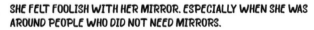

HELP WANTED

SHE FELT FOOLISH WITH HER MIRROR. ESPECIALLY WHEN SHE WAS AROUND PEOPLE WHO DID NOT NEED MIRRORS.

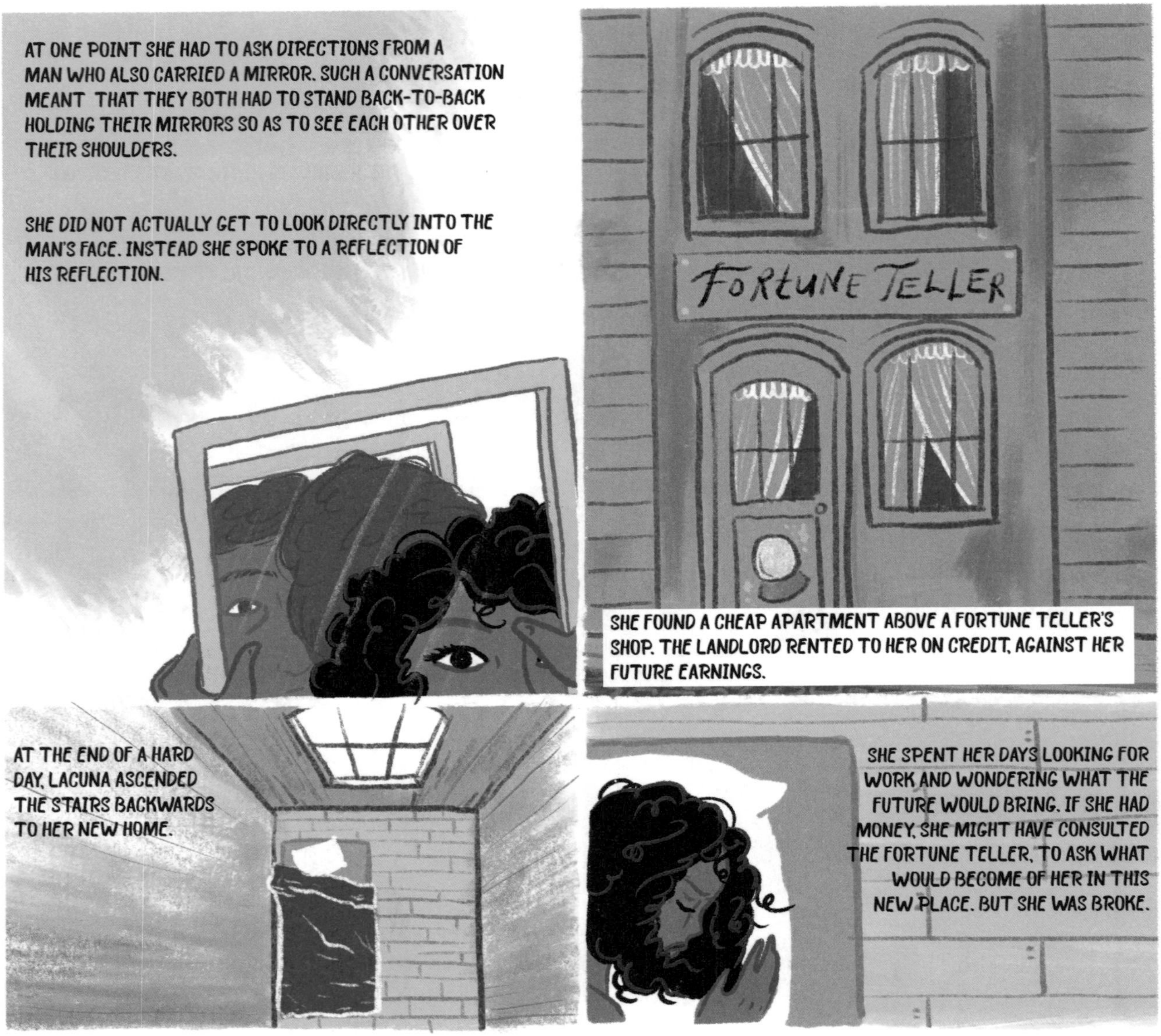
AT ONE POINT SHE HAD TO ASK DIRECTIONS FROM A MAN WHO ALSO CARRIED A MIRROR. SUCH A CONVERSATION MEANT THAT THEY BOTH HAD TO STAND BACK-TO-BACK HOLDING THEIR MIRRORS SO AS TO SEE EACH OTHER OVER THEIR SHOULDERS.
SHE DID NOT ACTUALLY GET TO LOOK DIRECTLY INTO THE MAN'S FACE. INSTEAD SHE SPOKE TO A REFLECTION OF HIS REFLECTION.
FORTUNE TELLER
SHE FOUND A CHEAP APARTMENT ABOVE A FORTUNE TELLER'S SHOP. THE LANDLORD RENTED TO HER ON CREDIT, AGAINST HER FUTURE EARNINGS.
AT THE END OF A HARD DAY, LACUNA ASCENDED THE STAIRS BACKWARDS TO HER NEW HOME.
SHE SPENT HER DAYS LOOKING FOR WORK AND WONDERING WHAT THE FUTURE WOULD BRING. IF SHE HAD MONEY, SHE MIGHT HAVE CONSULTED THE FORTUNE TELLER, TO ASK WHAT WOULD BECOME OF HER IN THIS NEW PLACE. BUT SHE WAS BROKE.

SHE KNEW THAT THIS PLACE WAS BETTER THAN THE GREAT SWAMP OF INK. BUT IT WASN'T WHAT SHE HAD EXPECTED AT ALL.

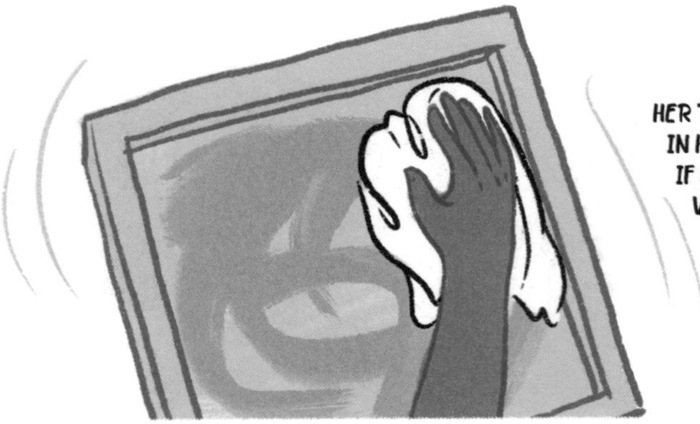

HER THOUGHTS CIRCLED AROUND IN HER MIND. SHE WASN'T SURE IF SHE WAS HAPPY OR SAD. SHE WAS PUZZLED. BUT SHE ALSO HAD AN IDEA FOR HOW SHE COULD MAKE A LIVING.

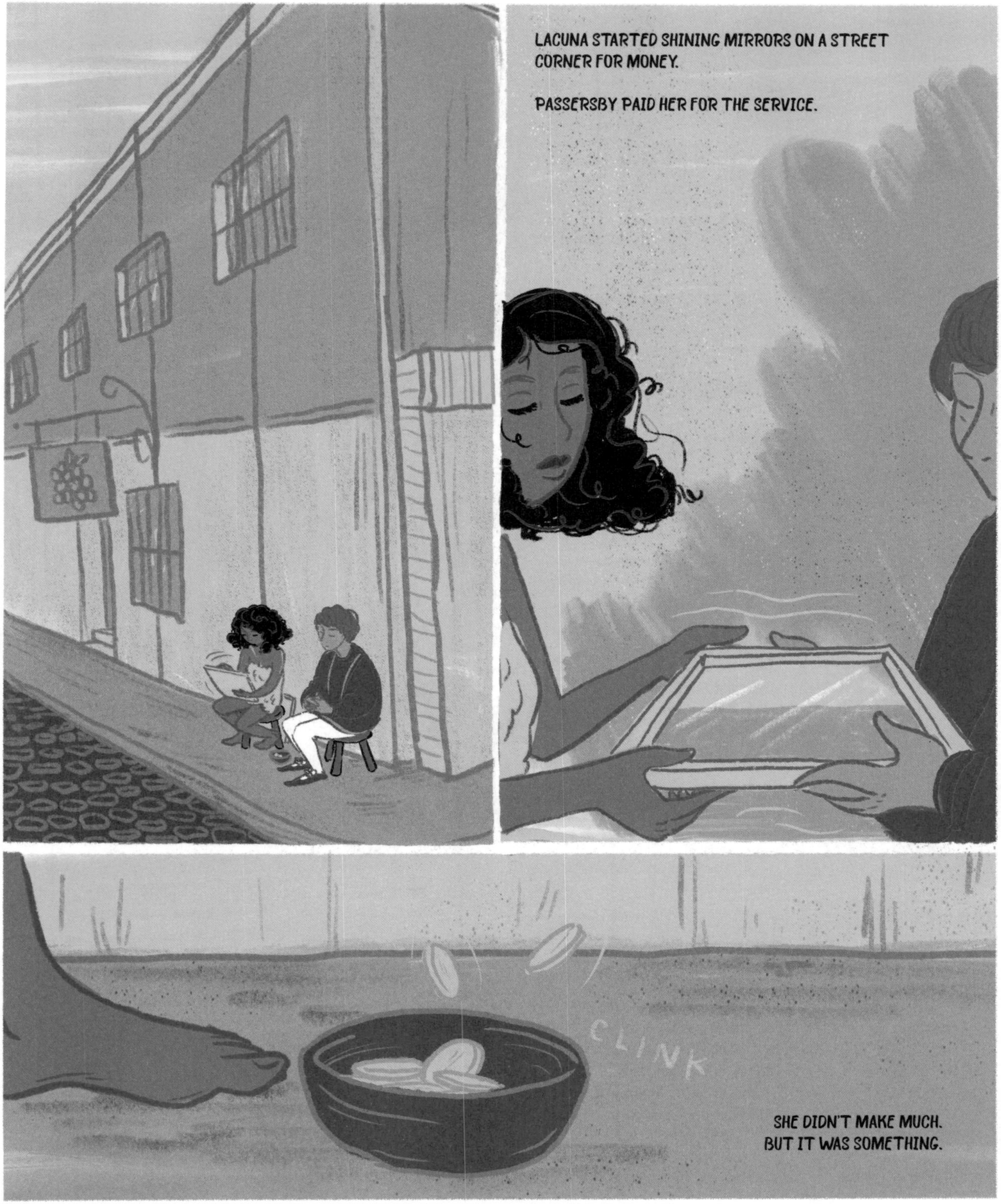
LACUNA STARTED SHINING MIRRORS ON A STREET CORNER FOR MONEY.
PASSERSBY PAID HER FOR THE SERVICE.
CLINK
SHE DIDN'T MAKE MUCH.
BUT IT WAS SOMETHING.

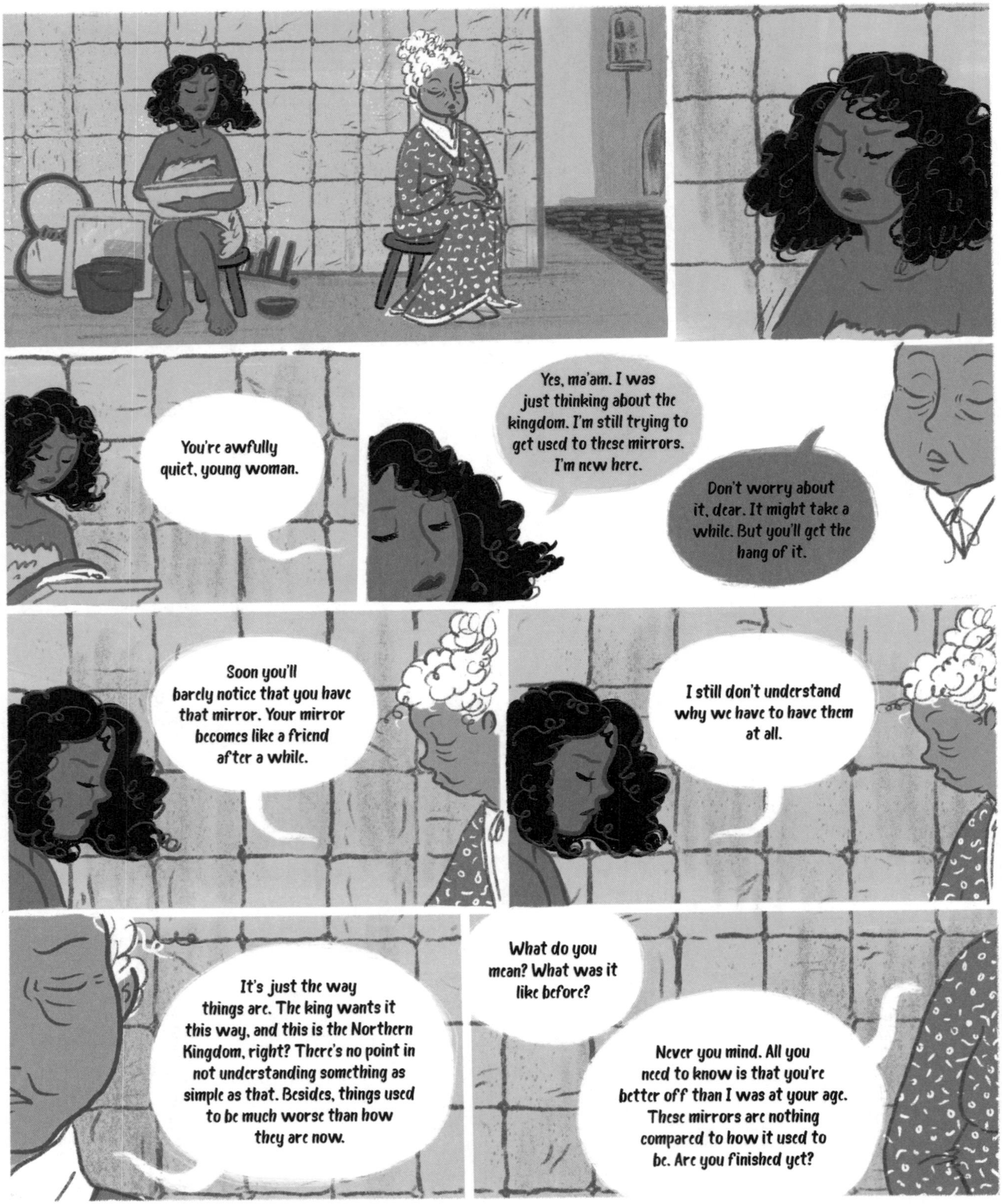

You're awfully quiet, young woman.
Yes, ma'am. I was just thinking about the kingdom. I'm still trying to get used to these mirrors. I'm new here.
Don't worry about it, dear. It might take a while. But you'll get the hang of it.
Soon you'll barely notice that you have that mirror. Your mirror becomes like a friend after a while.
I still don't understand why we have to have them at all.
It's just the way things are. The king wants it this way, and this is the Northern Kingdom, right? There's no point in not understanding something as simple as that. Besides, things used to be much worse than how they are now.
What do you mean? What was it like before?
Never you mind. All you need to know is that you're better off than I was at your age. These mirrors are nothing compared to how it used to be. Are you finished yet?

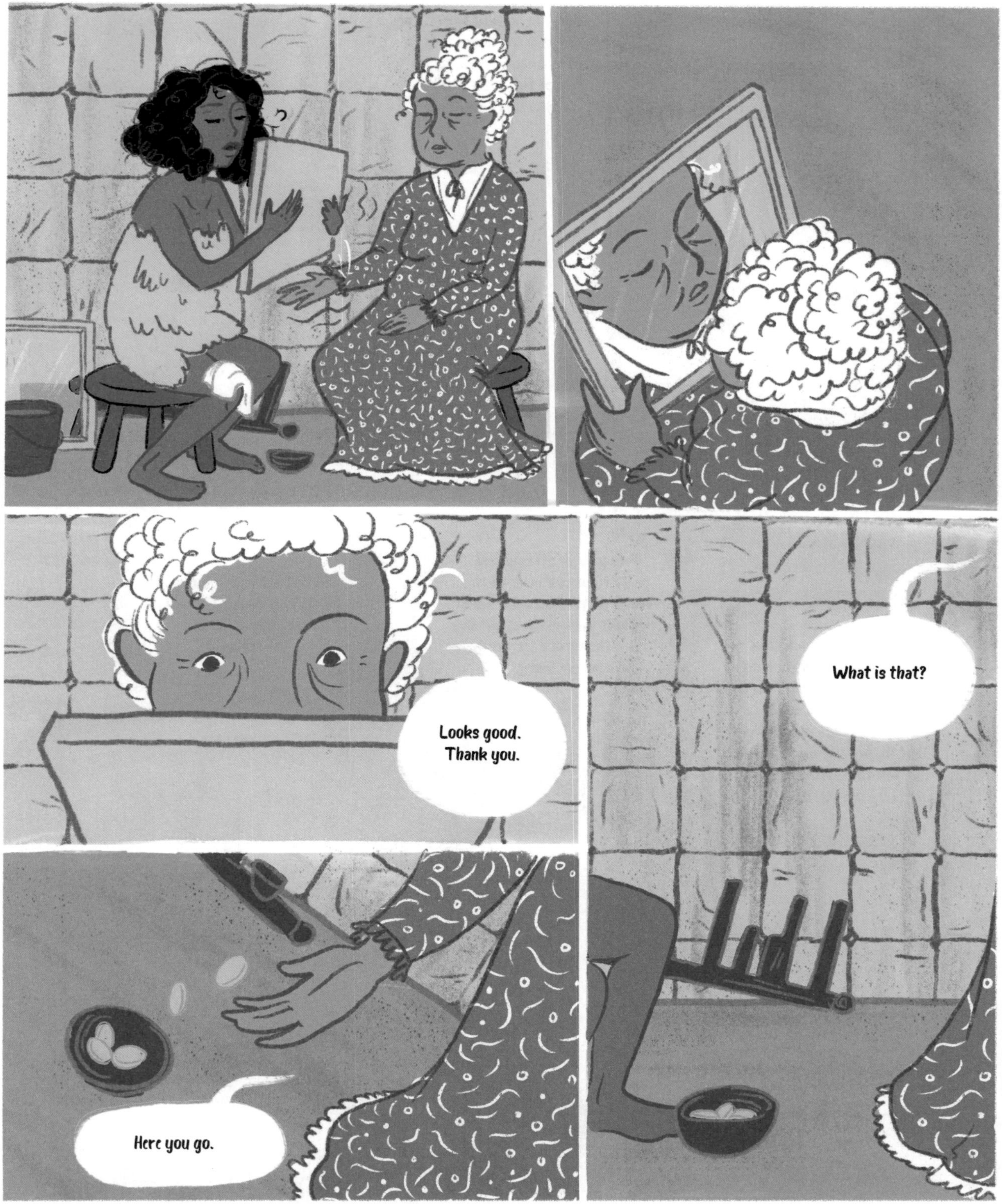
Looks good.
Thank you.
What is that?
Here you go.

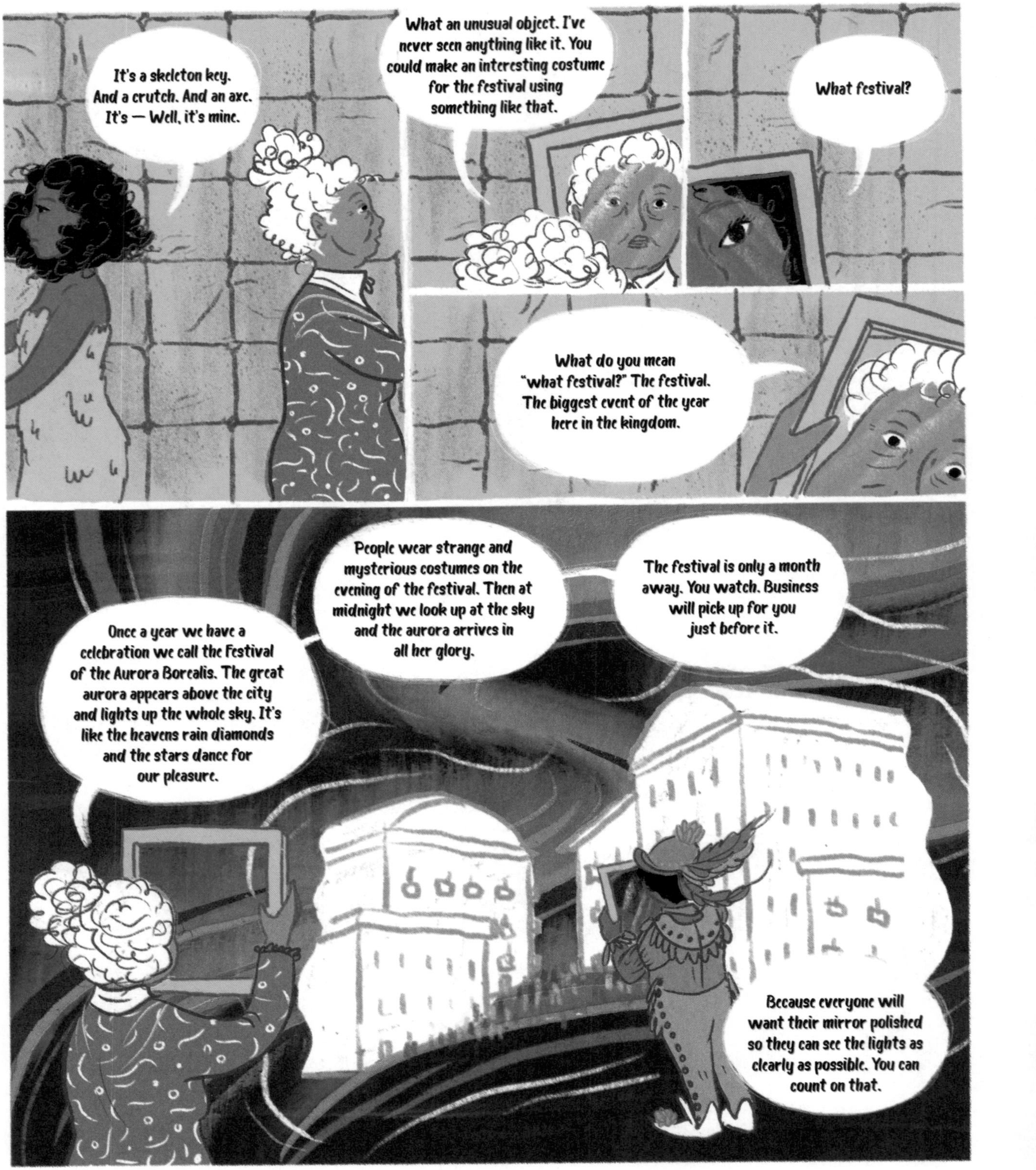
It's a skeleton key. And a crutch. And an axe. It's — Well, it's mine.
What an unusual object. I've never seen anything like it. You could make an interesting costume for the festival using something like that.
What festival?
What do you mean "what festival?" The festival. The biggest event of the year here in the kingdom.
Once a year we have a celebration we call the Festival of the Aurora Borealis. The great aurora appears above the city and lights up the whole sky. It's like the heavens rain diamonds and the stars dance for our pleasure.
People wear strange and mysterious costumes on the evening of the festival. Then at midnight we look up at the sky and the aurora arrives in all her glory.
The festival is only a month away. You watch. Business will pick up for you just before it.
Because everyone will want their mirror polished so they can see the lights as clearly as possible. You can count on that.

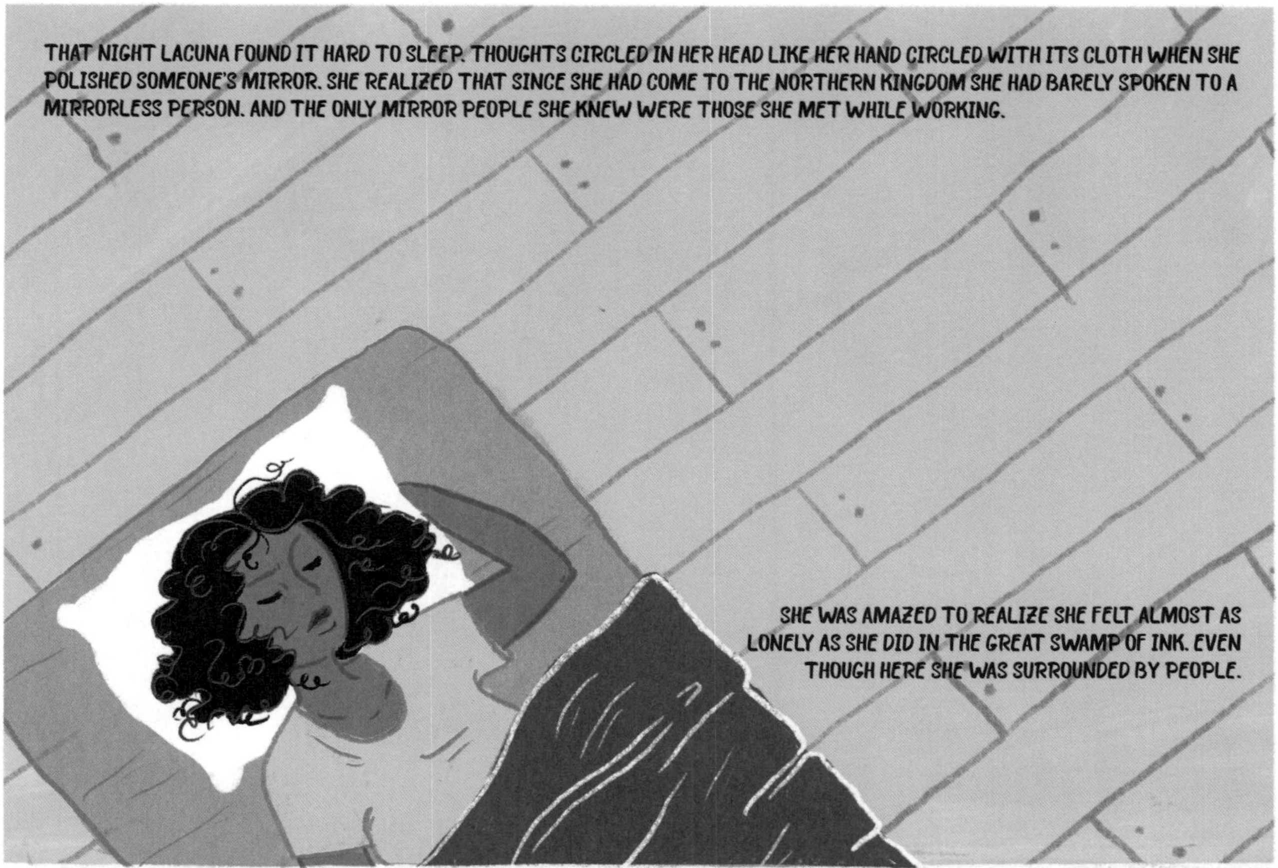
THAT NIGHT LACUNA FOUND IT HARD TO SLEEP. THOUGHTS CIRCLED IN HER HEAD LIKE HER HAND CIRCLED WITH ITS CLOTH WHEN SHE POLISHED SOMEONE'S MIRROR. SHE REALIZED THAT SINCE SHE HAD COME TO THE NORTHERN KINGDOM SHE HAD BARELY SPOKEN TO A MIRRORLESS PERSON. AND THE ONLY MIRROR PEOPLE SHE KNEW WERE THOSE SHE MET WHILE WORKING.
SHE WAS AMAZED TO REALIZE SHE FELT ALMOST AS LONELY AS SHE DID IN THE GREAT SWAMP OF INK. EVEN THOUGH HERE SHE WAS SURROUNDED BY PEOPLE.

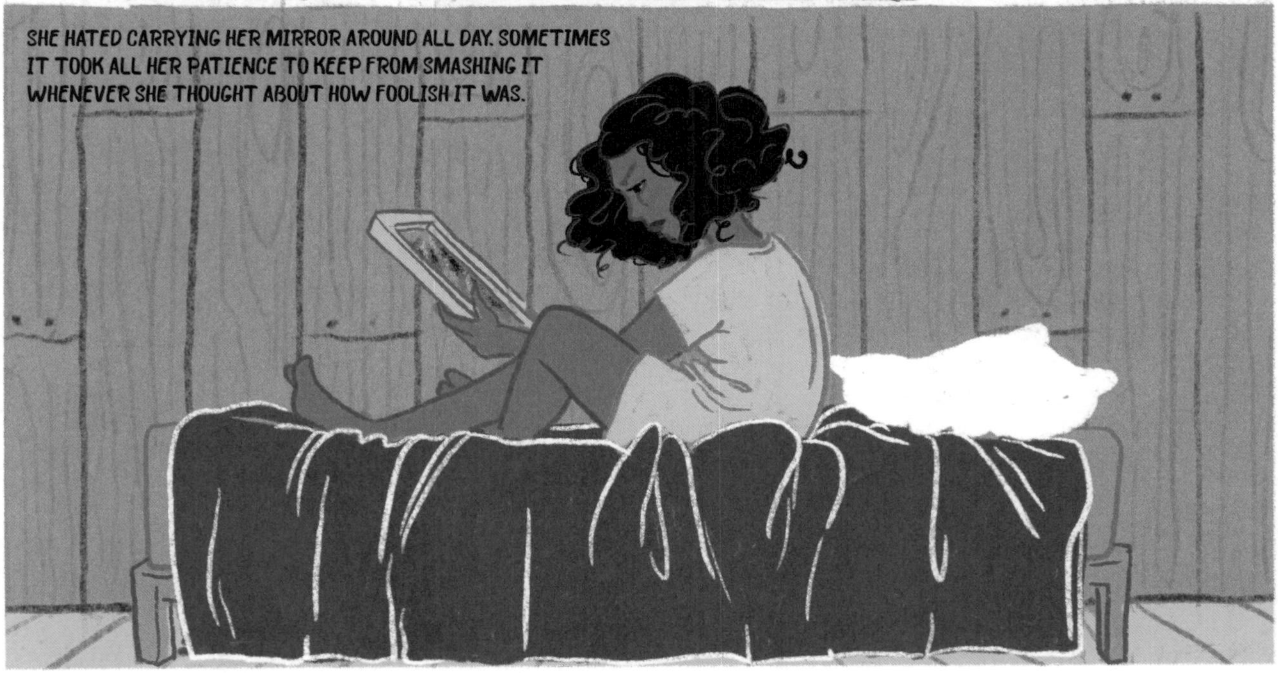
SHE HATED CARRYING HER MIRROR AROUND ALL DAY. SOMETIMES IT TOOK ALL HER PATIENCE TO KEEP FROM SMASHING IT WHENEVER SHE THOUGHT ABOUT HOW FOOLISH IT WAS.

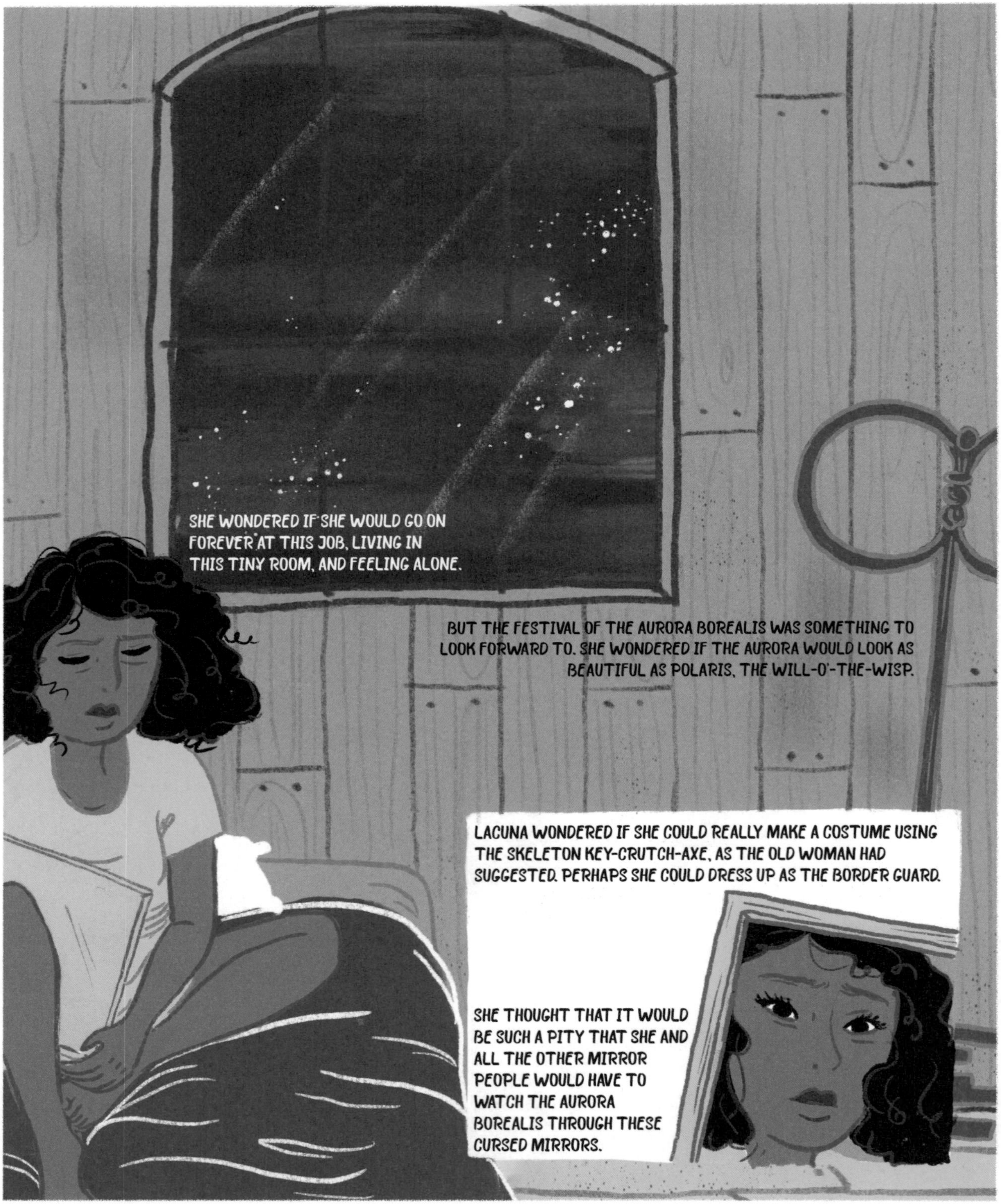
SHE WONDERED IF SHE WOULD GO ON FOREVER AT THIS JOB, LIVING IN THIS TINY ROOM, AND FEELING ALONE.
BUT THE FESTIVAL OF THE AURORA BOREALIS WAS SOMETHING TO LOOK FORWARD TO. SHE WONDERED IF THE AURORA WOULD LOOK AS BEAUTIFUL AS POLARIS, THE WILL-O'-THE-WISP.
LACUNA WONDERED IF SHE COULD REALLY MAKE A COSTUME USING THE SKELETON KEY-CRUTCH-AXE, AS THE OLD WOMAN HAD SUGGESTED. PERHAPS SHE COULD DRESS UP AS THE BORDER GUARD.
SHE THOUGHT THAT IT WOULD BE SUCH A PITY THAT SHE AND ALL THE OTHER MIRROR PEOPLE WOULD HAVE TO WATCH THE AURORA BOREALIS THROUGH THESE CURSED MIRRORS.

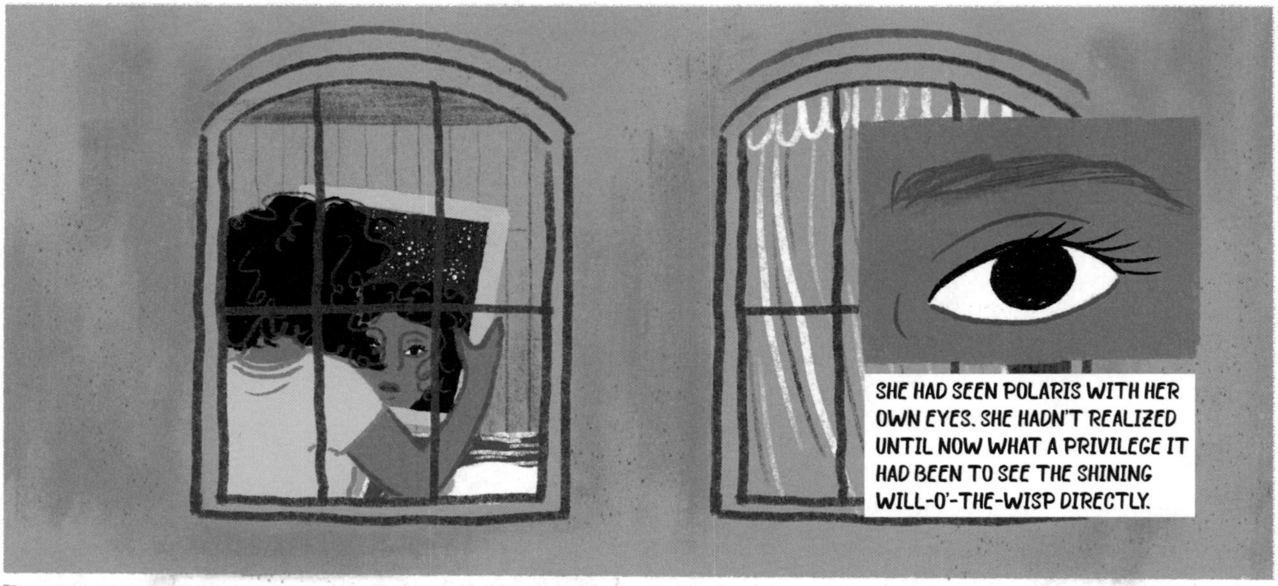
SHE HAD SEEN POLARIS WITH HER OWN EYES. SHE HADN'T REALIZED UNTIL NOW WHAT A PRIVILEGE IT HAD BEEN TO SEE THE SHINING WILL-O'-THE-WISP DIRECTLY.

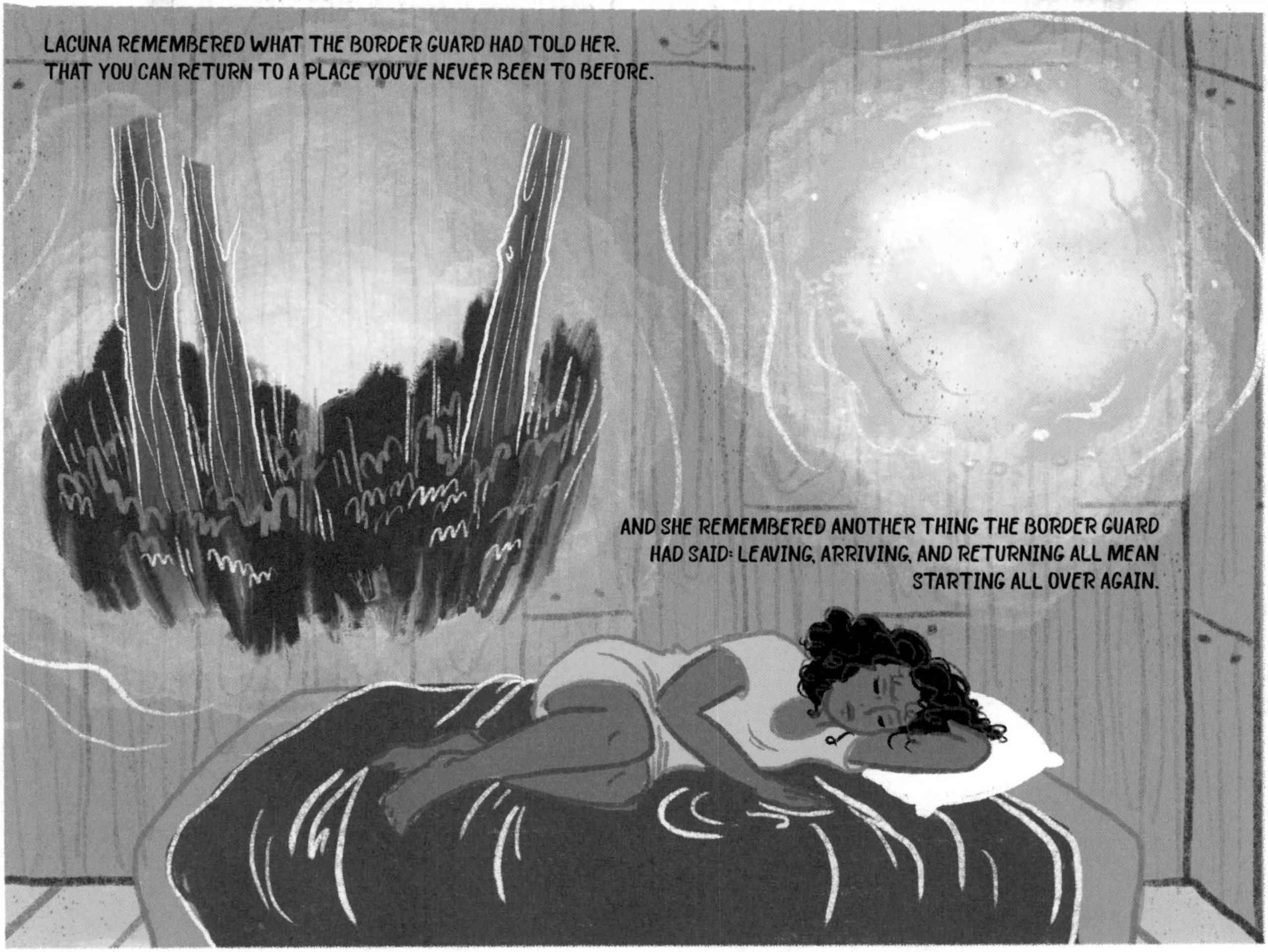
LACUNA REMEMBERED WHAT THE BORDER GUARD HAD TOLD HER. THAT YOU CAN RETURN TO A PLACE YOU'VE NEVER BEEN TO BEFORE.
AND SHE REMEMBERED ANOTHER THING THE BORDER GUARD HAD SAID: LEAVING, ARRIVING, AND RETURNING ALL MEAN STARTING ALL OVER AGAIN.

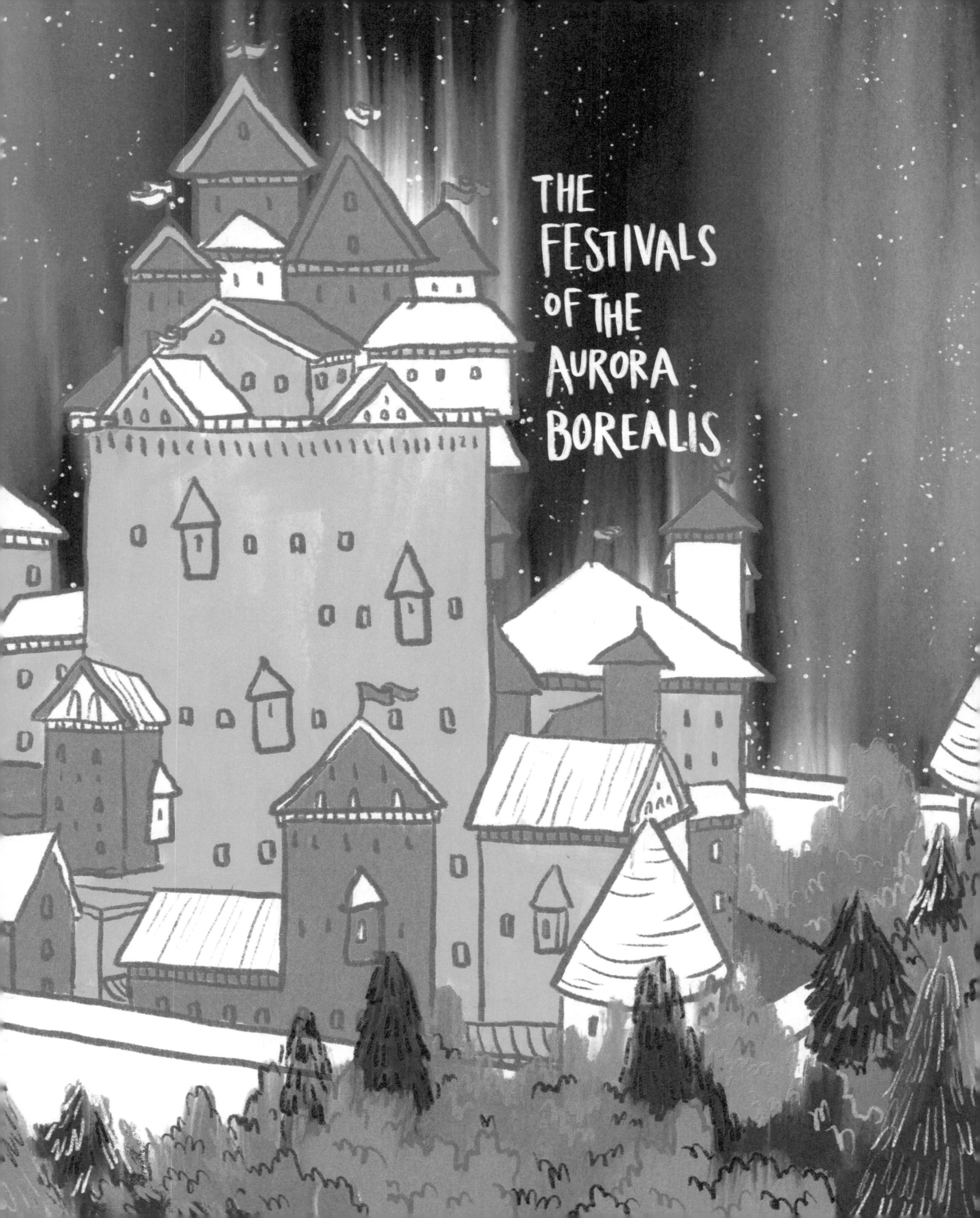
THE FESTIVALS OF THE AURORA BOREALIS

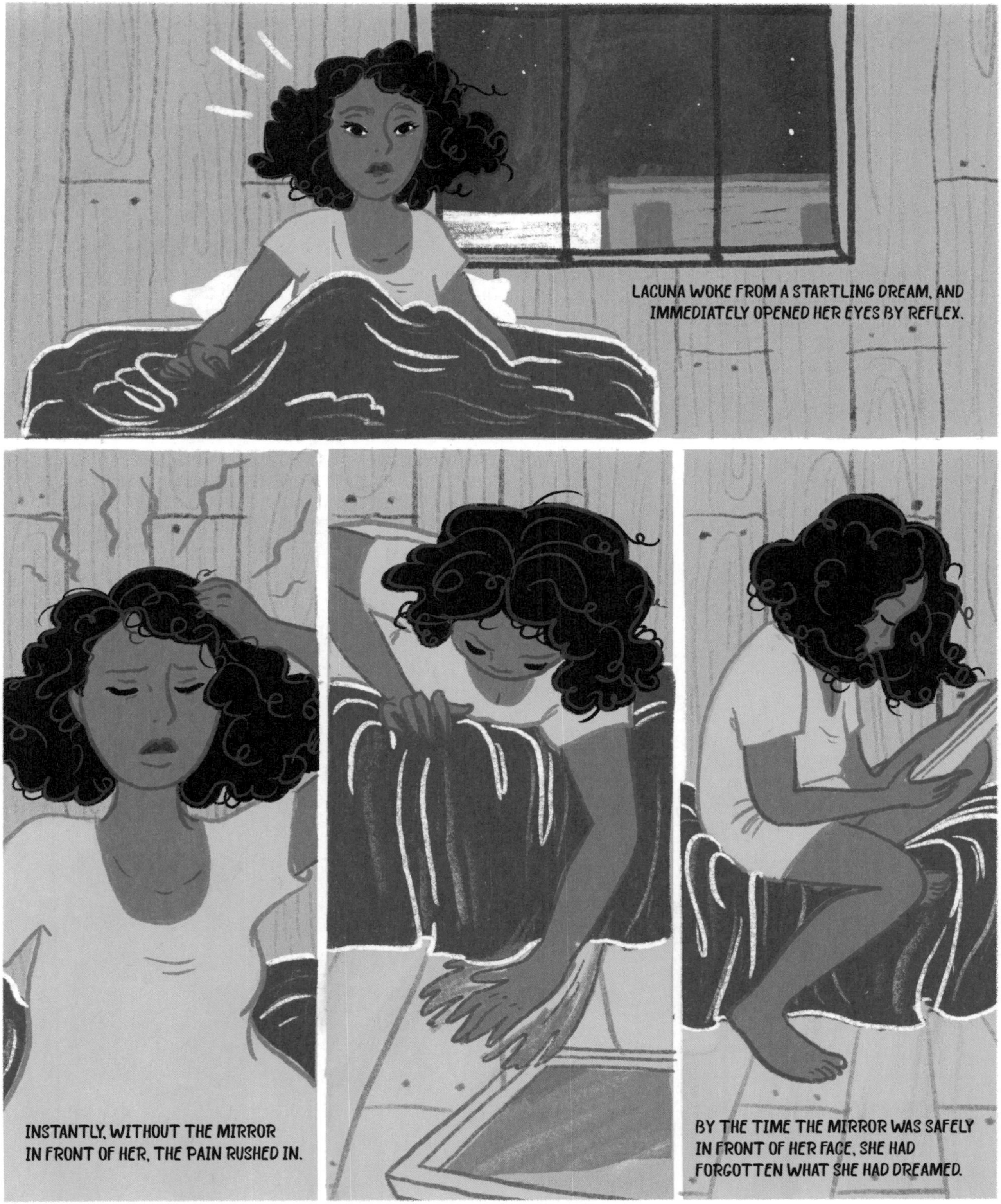
LACUNA WOKE FROM A STARTLING DREAM, AND IMMEDIATELY OPENED HER EYES BY REFLEX.
INSTANTLY, WITHOUT THE MIRROR IN FRONT OF HER, THE PAIN RUSHED IN.
BY THE TIME THE MIRROR WAS SAFELY IN FRONT OF HER FACE, SHE HAD FORGOTTEN WHAT SHE HAD DREAMED.

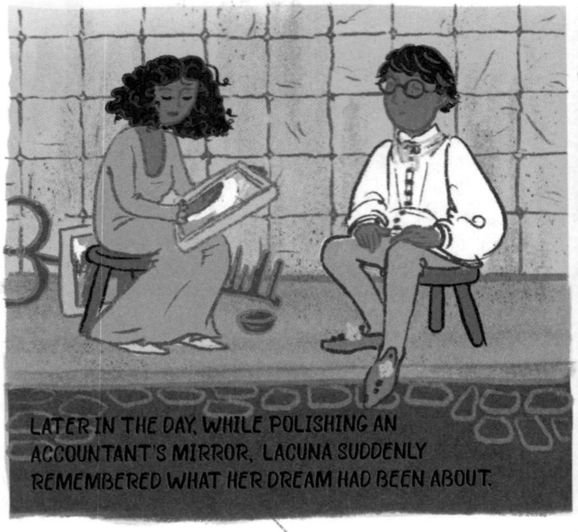
LATER IN THE DAY, WHILE POLISHING AN ACCOUNTANT'S MIRROR, LACUNA SUDDENLY REMEMBERED WHAT HER DREAM HAD BEEN ABOUT.

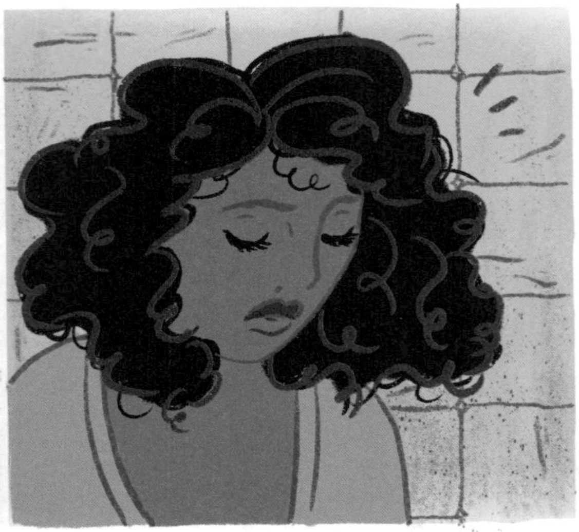

SHE HAD DREAMED OF A VAST SHEET OF ICE. LACUNA WORE A PAIR OF SKATES AND GLIDED EFFORTLESSLY ACROSS ITS SURFACE. SHE FELT AS IF SHE WERE FLYING. SHE FELT JUST AS SHE DID WHEN POLARIS HAD CARRIED HER THROUGH THE AIR, AWAY FROM THE GREAT SWAMP OF INK.

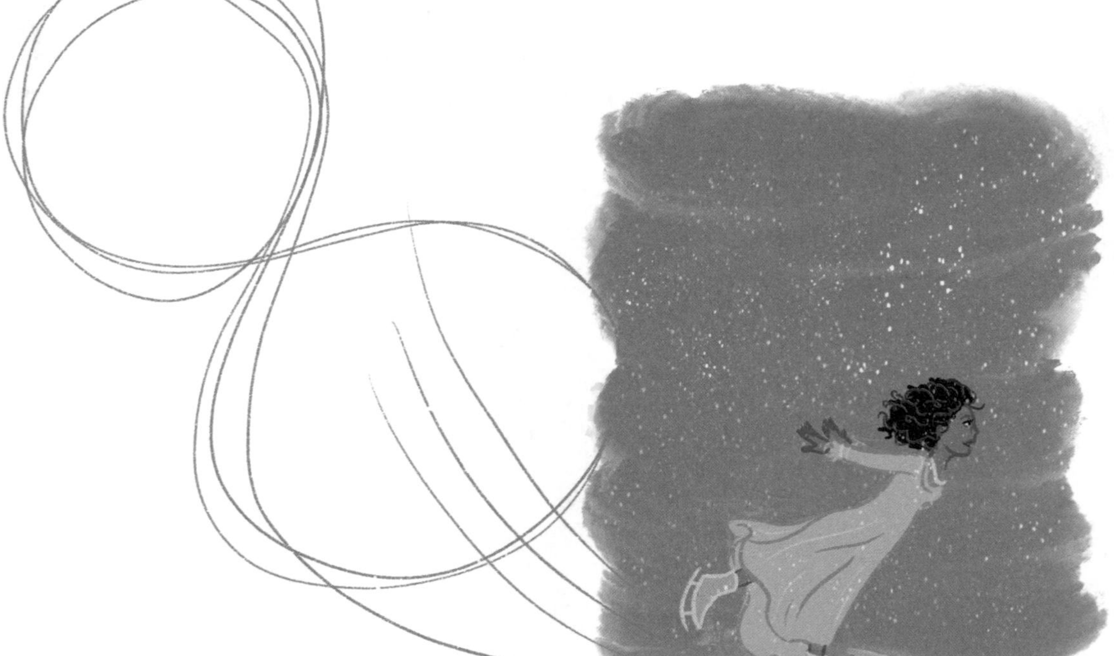

LACUNA SKATED IN LARGE FIGURE-EIGHTS, LOOPING A BROAD CURVE, THEN ARCING BACK ACROSS HER PREVIOUS PATH. HER SKATES CUT A MASSIVE FIGURE INTO THE ICE.

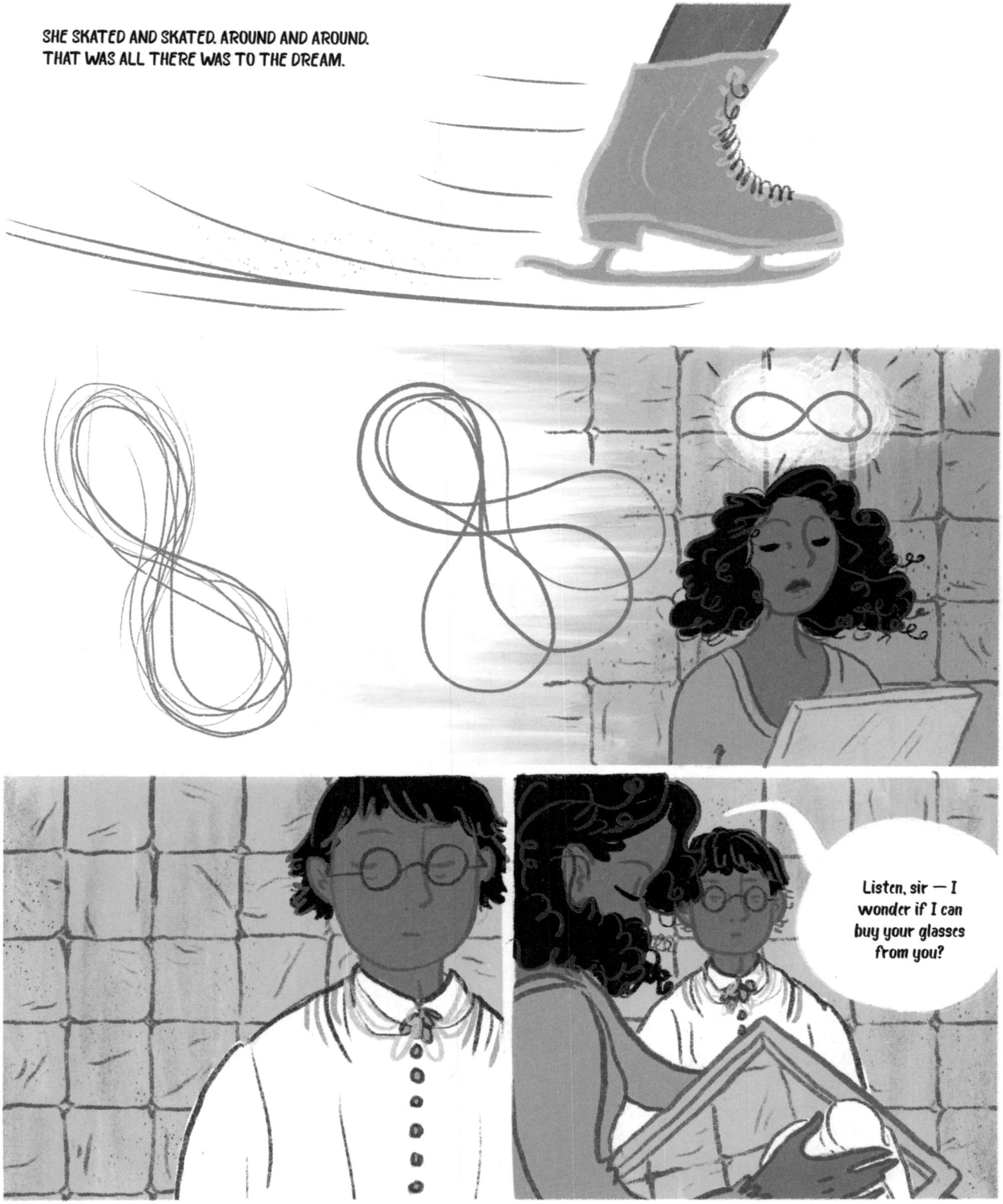
SHE SKATED AND SKATED. AROUND AND AROUND.
THAT WAS ALL THERE WAS TO THE DREAM.
Listen, sir — I wonder if I can buy your glasses from you?

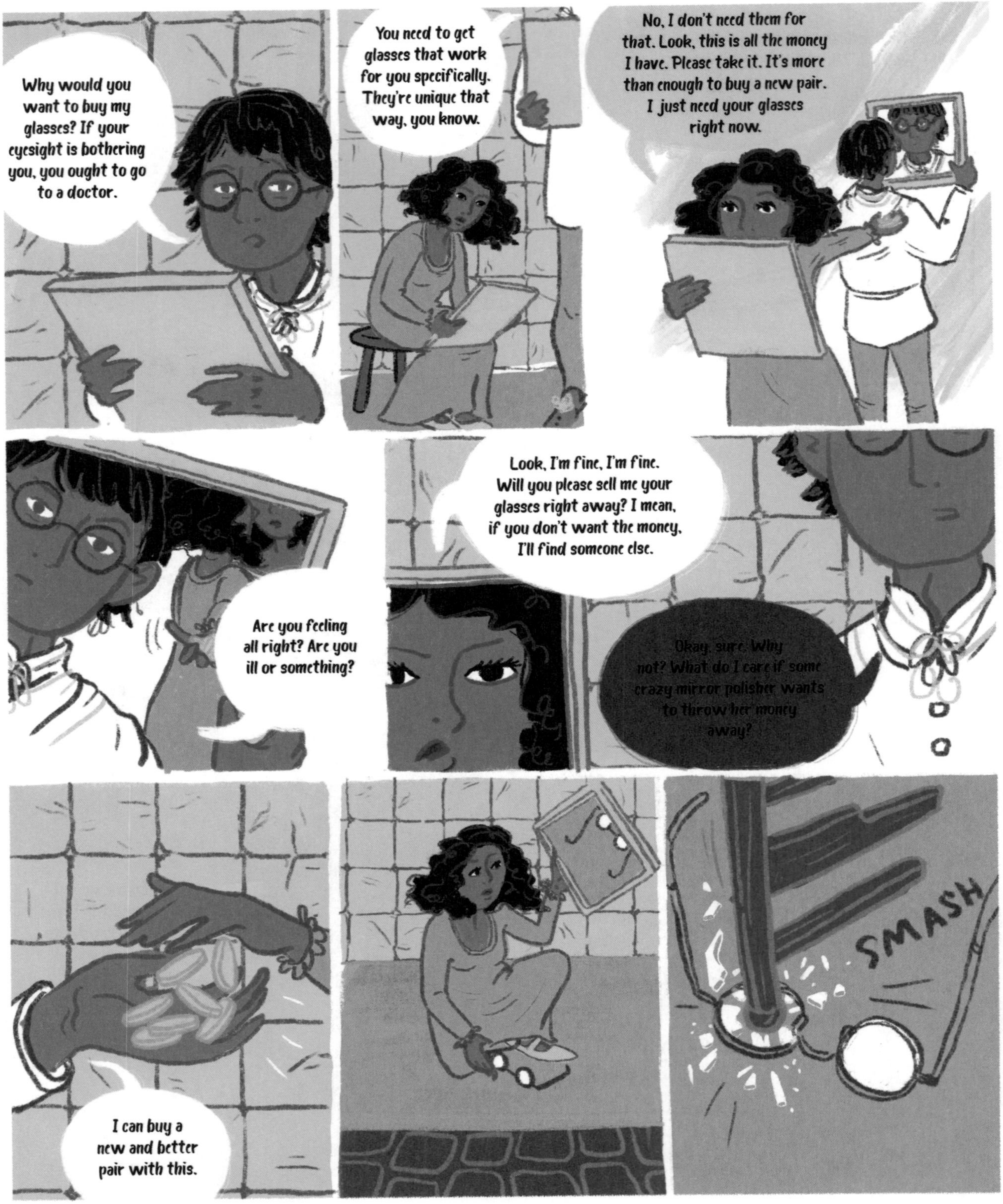
Why would you want to buy my glasses? If your eyesight is bothering you, you ought to go to a doctor.
You need to get glasses that work for you specifically. They're unique that way, you know.
No, I don't need them for that. Look, this is all the money I have. Please take it. It's more than enough to buy a new pair. I just need your glasses right now.
Are you feeling all right? Are you ill or something?
Look, I'm fine, I'm fine. Will you please sell me your glasses right away? I mean, if you don't want the money, I'll find someone else.
Okay, sure. Why not? What do I care if some crazy mirror polisher wants to throw her money away?
I can buy a new and better pair with this.
SMASH

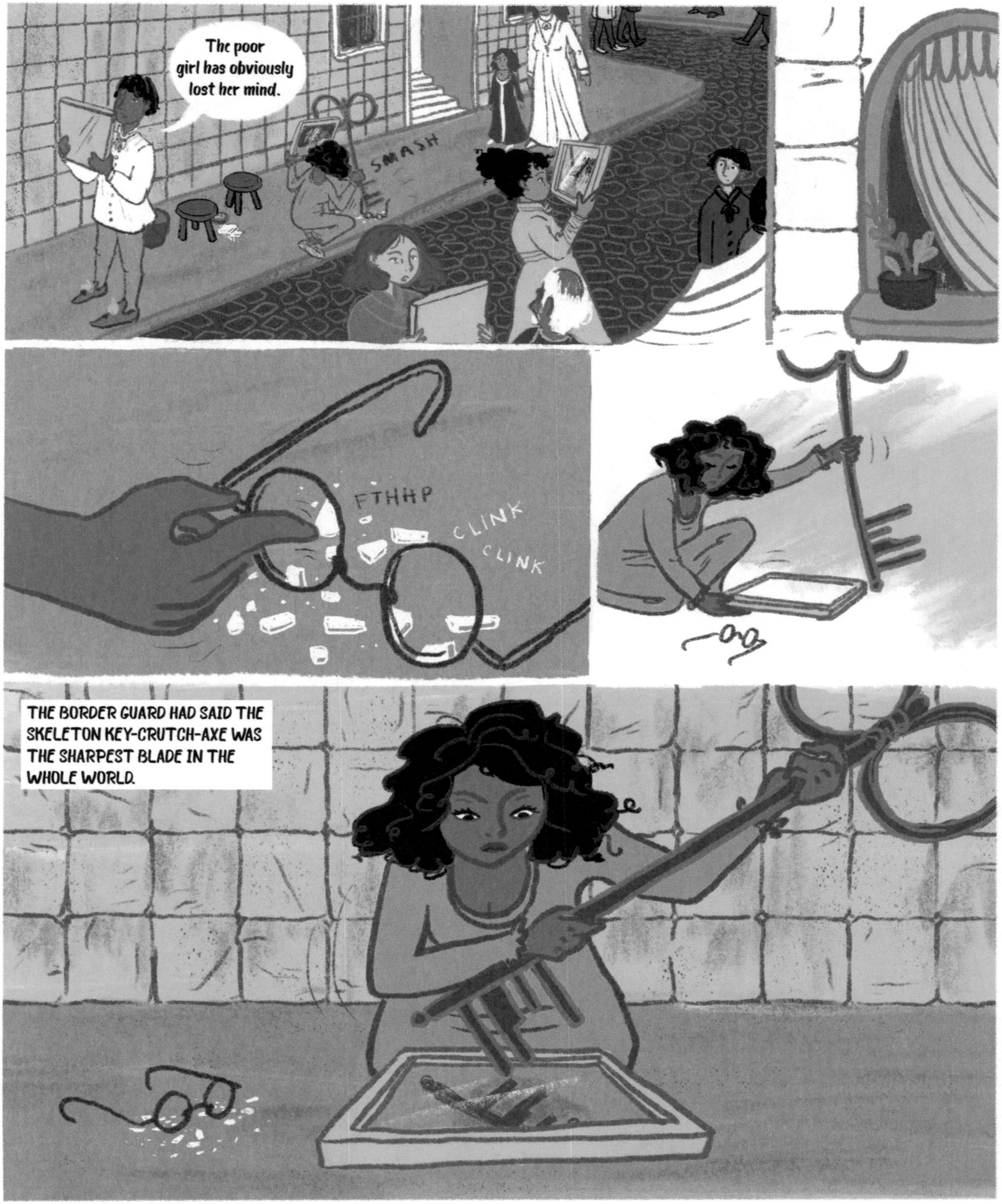
The poor girl has obviously lost her mind.
SMASH
FTHHP
CLINK
CLINK
THE BORDER GUARD HAD SAID THE SKELETON KEY-CRUTCH-AXE WAS THE SHARPEST BLADE IN THE WHOLE WORLD.

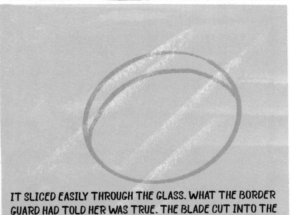

IT SLICED EASILY THROUGH THE GLASS. WHAT THE BORDER GUARD HAD TOLD HER WAS TRUE. THE BLADE CUT INTO THE GLASS JUST AS EASILY AS IF SHE WERE DIPPING IT INTO THE SURFACE OF A POND.

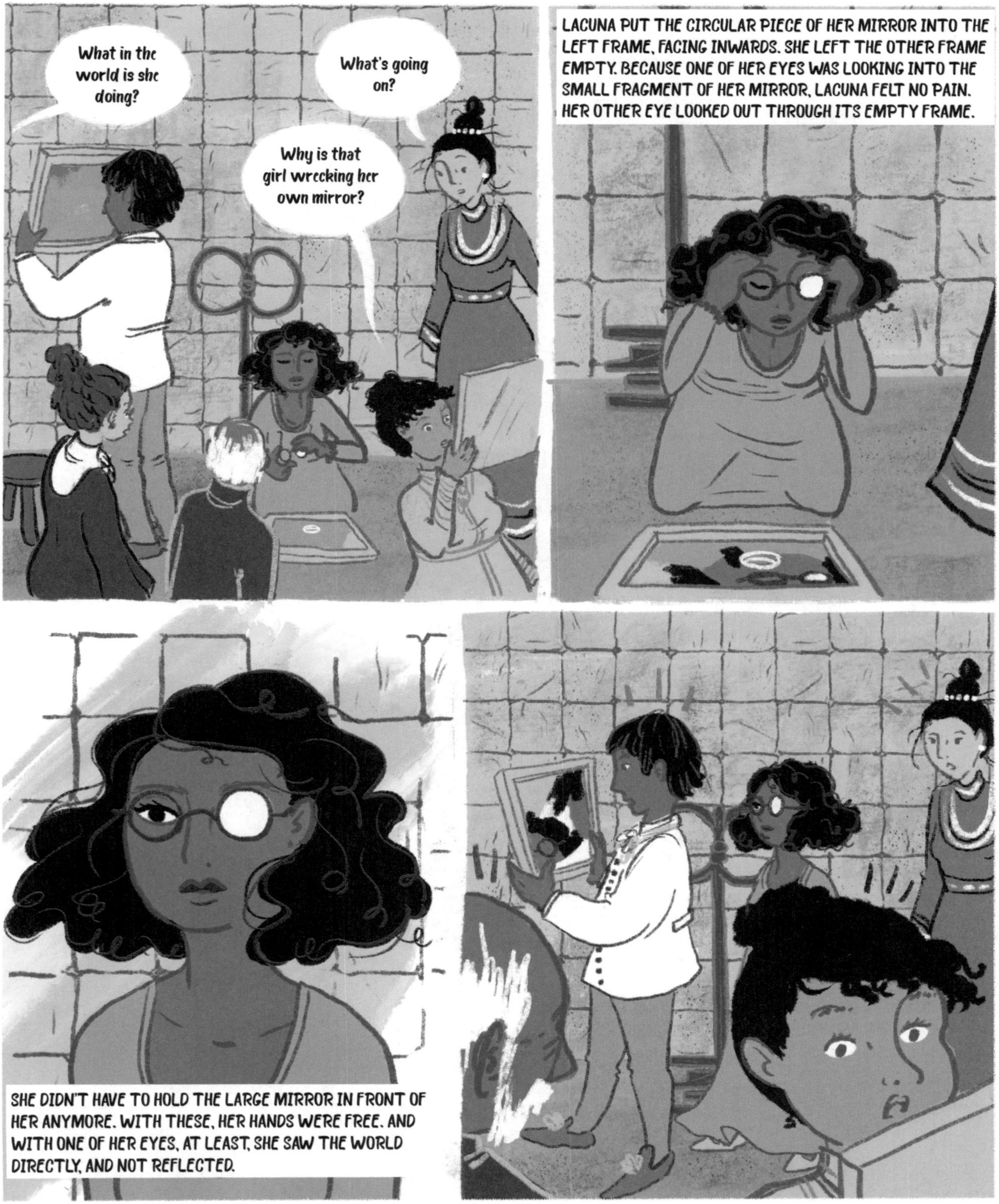
What in the world is she doing?
What's going on?
Why is that girl wrecking her own mirror?
LACUNA PUT THE CIRCULAR PIECE OF HER MIRROR INTO THE LEFT FRAME, FACING INWARDS. SHE LEFT THE OTHER FRAME EMPTY. BECAUSE ONE OF HER EYES WAS LOOKING INTO THE SMALL FRAGMENT OF HER MIRROR, LACUNA FELT NO PAIN. HER OTHER EYE LOOKED OUT THROUGH ITS EMPTY FRAME.
SHE DIDN'T HAVE TO HOLD THE LARGE MIRROR IN FRONT OF HER ANYMORE. WITH THESE, HER HANDS WERE FREE. AND WITH ONE OF HER EYES, AT LEAST, SHE SAW THE WORLD DIRECTLY, AND NOT REFLECTED.

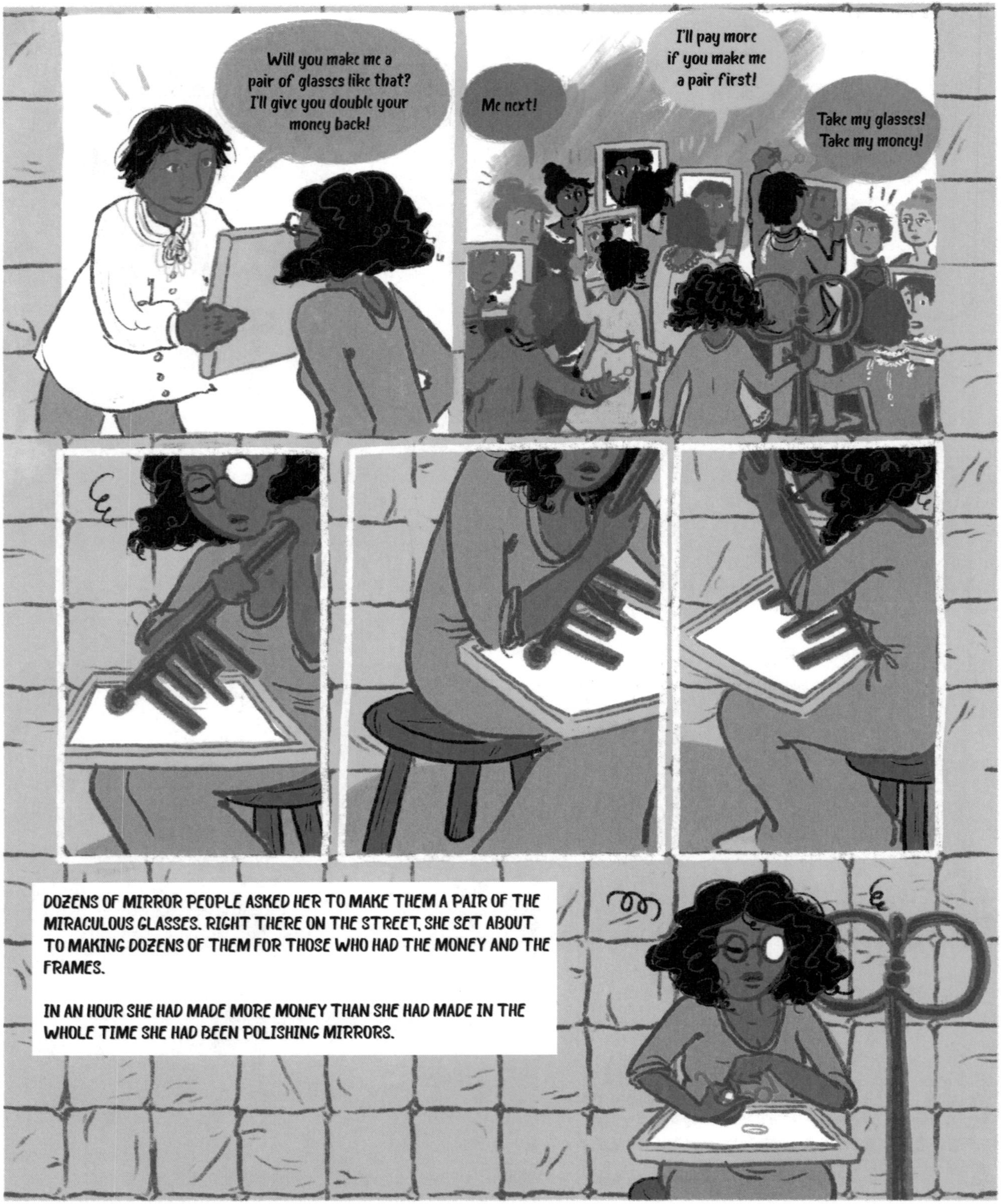
Will you make me a pair of glasses like that? I'll give you double your money back!
Me next!
I'll pay more if you make me a pair first!
Take my glasses! Take my money!
DOZENS OF MIRROR PEOPLE ASKED HER TO MAKE THEM A PAIR OF THE MIRACULOUS GLASSES. RIGHT THERE ON THE STREET, SHE SET ABOUT TO MAKING DOZENS OF THEM FOR THOSE WHO HAD THE MONEY AND THE FRAMES.
IN AN HOUR SHE HAD MADE MORE MONEY THAN SHE HAD MADE IN THE WHOLE TIME SHE HAD BEEN POLISHING MIRRORS.

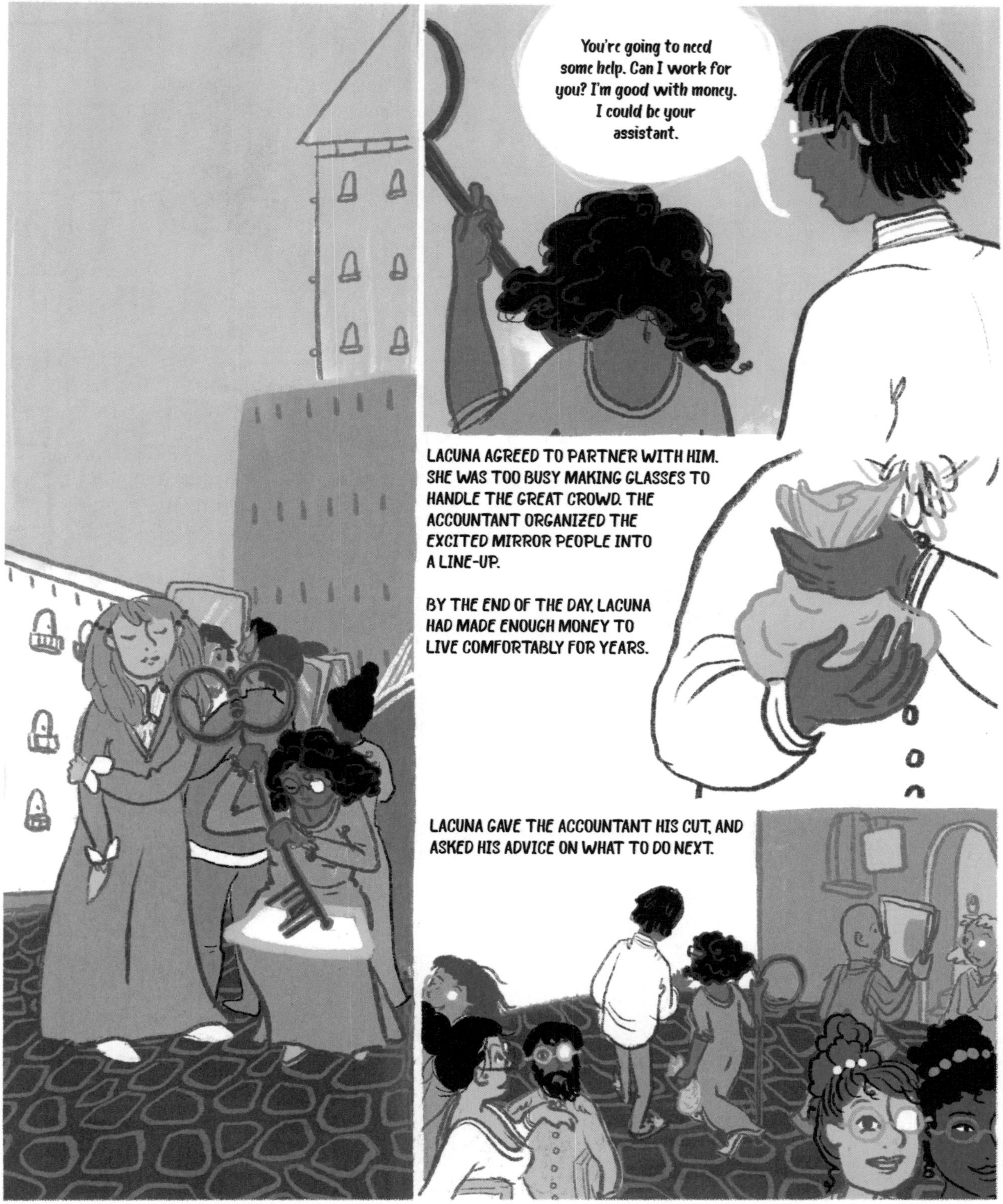
You're going to need some help. Can I work for you? I'm good with money. I could be your assistant.
LACUNA AGREED TO PARTNER WITH HIM. SHE WAS TOO BUSY MAKING GLASSES TO HANDLE THE GREAT CROWD. THE ACCOUNTANT ORGANIZED THE EXCITED MIRROR PEOPLE INTO A LINE-UP.
BY THE END OF THE DAY, LACUNA HAD MADE ENOUGH MONEY TO LIVE COMFORTABLY FOR YEARS.
LACUNA GAVE THE ACCOUNTANT HIS CUT, AND ASKED HIS ADVICE ON WHAT TO DO NEXT.

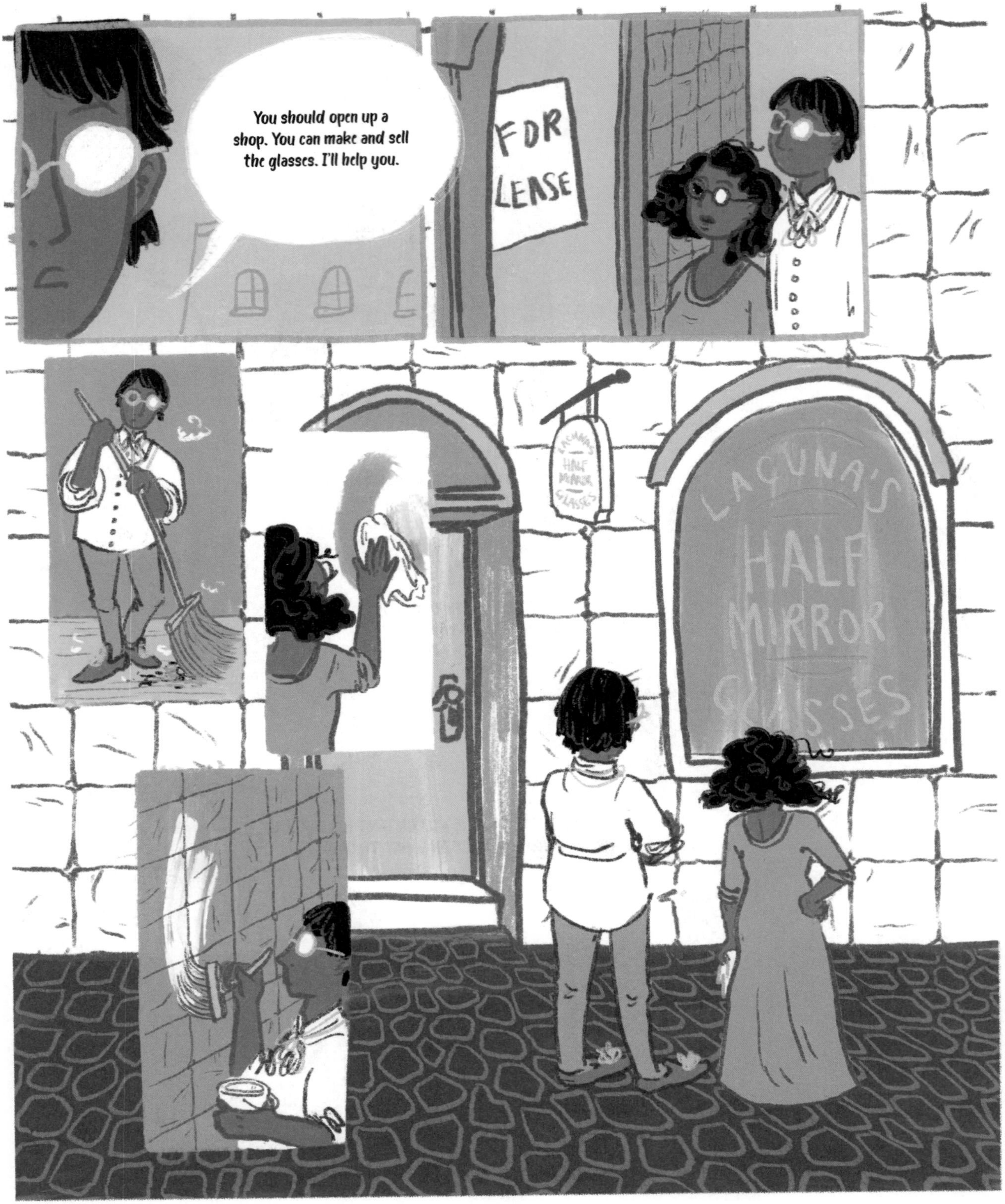

You should open up a shop. You can make and sell the glasses. I'll help you.
FOR LEASE
LAGUNA'S HALF MIRROR GLASSES
LAGUNA'S HALF MIRROR GLASSES

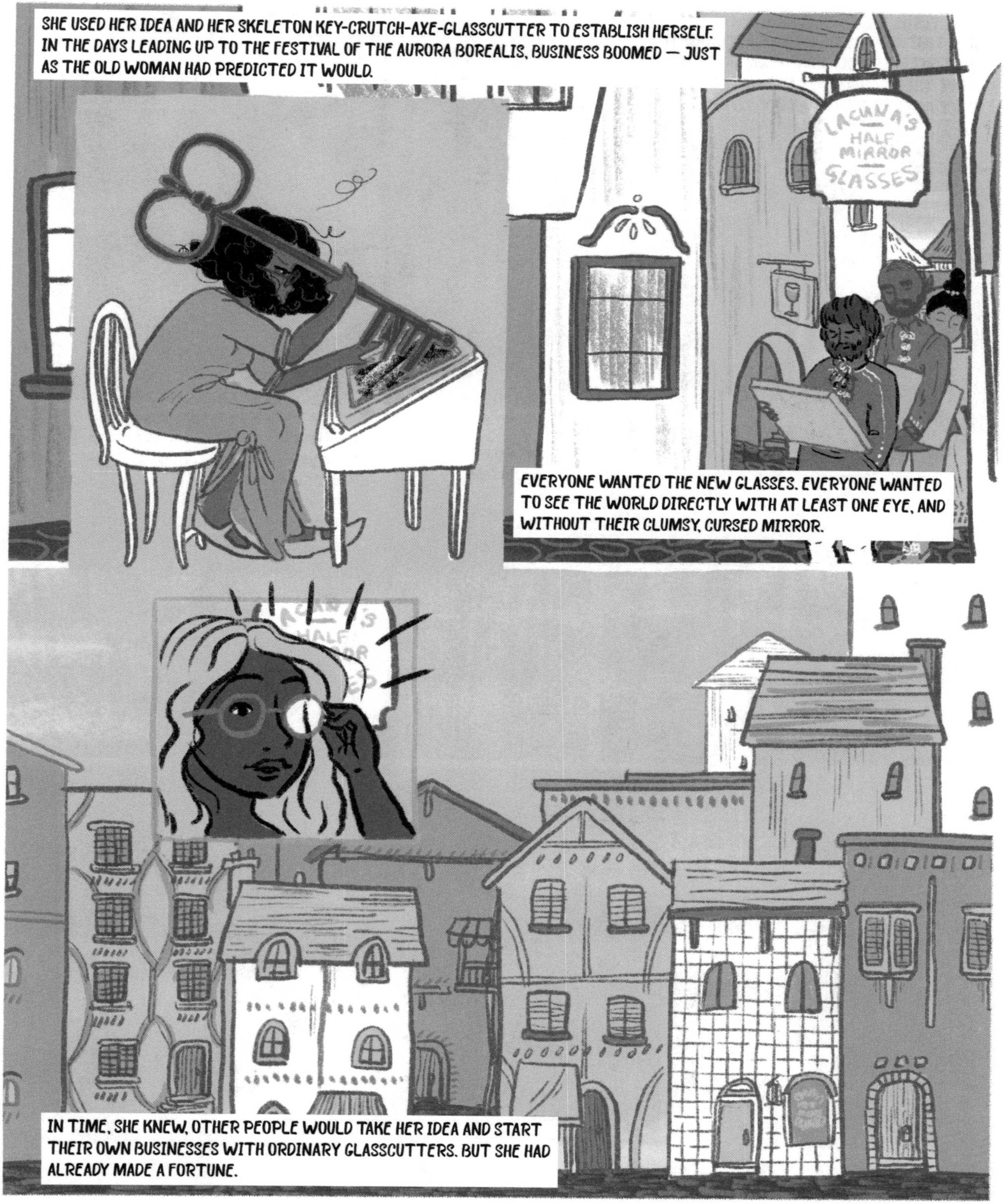
SHE USED HER IDEA AND HER SKELETON KEY-CRUTCH-AXE-GLASSCUTTER TO ESTABLISH HERSELF. IN THE DAYS LEADING UP TO THE FESTIVAL OF THE AURORA BOREALIS, BUSINESS BOOMED — JUST AS THE OLD WOMAN HAD PREDICTED IT WOULD.
LACUNA'S HALF MIRROR GLASSES
EVERYONE WANTED THE NEW GLASSES. EVERYONE WANTED TO SEE THE WORLD DIRECTLY WITH AT LEAST ONE EYE, AND WITHOUT THEIR CLUMSY, CURSED MIRROR.
IN TIME, SHE KNEW, OTHER PEOPLE WOULD TAKE HER IDEA AND START THEIR OWN BUSINESSES WITH ORDINARY GLASSCUTTERS. BUT SHE HAD ALREADY MADE A FORTUNE.

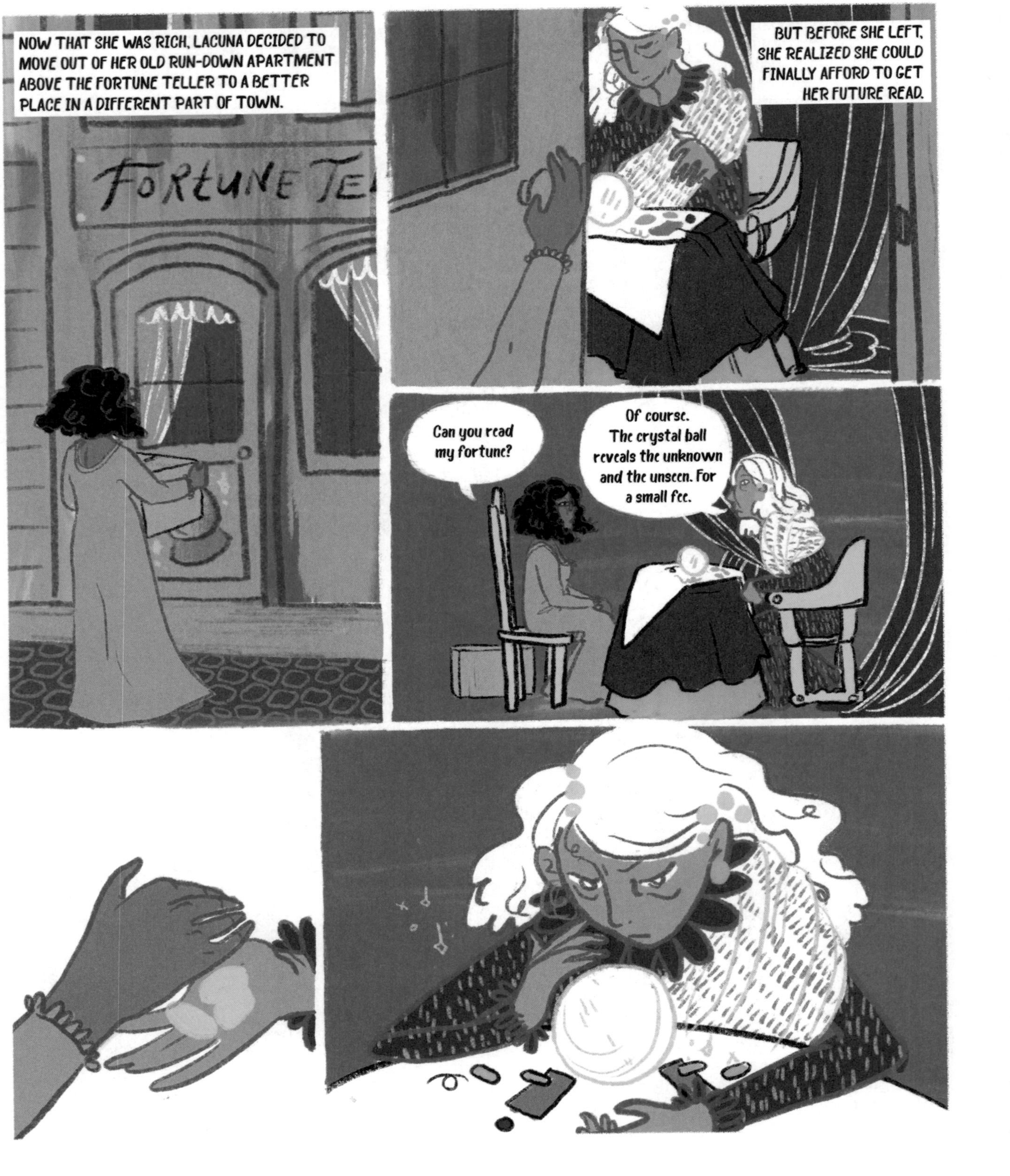
NOW THAT SHE WAS RICH, LACUNA DECIDED TO MOVE OUT OF HER OLD RUN-DOWN APARTMENT ABOVE THE FORTUNE TELLER TO A BETTER PLACE IN A DIFFERENT PART OF TOWN.
FORTUNE TEL
BUT BEFORE SHE LEFT, SHE REALIZED SHE COULD FINALLY AFFORD TO GET HER FUTURE READ.
Can you read my fortune?
Of course. The crystal ball reveals the unknown and the unseen. For a small fee.

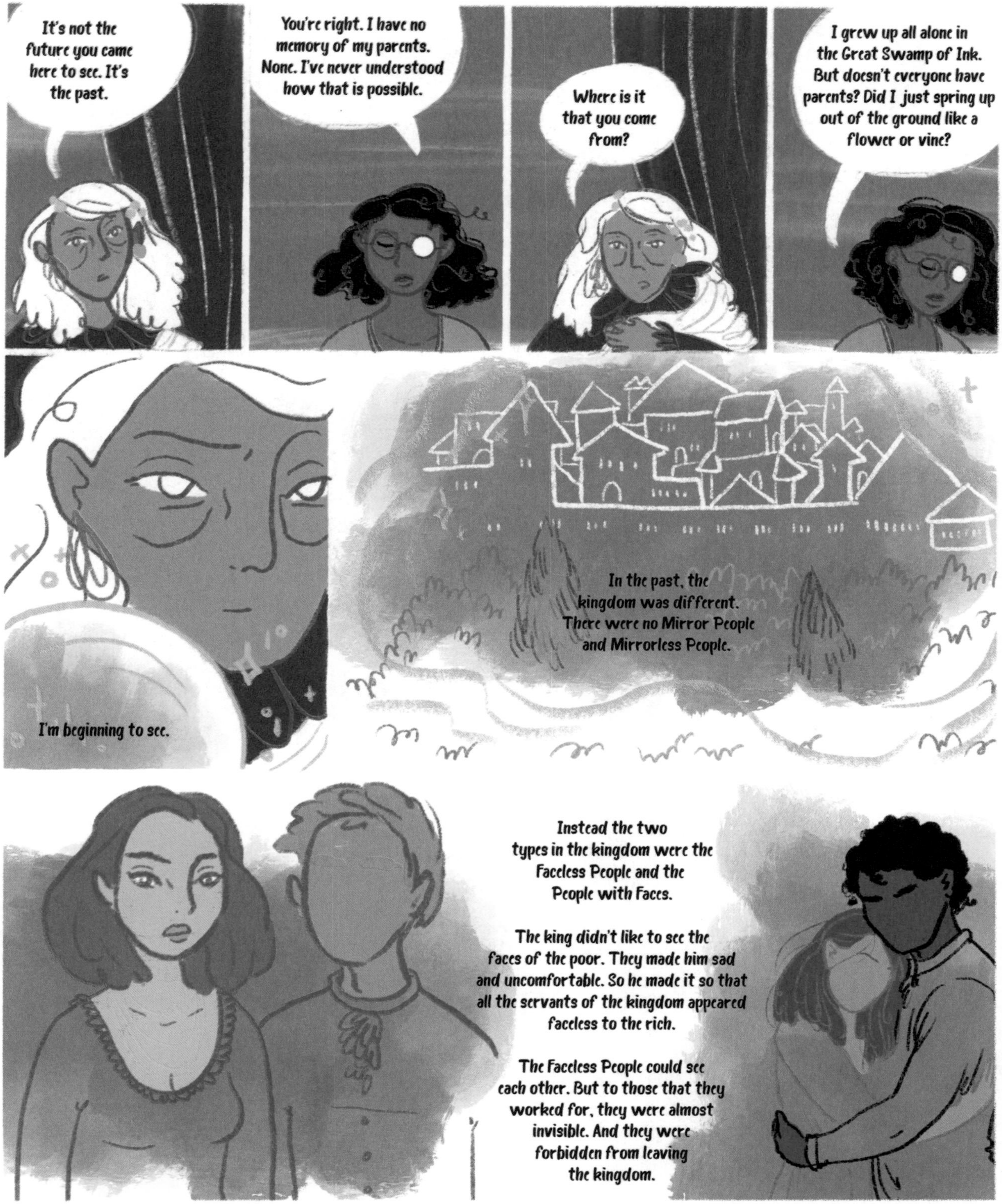
It's not the future you came here to see. It's the past.
You're right. I have no memory of my parents. None. I've never understood how that is possible.
Where is it that you come from?
I grew up all alone in the Great Swamp of Ink. But doesn't everyone have parents? Did I just spring up out of the ground like a flower or vine?
I'm beginning to see.
In the past, the kingdom was different. There were no Mirror People and Mirrorless People.
Instead the two types in the kingdom were the Faceless People and the People with Faces.
The king didn't like to see the faces of the poor. They made him sad and uncomfortable. So he made it so that all the servants of the kingdom appeared faceless to the rich.
The Faceless People could see each other. But to those that they worked for, they were almost invisible. And they were forbidden from leaving the kingdom.

Some found ways to escape,
as captive people do.

Sometimes guards would look for them, to make them
return. So those who escaped went far away. To other
lands. To distant mountains. Or to places where
no one else wanted to live.

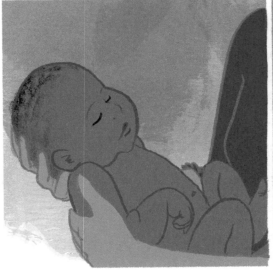

The children born outside the walls of the
kingdom were not cursed in the way they were.

But their parents still bore the effects of the spell.
They were faceless to their own children.

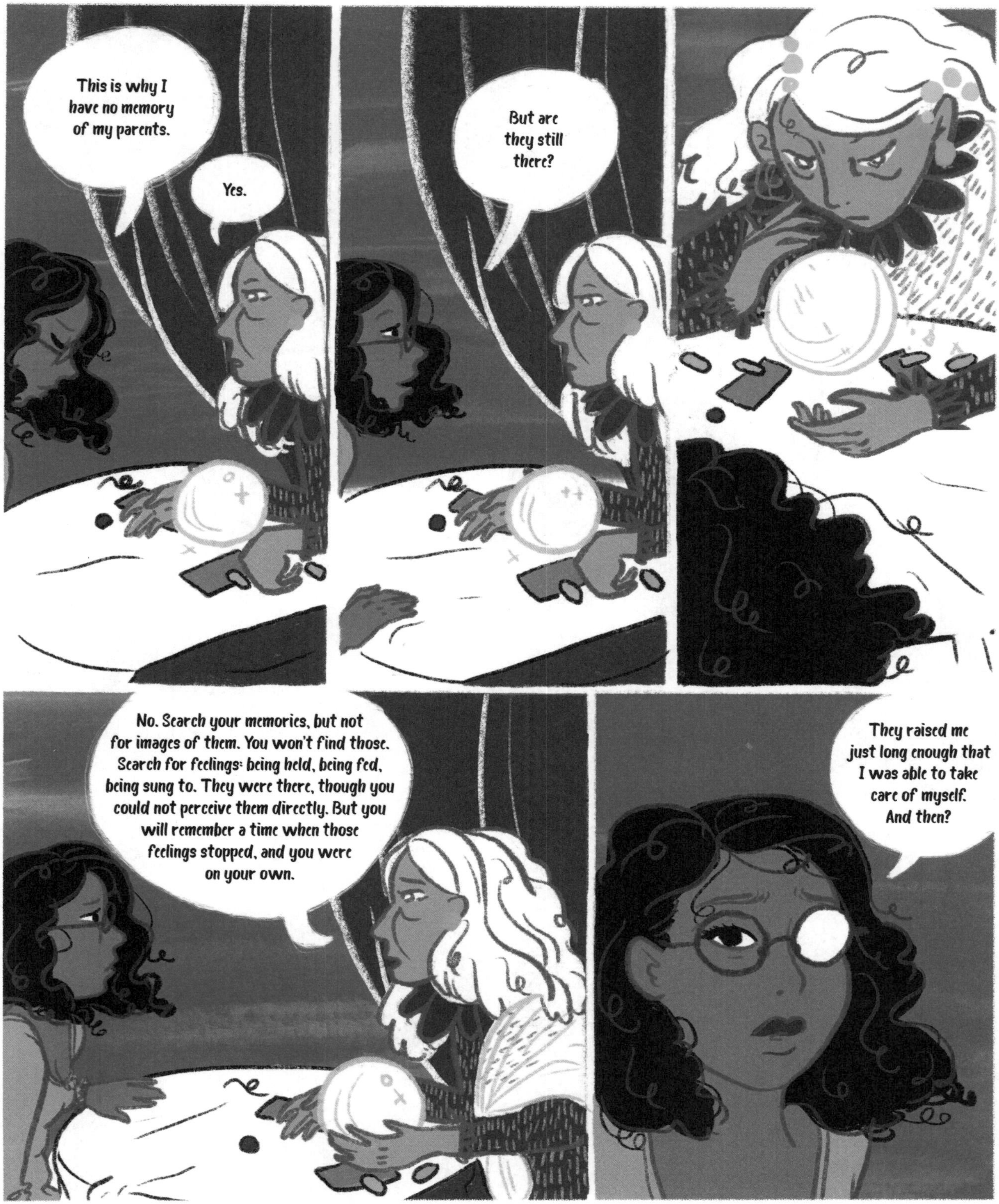
This is why I have no memory of my parents.
Yes.
But are they still there?
No. Search your memories, but not for images of them. You won't find those. Search for feelings: being held, being fed, being sung to. They were there, though you could not perceive them directly. But you will remember a time when those feelings stopped, and you were on your own.
They raised me just long enough that I was able to take care of myself. And then?

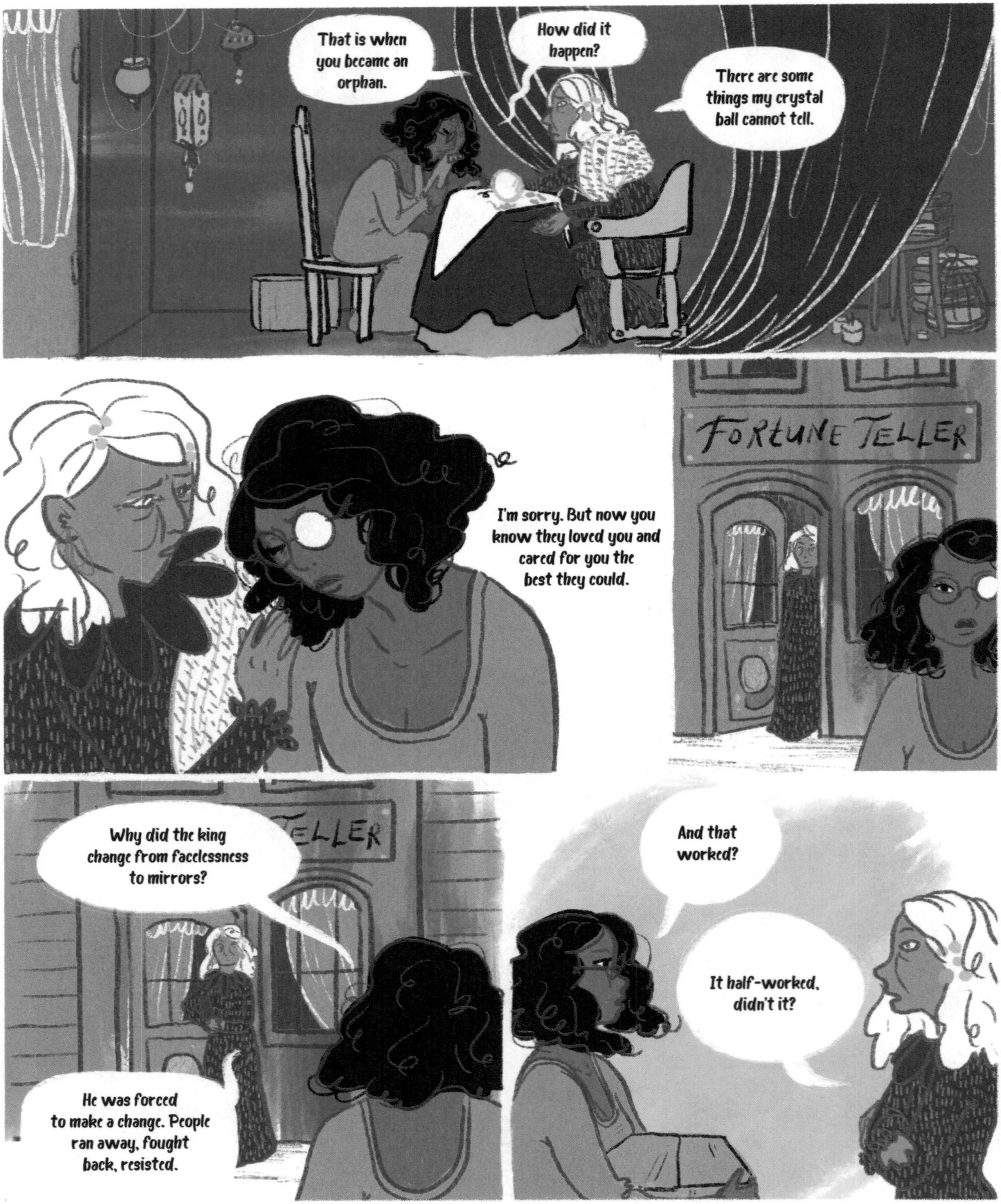

That is when you became an orphan.
How did it happen?
There are some things my crystal ball cannot tell.
I'm sorry. But now you know they loved you and cared for you the best they could.
FORTUNE TELLER
Why did the king change from facelessness to mirrors?
He was forced to make a change. People ran away, fought back, resisted.
And that worked?
It half-worked, didn't it?

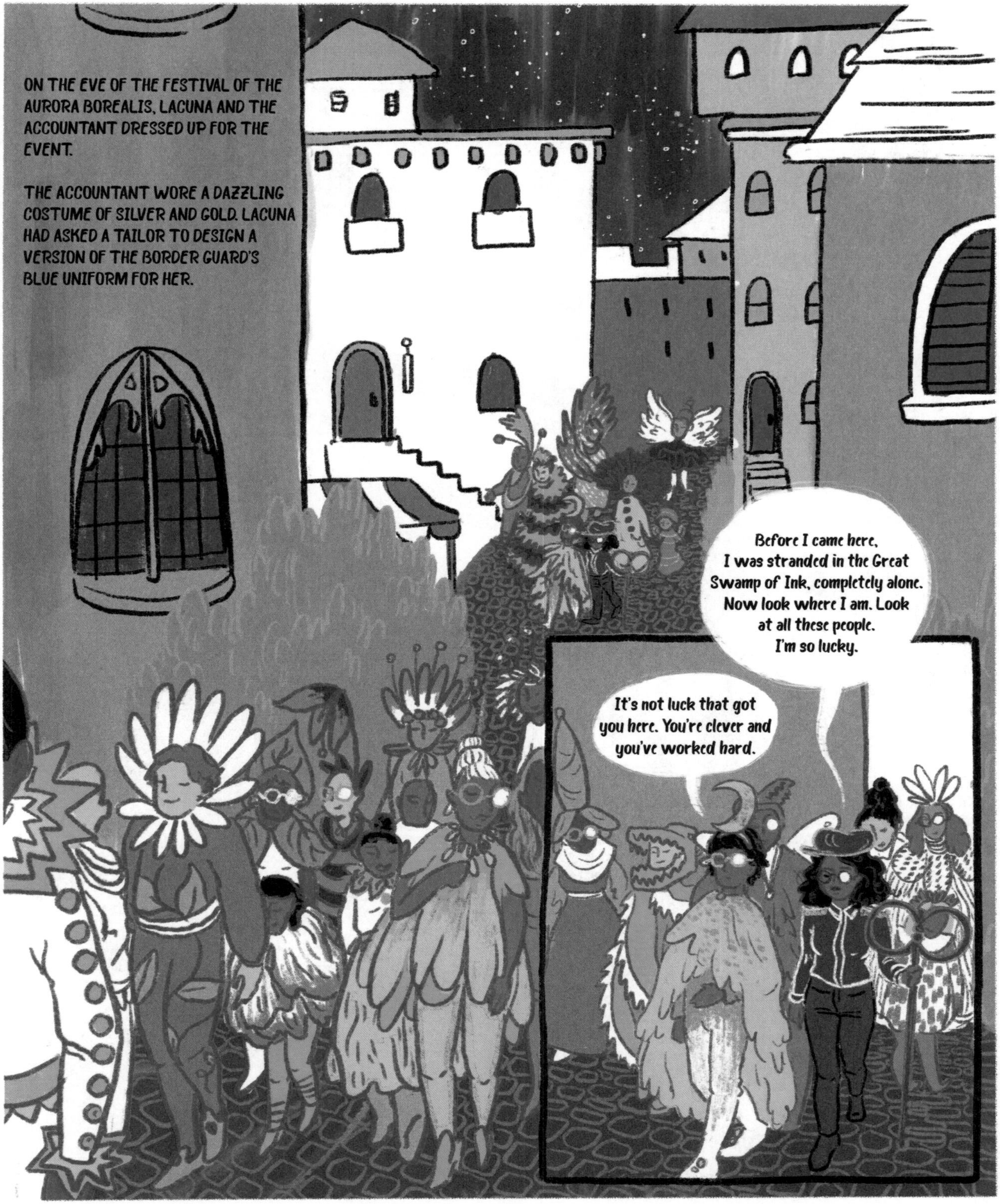
ON THE EVE OF THE FESTIVAL OF THE AURORA BOREALIS, LACUNA AND THE ACCOUNTANT DRESSED UP FOR THE EVENT.
THE ACCOUNTANT WORE A DAZZLING COSTUME OF SILVER AND GOLD. LACUNA HAD ASKED A TAILOR TO DESIGN A VERSION OF THE BORDER GUARD'S BLUE UNIFORM FOR HER.
Before I came here, I was stranded in the Great Swamp of Ink, completely alone. Now look where I am. Look at all these people. I'm so lucky.
It's not luck that got you here. You're clever and you've worked hard.

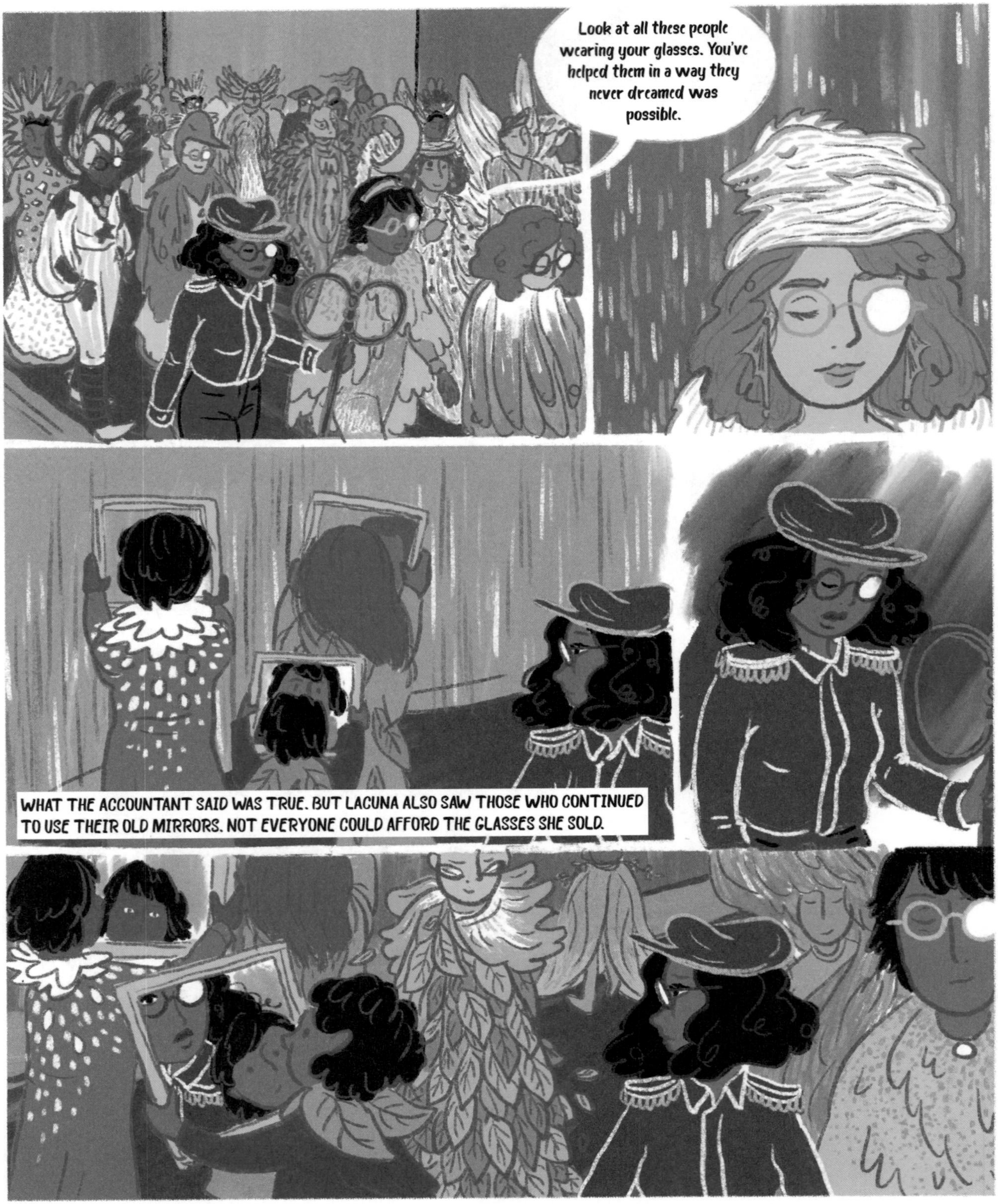
Look at all these people wearing your glasses. You've helped them in a way they never dreamed was possible.
WHAT THE ACCOUNTANT SAID WAS TRUE. BUT LACUNA ALSO SAW THOSE WHO CONTINUED TO USE THEIR OLD MIRRORS. NOT EVERYONE COULD AFFORD THE GLASSES SHE SOLD.

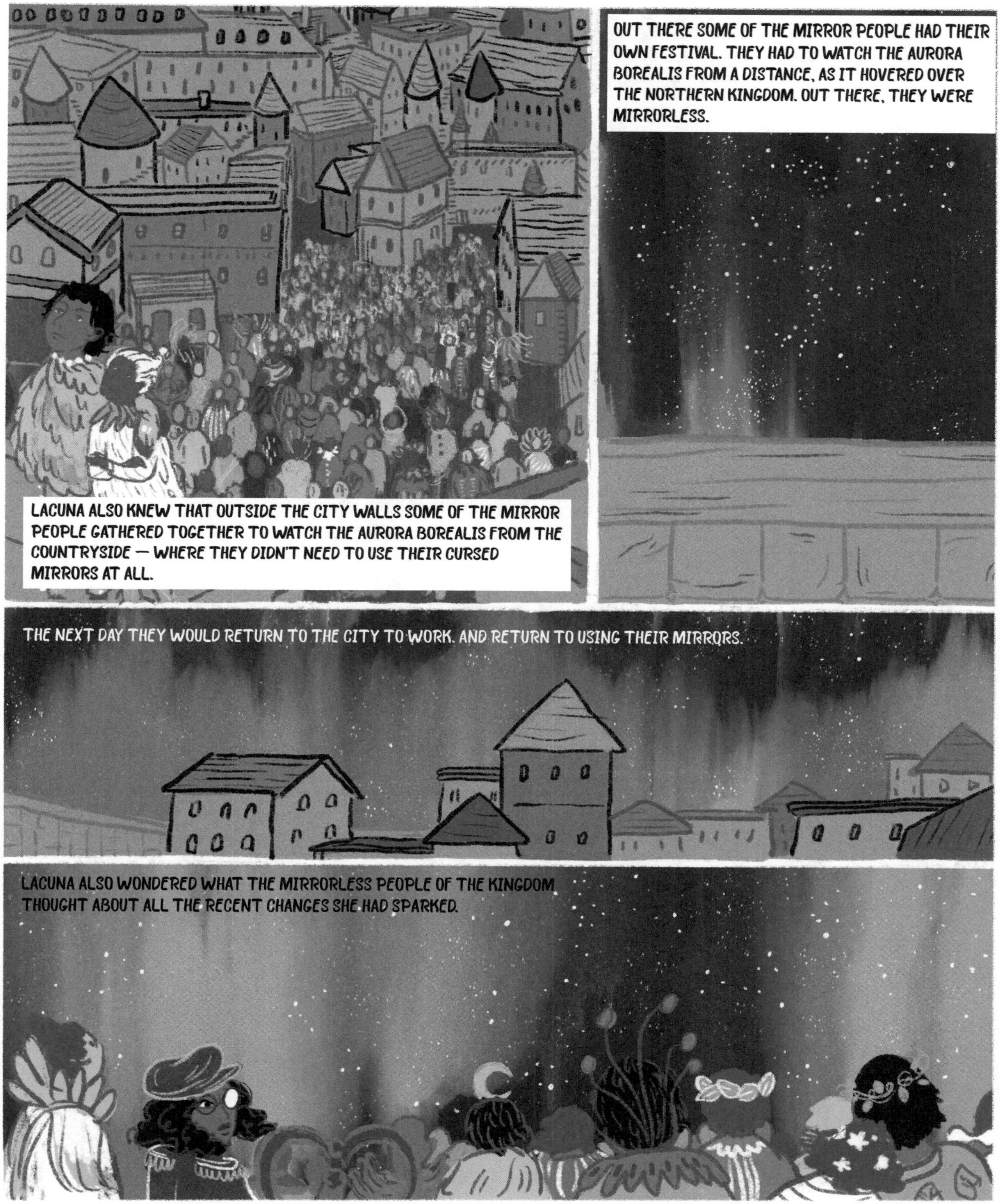
LACUNA ALSO KNEW THAT OUTSIDE THE CITY WALLS SOME OF THE MIRROR PEOPLE GATHERED TOGETHER TO WATCH THE AURORA BOREALIS FROM THE COUNTRYSIDE — WHERE THEY DIDN'T NEED TO USE THEIR CURSED MIRRORS AT ALL.
OUT THERE SOME OF THE MIRROR PEOPLE HAD THEIR OWN FESTIVAL. THEY HAD TO WATCH THE AURORA BOREALIS FROM A DISTANCE, AS IT HOVERED OVER THE NORTHERN KINGDOM. OUT THERE, THEY WERE MIRRORLESS.
THE NEXT DAY THEY WOULD RETURN TO THE CITY TO WORK, AND RETURN TO USING THEIR MIRRORS.
LACUNA ALSO WONDERED WHAT THE MIRRORLESS PEOPLE OF THE KINGDOM THOUGHT ABOUT ALL THE RECENT CHANGES SHE HAD SPARKED.

SHE WONDERED ABOUT ALL THESE THINGS. BUT HER THOUGHTS JUST CIRCLED IN HER HEAD, AROUND AND AROUND, LIKE THE ALABASTER WALLS OF THE CITY.

LACUNA STOOD THERE, AMONG PEOPLE AT LAST ...

... GAZING AT THE SKY, THE AURORA, AND THE KINGDOM WITH ONE HALF OF HER VISION ...

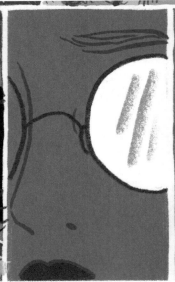

... STARING AT HER OWN OPEN EYE WITH THE OTHER.

110

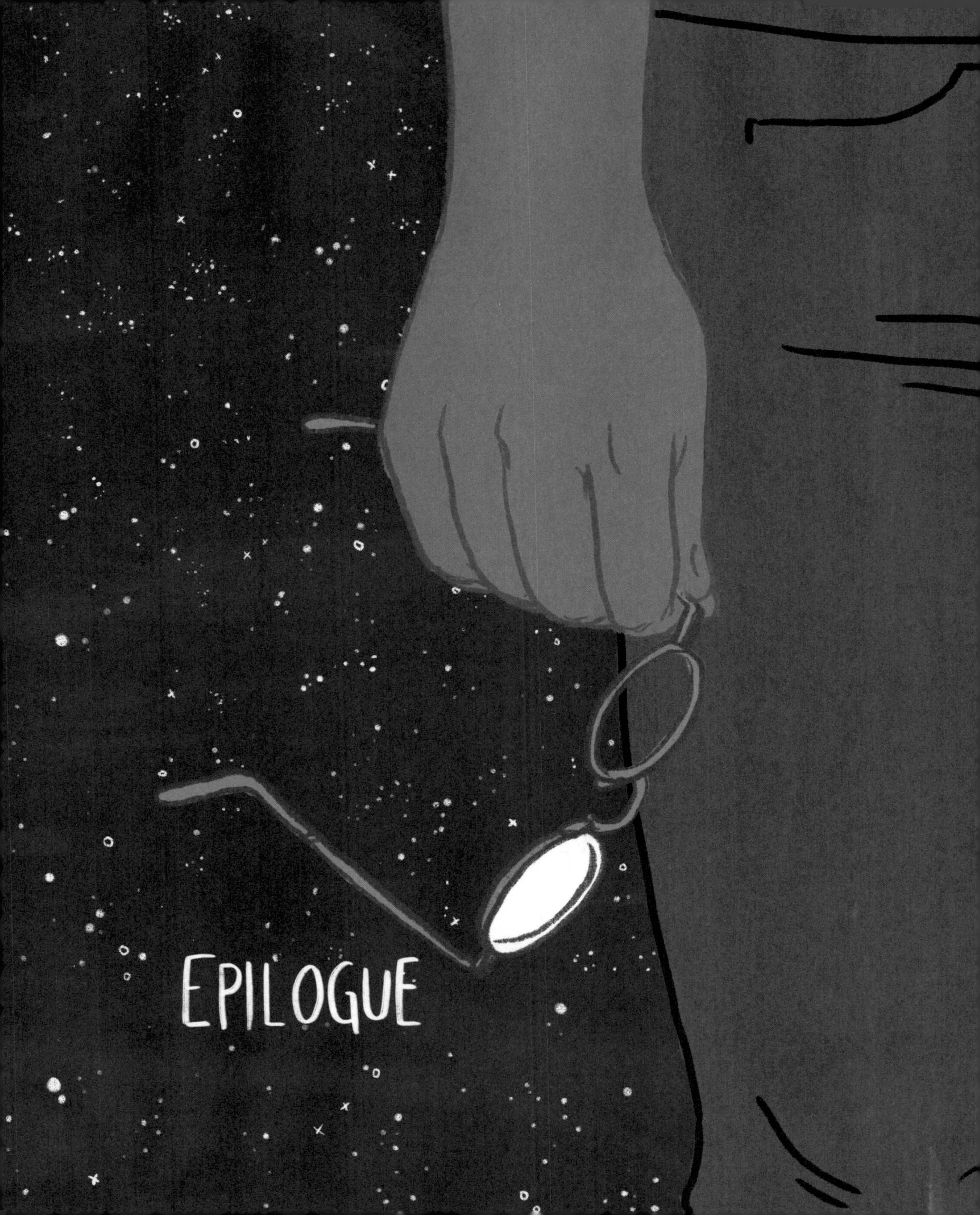
EPILOGUE

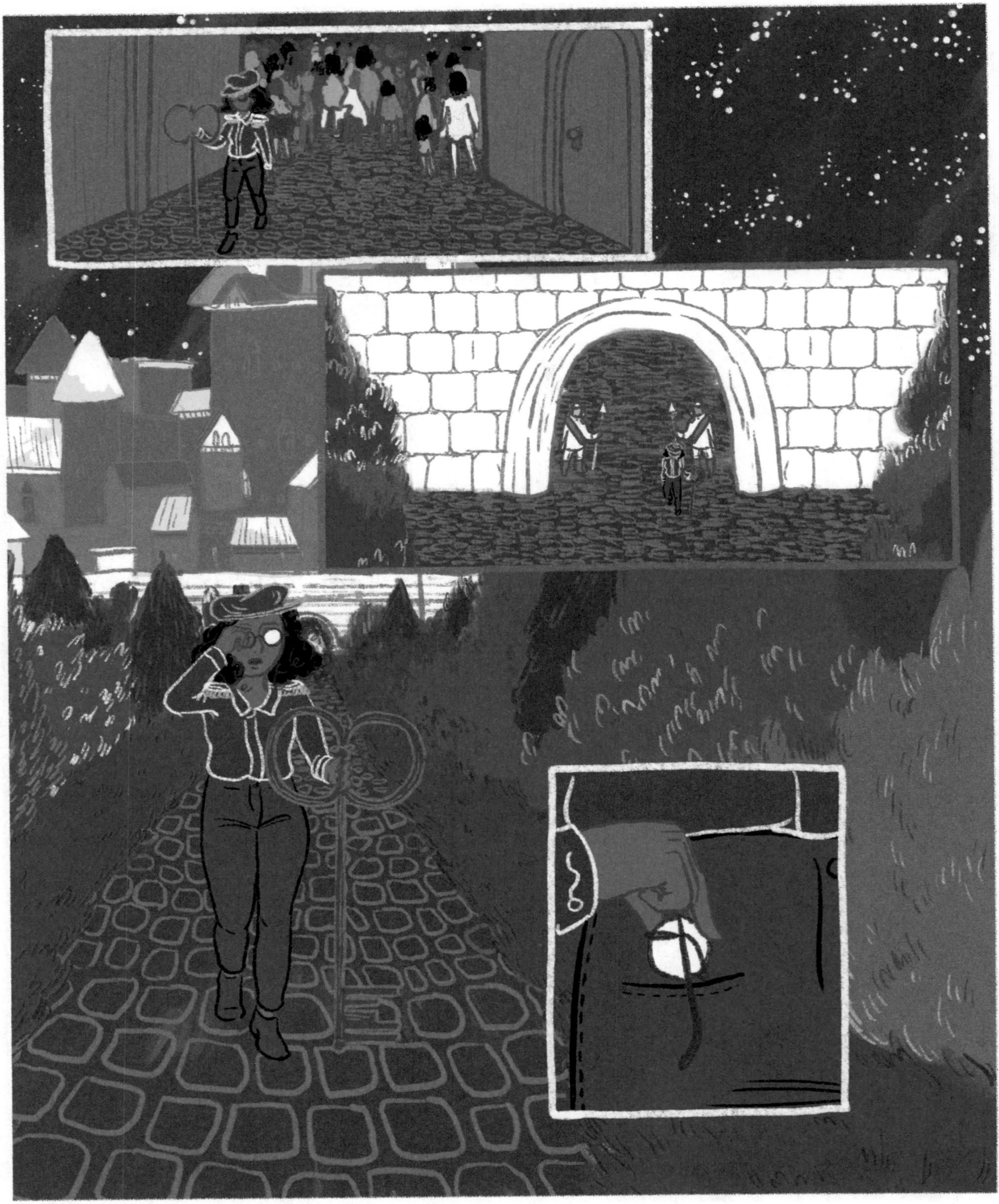

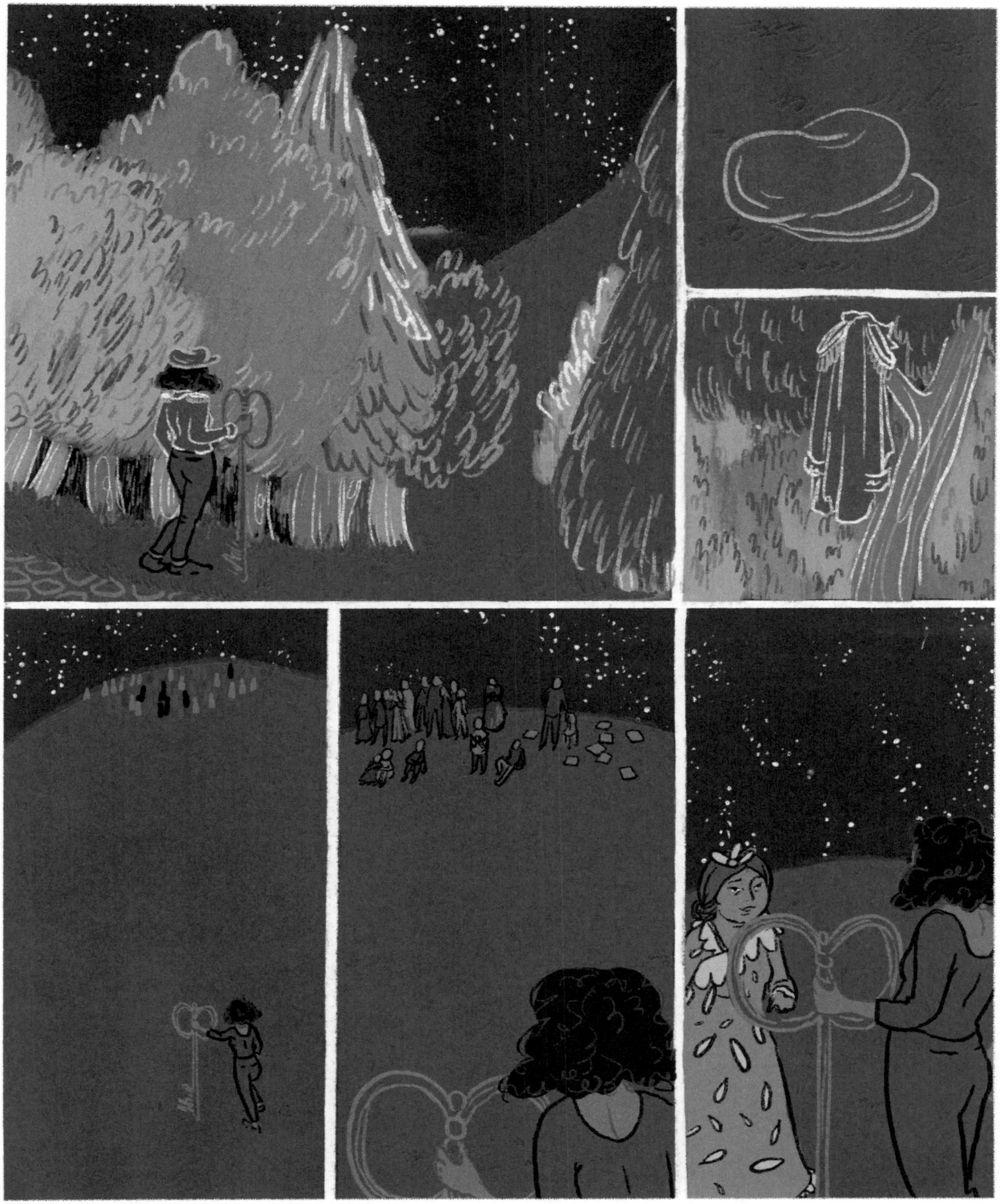

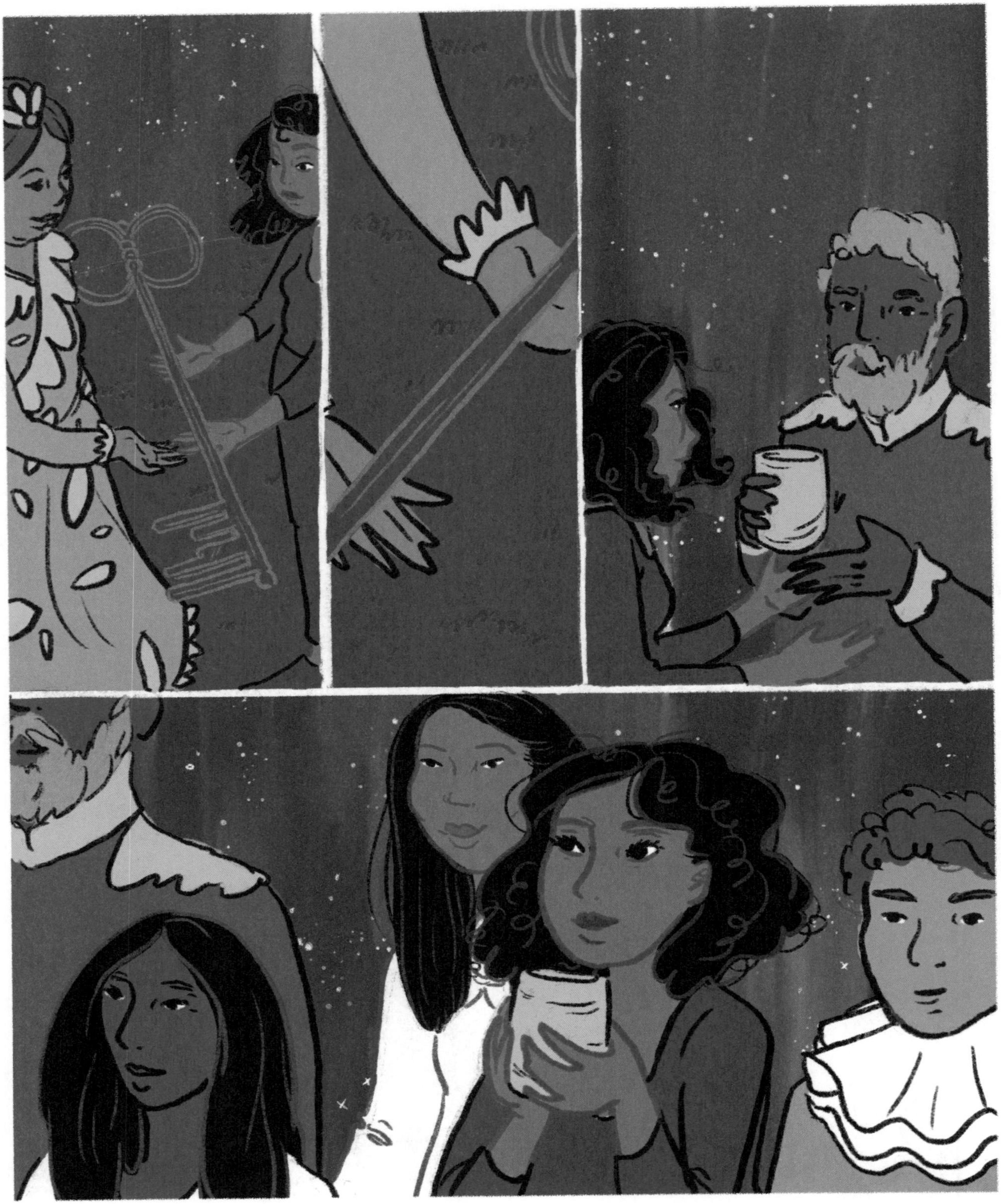

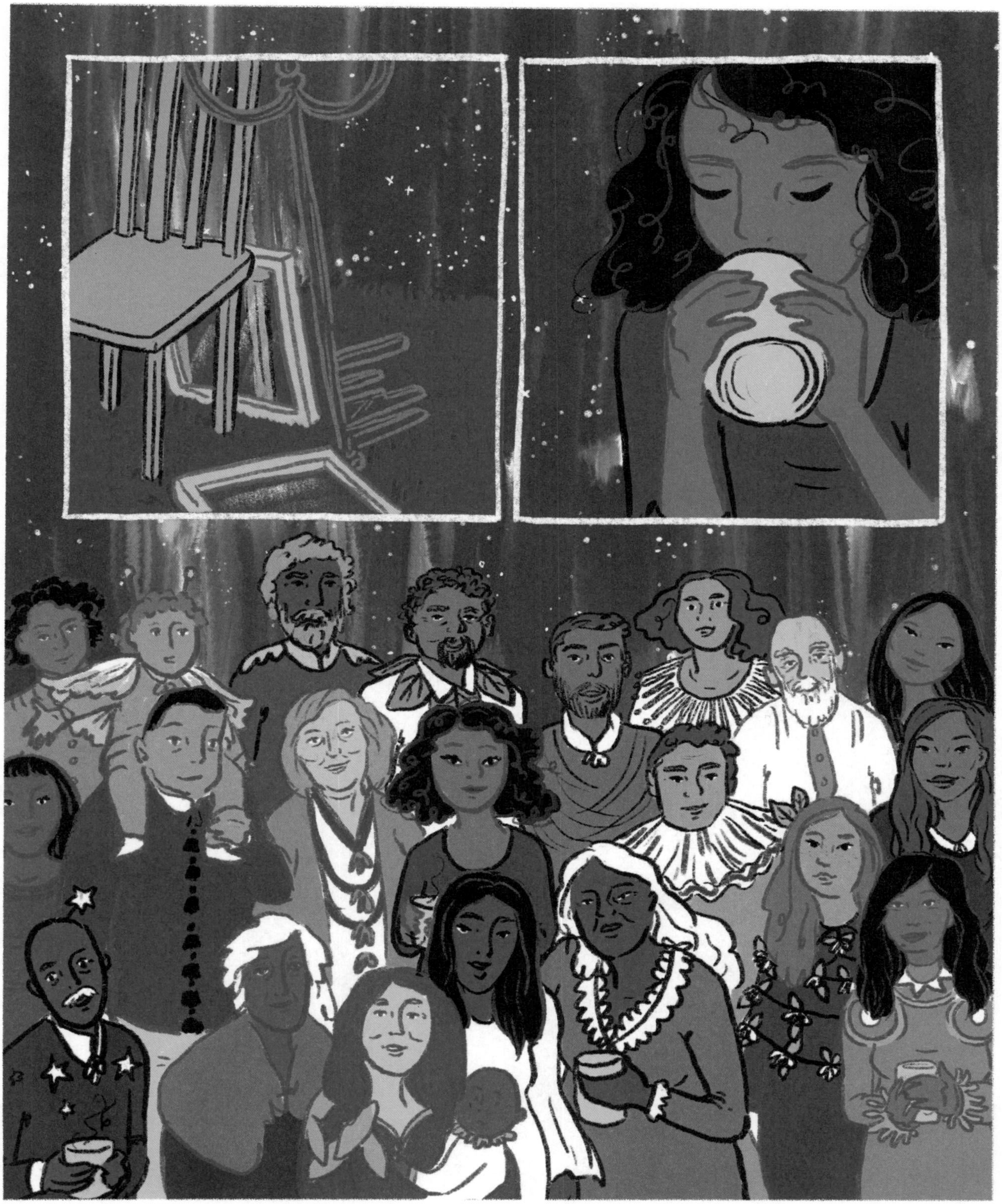

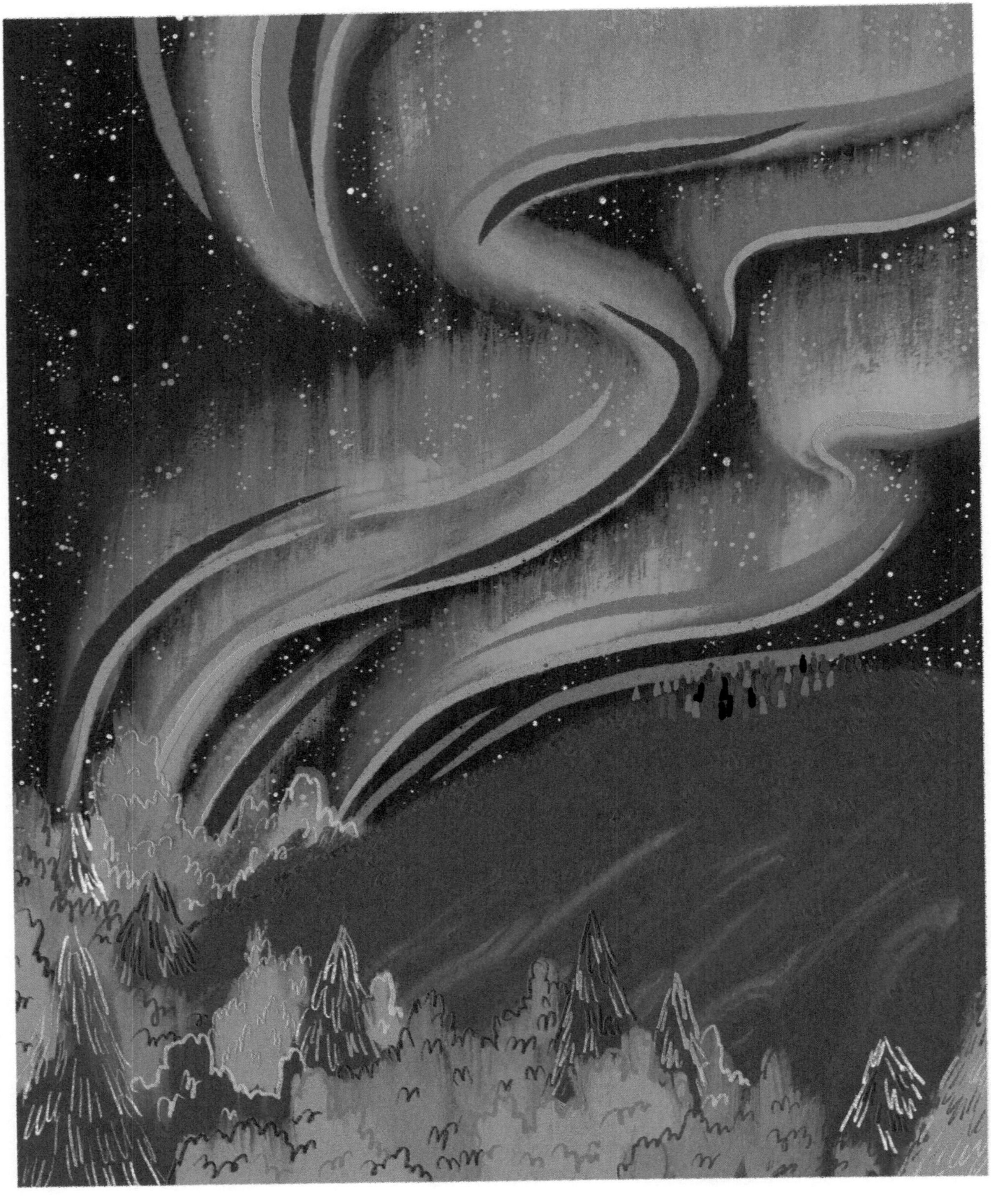

END

Photo: Erin Flegg

Photo: Erin Flegg

WAYDE COMPTON is the author of four books and the editor of two anthologies. His collection of short stories, *The Outer Harbour*, won the City of Vancouver Book Award in 2015, and he won a National Magazine Award for Fiction in 2011. Compton teaches Creative Writing at Douglas College. *The Blue Road* is based on a passage that first appeared in his debut poetry book *49th Parallel Psalm*.
waydecompton.com

APRIL DELA NOCHE MILNE is a Filipino Canadian artist based in Vancouver. She studied fine arts at Langara College and graduated with a BFA in illustration from Emily Carr University of Art + Design. Her illustrations have been featured in *Ricepaper*, *EVENT*, and *Briarpatch* magazines. *The Blue Road* is her first graphic novel.
aprilmilne.com